What Are the Odds

What Are the Odds

DAVID LIST

BLACK STONE
PUBLISHING

Copyright © 2024 by David List
Published in 2024 by Blackstone Publishing
Cover and book design by Kristen M. Gully

The characters and events in this book are fictitious.
Any similarity to real persons, living or dead, is coincidental
and not intended by the author.

Printed in the United States of America

First edition: 2024
ISBN 979-8-212-33721-2
Fiction / Mystery & Detective / International Crime & Mystery

Version 1

Blackstone Publishing
31 Mistletoe Rd.
Ashland, OR 97520

www.BlackstonePublishing.com

For Alley, Casey, Moose, and Hammer

Sometimes it takes a long time to play like yourself.
Miles Davis

But your solitude will be a support and a home for
you, even in the midst of very unfamiliar circumstances, and from it you will find all your paths.
Rainer Maria Rilke

PROLOGUE

Desolate. The only sound is the whispering wind. The only feeling is emptiness. The only sensation, fear. Dust devils spin counterclockwise as they waltz across the dry, dusty rolling hills—long believed by many to be ghosts or spirits of the dead. To Chicanos, they are simply known as *el Diablo*, the Devil. To the Navajo, *chiindii* spinning counterclockwise are bad spirits, while those spinning clockwise are good. In African folklore, *Nums* are shape-shifting demons or sorcerers possessing human souls. And in the Good Book, Genesis 3:19 reminds the faithful, "For dust you are, and to dust you shall return."

One dances over a pool of fresh blood, leaving no doubt that something horrific, something violent, something deadly, happened here. The blood drains off one side and dwindles to drops that end at the feet of two men standing at the edge of a massive deep ditch. Dry, crusty dirt clings to bloody cuts. Extension cords bind their hands behind their backs, choking the life from their swollen fingers. But most striking is that they are both buck naked except for their shoes.

Former NYPD detective Raymond Dawson, the guy on the left in the worn utility boots, blinks dust from his eyes. From his powerful physique for a guy in his early forties, it's safe to say he's tough as nails.

Yet here he is, bloodied, bound, and buck naked at the edge of a massive deep ditch in the middle of God knows where, trying to wrap his head around how a romantic weekend getaway to propose again to his second ex-wife went this far off the rails. But then again, from the three bullet hole scars on his back, each labeled with a tat, perhaps it isn't that hard for him to understand. The one near his right shoulder reads *9mm*. The one an inch above his waist, *.44*. And the third, the near kill shot at his heart, reads *1st wife*.

Former Amco Oil executive Wilbur Bailey, the guy next to Ray in the torn canvas loafers, furrows his brow and squints his eyes, lost in thought. He's also in his early forties, but from his skinny, toneless frame and über-white skin, beet red from its introduction to the sun, it's safe to say he's not as tough. There's one thing, though, Wilbur knows for sure—being bloodied, bound, and buck naked at the edge of a massive deep ditch in the middle of God knows where was not on his list of "THE EIGHT EXOTIC WAYS TO CLEANSE NEGATIVE ENERGY FROM THE BODY."

A scorpion scurries over Wilbur's loafer and into the ditch, perhaps heading to its burrow under one of the many vehicles lining it—most of them metal carcasses, others partially stripped. Or perhaps it's on its way to a crevice inside the rusted shipping container on the far side, catty-corner to several rows of stacked oil barrels.

"One in three hundred thirty-seven million eight hundred fifty-six thousand four hundred and two. The odds our paths would cross—give or take," Wilbur says, his voice low.

Ray's eyes, fixed straight ahead, reflect stoic indifference. "One in one. The odds I'll kill you myself if you don't shut the fuck up."

A moment later, both men turn their focus to a gangly dark-skinned thug with a close-cropped beard in worn, bloodstained utility workwear, who's climbing toward them from within the ditch. With each step, the assault rifle slung over his shoulder sways over a red, white, and green patch bearing the initials CDN, and its butt clanks against a bloody machete tucked in his waist.

He stops before Ray and Wilbur. His paranoid eyes dart back and forth between them, and he holds up two recently severed heads by their hair. Blood drips from their necks. One still has a lit, half-smoked cigarillo dangling from its lips.

"These the men who robbed you?"

ONE

"I didn't want this case," booms IRS Criminal Investigation Special Agent Phil Dancourt's deep, gravelly Texan voice. In his loose-fitting sober gray suit and sidearm at this belt, he ambles past the lecture title displayed on the massive HD screen inside FLETC's state-of-the-art lecture hall.

Standing in the front of the hall, Phil shields his eyes from the bright lights upon him and peers out at this year's group of IRS special agent trainees that fill the room. Still, with the lights over the tiered seating area dimmed, it's tough for him to see all the young, eager faces beyond those in the first eight or ten rows. It doesn't matter, though. He knows there are 403 of them—a record number for a graduating class, surpassing last year's record of 312 and the annual average of 298.

Despite the multitude of bodies, the lecture hall's temperature never deviates from seventy degrees—the optimal temperature, based on several scientific studies, to keep the brain at its peak sharpness. In a room that's too cold or too hot, part of the brain becomes focused on maintaining the body's temperature, either cooling or heating, in turn reducing focus on the task at hand. And when the nature of your chosen career dictates that any day could be your last on earth, peak focus is a sixth vital organ.

Staying focused, though, won't be an issue for the 403 agent trainees in the hall today. It's a day they've been fervently awaiting—the privileged few who are about to hear, directly from the horse's mouth, the unvarnished, harrowing, and outrageous events of three months ago. Events that led to the unlikely conclusion of Case #1A, making it an immediate GOAT across all thin lines of FLETC's law enforcement community.

From the moment Phil arrived in Glynco, Georgia, to talk to the trainees at the Federal Law Enforcement Training Center, or FLETC as it's known to those in the biz, it seemed like only yesterday when he'd pulled into the facility as a trainee himself.

The modern, high-tech campus sprawled across 1,600 acres makes FLETC the largest law enforcement training organization in the United States—a town unto itself, with a dedicated zip code and unrivaled facilities that, each year, gives birth to seventy thousand federal agents across ninety different law enforcement organizations.

"You wouldn't believe your eyes," a young and enthusiastic Phil had said to his father back when he'd told him about the dorms, gyms, administrative structures, classrooms, library, interviewing suites, lecture halls, and mock courtrooms. "You should see the forensic labs," he said. "State of the art. One just for cybercrimes, and three others where they collect and analyze everything from hair, fiber, ballistics, and pathology to blood splatter, DNA, and all kinds of narcotics.

"And the precision shooting ranges . . . There are eighteen of them." These are where Phil and thousands of others like him, with a yearning to be in the field, hone their marksmanship skills. "It's like Disneyland with real guns, Dad," Phil told him and detailed how one indoor range has 146 separate firing points and how eight of the others are multipurpose, semi-enclosed ranges with 200 additional firing points.

Even now Phil was in awe of some of the facility's über-cool assets: its massive complex of driver training ranges, the physical combat technique facility and explosive range, its fully functional mock port of entry, and its mock neighborhood with thirty-four buildings—each equipped with cameras to record every training exercise.

"The best part, Dad," Phil said to him, "is the chefs. World class, and they serve around four thousand meals a day."

Closing in on fifty, Phil's thinning hair, gray beard, and tired eyes reflect the physical and emotional toll of twenty-plus years in the field. It's one of the many messages he conveys to the 403 trainees. The other side of the coin that many in the public overlook regarding those in law enforcement, let alone those with the IRS. But the steady diet of pain and suffering that IRS Criminal Investigation special agents inflict on fellow human beings or that's inflicted on them is engraved across Phil's stress-worn face, which is still dotted with cuts and bruises he'd sustained compliments of Case #1A.

"I was burnt out," he says. "Twenty years in the field had worn me down. But my boss, Callahan, was in line for the state's top finance gig if Governor Hargrove was reelected. For this case, Callahan needed a guy with good stats. And I had good stats."

He sits on the stool and pulls out his Banana Nut Bread e-cig while he collects his thoughts.

"Soon you'll all be full-fledged IRS special agents," Phil says. "Top of the food chain. Armed and with powers that place you among the most powerful in the US government. You have two main objectives, neither of which you can fail. First, make your stats: the number of seizures, levies, and most important, closed cases. Second, use all means necessary to instill fear of the IRS in the minds of the public."

From the rigid stillness on the young, eager faces gazing at him, it's clear Phil has captured their attention.

"How?" he says, exhaling his first vape blast of Banana Nut Bread. "Take down anyone who tries to fuck us."

He thumbs at the screen. "Amco Oil. Founded in 1920 in Kansas, it was sold in 2000 to Venezuela along with Rio Bravo, its refinery along the Texas-Mexico border." He pulls up a photo of Rio Bravo on the screen. "This behemoth can refine upward of five hundred thousand barrels of crude oil a day," he says of the imposing 1,400-acre complex of pipes, tanks, and towers.

"When Venezuela's economy tanked, the country borrowed billions from Russia, using Amco as collateral. And when they couldn't pay it back, Russia took it over and put this guy in charge." Phil pulls up a photo and looks back at the screen, along with the trainees.

"Mika Salko," he announces, letting the name sink in.

Mika Salko was born in Moscow to a Russian father, Vadim, and an American mother, Denise, who met on the beach in Nice. She was a student in a foreign exchange program, and he was visiting his father, a Russian multibillionaire with a magnificent stone villa overlooking Villefranche Bay and the sea beyond.

At first, Denise paid no attention to Vadim when she and her friends planted themselves on the rocky beach about twenty feet away from where he lounged on a beach chair.

But ten or so minutes later, Denise cast her gaze his way, intrigued by his reading what looked to be a thousand-page book as well as irritated by the indecently loud live broadcast of Richard Strauss's *Arabella* that blared from his transistor radio.

"Hi," Vadim mouthed with a smile and a wave when he caught Denise checking him out.

"You mind turning your radio down?" she said.

Vadim turned the radio down and his ego up—his smile a bit brighter, his chest a bit puffier. The ensuing conversation led to their meeting later in the day for a drink. Which led to dinner together the following night.

Many a weekend thereafter was spent at Vadim's $15 million condo in central Moscow, where he was a standout structural engineer whose blueprints helped make the 1,800-mile-long oil pipeline from Russia to China a reality.

After two years of dating, they married.

Soon after, Vadim bought a second home: a seven-story, twenty-thousand-square-foot, $55 million townhouse on New York

City's Upper East Side—across town from where Denise's parents had a rent-controlled apartment. And thanks to Vadim's family's connections, he went from being a green card holder to a full-fledged American citizen faster than a proverbial New York minute.

Two years later, Mika was born.

It didn't take long to see that he had inherited his father's piercing eyes and chiseled, classically Russian features. By the age of five, Mika was required to wear a jacket and tie at the family dinner table, where Vadim engaged him in debate and instilled in him the importance of a focused work ethic.

Mika, though, favored his grandfather. He admired the old man's values and hardline commitment to the motherland. Early on, he deciphered that it was his grandfather who provided the platinum spoon and afforded him and his parents a lifestyle that eluded most Russians and Americans alike.

Much of his childhood and early adult life was split between their New York mansion and the condo in Moscow, but Mika spent as much time as he could at his grandfather's estate in Moscow's ritziest suburb, Rublyovka—Russia's equivalent to Beverly Hills and Bel Air.

Many high-level government officials and billionaire businesspeople have homes there. Its streets are lush and tree-lined and without sidewalks. And the estates, which set residents back sixty to eighty million bucks, are hidden behind fortress-worthy walls laced with security cameras.

It's his grandfather whom Mika later credited for his success. His generosity and philanthropy secured Mika's entry into New York's prestigious Trinity School. The ten-grand-a-year tuition—a lot of money at the time and a far cry from the sixty grand it is today—was a mere pittance. What mattered is that 100 percent of the graduating class went on to attend four-year universities, many in the Ivy League.

To the pride of his parents and grandfather, Mika graduated from Trinity at the top of his class and attended Yale, where he cultivated an extraordinary array of rich and powerful connections. They ran the gamut from global corporate leaders, celebs, and politicians to Russian mafia thugs.

But it's the contacts he made with several of the highest-ranking Kremlin officials, whom he still counts among his closest friends, that causes many in the US government to take notice of him and raise the alarm.

Roughly twelve years ago, armed with inside information given to him by one of those close Russian allies—a first deputy chief of staff to the Presidential Executive Office—Mika invested heavily in several independent oil and gas companies. Lo and behold, several months later each of them was sold in blockbuster deals to Russia's state-owned oil company, Rosneft, which catapulted Mika into the ranks of the multibillionaires.

Salko was already on US intelligence's radar, but with his newfound bankroll, it wasn't long before they branded him a Russian oligarch, even suspecting he was a key source of the dark money behind several shadowy radical groups with ties to Russian military intelligence—groups allegedly behind everything from the 2014 covert invasion of Crimea by Russian troops disguised as Crimean militia to US election interference and the mysterious death of Amco's former CEO while vacationing in Chile two weeks after he spoke out against the Kremlin.

Amco's vast transportation network controlled 650 miles of pipeline, trucks, railcars, tankers, and fifty terminals in thirty-three states to distribute everything from gasoline, diesel, and heating oil to jet fuel.

Quiet chatter that made its way through the halls of Congress, the FBI, DOJ, DOD, State Department, and White House expressed anxiety over how placing a die-hard loyalist like Salko at the company's helm not only raised national security concerns but further cemented Russia's direct, unfettered access to America's lucrative energy market.

"Despite the numerous red flags, the narrative out of the White House was clear: the US and Russia are looking for ways to better their relations amid turbulent political winds," Phil says to the group. "And truth be told, Americans are in no rush to give up their Stoli, caviar, or Russian hookers and mail-order brides."

There's hearty laughter throughout the hall, a clear indication the trainees also know it's true.

"On a more serious note, the leaders of both countries surely grasp that they, and the world, stand a better chance of defeating terrorism once and for all if they stand together. So, like it or not, we might as well try to get along."

Phil sucks in another hit of Banana Nut Bread and exhales the cloud.

"Still, we knew Amco was cooking the books. Millions of dollars more than they let on were flowing in, but we couldn't figure out how it all worked and where it was coming from."

Phil glances back at the screen, and he replaces Mika's photo with a diagram resembling a genealogical tree. Instead of people, it details the flow of money from one shell company to another, each with the acronym IRS—Idle River Steam, India Rubber & Steel, Indigo Rail Systems, and so on. One by one, each company name fades and disappears.

"These guys were good. Old-school daisy-chain shit but with twenty-first-century technology," Phil says, and fires another round of Banana Nut Bread. "Five years into the investigation, I still had squat. Except for Wilbur Bailey. The one guy on the inside with a conscience."

All eyes in the audience shift to the screen and lock onto the close-up of Wilbur's face.

"I'd been on him for over a year," Phil says. "First pounding away at his conscience for helping Salko skirt the law, and later squeezing him with threats of fines and jail time for 'discrepancies' on his last several returns—some business expense write-offs that might have been otherwise."

Chuckles permeate the hall. "Flimsy bullshit, I know," Phil says. "The truth is that I had nothing on Wilbur Bailey, but that didn't matter. My gut said Bailey wanted to talk, that he needed to talk. But he was afraid of Salko. So we took a kill shot instead."

Memories flood in as Phil refills his lungs, and the vapor contrail follows close behind. "This brings us to the first takeaway of this case: Things don't always go as planned."

TWO

For as long as Ray Dawson can remember, he planned to follow his father into the Marine Corps and the NYPD and, along the way, like his dad, meet and marry the love of his life.

But he never planned on being shot three times in the back on three separate occasions in three different years—each scar a permanent reminder of pursuits that took unexpected turns south.

The first bullet almost took his life at age twenty-six, halfway through his fourth, and last, two-year tour in Afghanistan. The second nearly did so two months after he made detective. And the third . . .

After eight years in the corps, in the wee hours of July 4, a day Ray regards as his luckiest, he strode up the C-130's ramp for the last time. By his side was his newly adopted one-year-old shepherd mix, Alley—her namesake linked to the trash-strewn alley where he'd found her the day before, bound to a pipe with barbed wire.

Wasting no time when he arrived home, he breezed through six months in the New York City Police Academy and officially became a cop assigned to Narcotics in the Bronx's Forty-First Precinct, where over the next year and a half, he rocketed to detective third grade.

Through it all, rain or shine, hot or cold, Ray's Saturday mornings were reserved for Alley. She burst into New York City life as if she had been there forever, and they've yet to miss an early Saturday morning in the park but for one when Ray had the flu.

He loved the quiet about an hour before the arrival of the brigade of other dog owners, when it was just him and Alley and a tennis ball. He loved to watch her take off like a rocket to fetch it—unaware that he, too, was being watched.

"No, he's always there alone," Aileen O'Malley told her friends, confident he was single. "And I bet he's a great guy. You should see the way he is with his dog."

Since starting at the boutique six weeks ago, Saturdays were the one morning she arrived early, an hour before her coworker, and sipped on her skinny vanilla latte while she watched Ray play with his dog in the park across the street.

With each passing Saturday, she imagined herself with him and envisioned him being an athlete, strong and tough. Or a doctor, smart, caring, and compassionate. Or something creative, an action film actor. Whatever. He felt right. Arousing. And on a crisp October morning, with a nudge from her friends, she mustered up the guts to amble over with her latte, a black coffee, and a beef-flavored bone.

In general, people are drawn to Ray. Sure, his bullshit meter, with its hair trigger, is a bit intense for some—especially those on the wrong end of it. But between growing up in New York City and having a decorated streetwise cop for a dad, Ray's a bloodhound when it comes to sniffing out BS. And like most New Yorkers, he has no patience for it.

But those lucky enough to get to know him below the surface can't help but be seduced by his infectious, disarming personality coupled with his killer smile and innate desire to help others. Especially the ladies. Especially Aileen O'Malley.

It's no secret that kids of alcoholics often marry someone with the same affliction—despite conscious thoughts and self-promises never to do so. In Aileen's case, the same can be said when it comes to cops.

Growing up, she longed for more attention from her father. He was a cop in Bay Ridge, Brooklyn's Sixty-Eighth Precinct, and spent most of his time on the job—whether he was home or not. It often left him on edge, and his patience for her was thin at best. Over the years, Aileen's unmet desire for attention crystallized into anger and resentment, and she vowed to set her life on a different path. She'd never end up with a guy like that, especially if he was a cop.

Whoa, Ray thought when he caught sight of the fiery redhead with emerald eyes and a killer figure. But as she made her way across the park, he drew up his guard the moment he realized she was heading straight for him.

"You strike me as a black coffee kind of guy," Aileen said with a smile, and held out the cup. "I work across the street."

Leery but intrigued, Ray studied her. *Beautiful smile*, he thought, unsure whether it was her striking red hair or the pink undertones of her flawless skin that made her teeth the brightest white he'd ever seen.

"Thanks," he said, and took the coffee as Alley ran up and dropped her ball at his feet.

"She's a beauty. Like a little deer," Aileen said and held up the bone. "May I?"

"Sure. Be a friend for life," Ray said with his most winning smile.

When Alley sat and raised her paw, Aileen gave her the bone and smiled. "I'm counting on it."

Later that night, over dinner and drinks at an intimate joint in the East Village, where she lived, Aileen did her best to keep her anxious inner voice at bay to mask how floored she was when Ray told her he was a cop. And she laughed when she told him about her father and the vow she made never to date a cop.

But I like him. And he's hot, she thought as she looked into his eyes.

Despite her effort to conceal it, Ray picked up on the unease in her voice when she spoke about her father, but he brushed it off.

I like her, he told himself. *She looks great. Incredible ass.* He smiled and turned on the charm.

"Our date was amazing," Aileen later told her friends. "But can you believe he's a cop? I mean, what are the odds?"

They went on their second date a few days later. Their third, the following Saturday, and so on. With each date, the more Aileen buried her fears. By mid-November, she and Ray were exclusive, and one year from the day they met, on a beautiful October evening, wedding bells rang.

Their life together couldn't have gotten off to a better start.

But four or so months after the wedding, cracks appeared. Fears seeped to the surface. Old wounds opened. And as Ray's caseload doubled, the wider the cracks became.

Lack of time for each other, though, wasn't the heart of their problem, but it enabled them to ignore more intimate, deep-rooted issues and allowed frustration and anger to percolate below the surface.

Within six months, the barbs began to land with heavyweight jab force.

Before either of them knew it, the rounds took a toll. And on a drizzly, cooler-than-usual, May evening—seven months after they vowed that for better or worse, for richer or poorer, and in sickness and health, they would love and cherish each other for the rest of their lives—a telltale sign their life together was destined for the used-to-be heap rang the bell for what proved to be the twelfth and final round.

It was a sign that Ray was sure had come from above.

It was subtle at first, but they both felt the tension brewing as they walked to a restaurant for dinner. It had been brewing for a while—whatever *it* was this time.

Maybe Aileen was irritated because Ray arrived at the boutique to meet her over an hour late.

Maybe the gang rape of an eleven-year-old girl, which caused Ray to be late, still had him on edge and on his phone while they walked.

Maybe Aileen was still hurt and angry that Ray had forgotten her birthday two months ago.

Maybe Ray was frustrated by the impact their recurring arguments were having on their sex life.

Maybe they both just weren't ready for the permanence of marriage. The finality of marriage.

Whatever . . . *It* was all kindling on a smoldering fire that was about to ignite.

The argument on the way home carried over into the apartment, where Aileen tripped on a runner and stumbled into the armoire on which Ray, only a moment before, had set his Glock down to take off his shirt.

The gun toppled off, and in the blink of an eye, it discharged when the trigger hit a marble-sized hardwood finial atop the chair's stile. The bullet tore through Ray's back, a half inch from his spine. A quarter inch from his heart.

In the end, they both realized their relationship was more of a whirlwind than a romance.

Six weeks later, on July 4, Ray signed the divorce papers—a day that perhaps set him on or kept him on a winding, invisible path toward Wilbur Bailey.

THREE

It took several months for Ray to settle into divorced life. No matter how hard he tried to look back and examine it, the marriage and its erosion were a big blur without clearly defined turning points. Nothing specific to hang its failure on. Just a slow burn till the doomed foundation gave.

Most of the time, his job kept his mind elsewhere. But in the solitude of his thoughts, his emotions surprised him. It wasn't that he didn't believe he and Aileen were better off now that they were apart, but there was no sense of relief. No joy at his newfound freedom. Only pain and guilt that the marriage had failed, and he was the first Dawson to ever allow that to happen. ·

The idea of meeting someone new seemed far away—not a worry he ever thought he'd have, let alone at age thirty-one. But little did Ray know that six months from the day he signed the divorce papers, a call on the job would take him to a paint-peeled, cracked wooden door inside an abandoned building being razed in the Bronx, through which would walk the women he was meant to be with for life.

7:15 a.m.

Despite the cold weather and the early hour, the construction site is already a buzz of activity. Between the crane, the bulldozer, the backhoe loader, and the jackhammers, chipping hammers, rotary hammers, hydraulic drills, rattle guns, and chop saws, the noise is deafening.

But residents living close by don't mind. Once this dilapidated tenement is razed, the new building will be the first new construction of low-income housing in the South Bronx's Longwood neighborhood in three years, an ongoing effort by the city to revitalize the community.

Titan Fitzgerald's thirty-one-year-old construction foreman, Stephanie Morego, a fluorescent high-visibility vest over her Berber-lined hooded flannel, and her wavy long brown hair secure under her hard hat, pops a couple of Tums and steps out from the mobile office trailer. The thermometer hanging next to the door reads thirty-three degrees, typical for a late December morning.

Off to the side, a young apprentice with a Santa hat pulled over his hard hat spray-paints a green line along the ground to indicate the sewer and drain lines below. But when he steps on a pile of rebar to avoid a gooey puddle left over from last night's rain, the pile shifts, and into the puddle he goes.

"¡Hijo de mil putas!" he laments, and jumps up covered in mud and muck.

"That's the Victor I know and love," Stephanie says in stride. "Embrace the suck. And let's get 'Watch-your-steps' on that pile—we don't need the DOB on our ass."

Victor smiles and gives her a thumbs-up.

A moment later, she clamps the steel carabiner on her waist belt to the hoist's grab rail. Twenty-mile-an-hour gusts whip through its see-through metal grates for walls as it clamors on its track six stories above where, late yesterday, an engineer discovered over a thousand pounds of potentially hazardous material buried behind bricks that were laid twenty years ago during a prior renovation—in an area of the building that sits four feet from the back of a school.

For Titan Fitzgerald, such a discovery risks a domino effect of schedule delays and budget overages. Stephanie, though, is known for running a tight ship, and because of her construction and leadership skills, she attracts many of the best crew in New York City.

"Morning, boss," the hazardous material supervisor says as Stephanie approaches, his four-member team standing behind him.

"Good morning," she says, and they go over the removal plan one more time. "You have everything you need?" When they all nod, she tells them, "You're all here because you deserve to be here. You've earned it. So, let's prove the suits wrong. Get it done by six . . . Beers on me."

"Might as well bust the cash out now, boss," the supervisor says, glancing back at his team. "We'll have it done by five."

Stephanie smiles, but no sooner do they disperse than the project manager's voice squawks from her walkie-talkie. "Boss, we got another problem."

Given the urgency in his voice, she hustles down the stairs to the ground level. A moment later, standing at the foot of the door of the old tenement's last barren room at the end of a long, dank, dimly lit hallway, Stephanie stares at a weathered black man in tattered clothing lying still in a pool of blood.

Those who don't know Stephanie Morego well might wonder how she ended up in construction in the Bronx. And those who do can't see her doing anything else.

She'd been around construction sites her whole life. Practically grew up on them. Her paternal grandparents emigrated to the US from Brazil in 1959 and settled in Astoria, Queens, New York. Her grandfather, an expert institutional and commercial sheet metal worker, was equally proficient in masonry and carpentry. But his greatest skill was leadership, and he became one of the first foremen at the burgeoning construction firm Titan Fitzgerald—a skill he instilled in his son, Stephanie's father, whom Titan considered to be their top master electrician.

Early on, her father knew Stephanie was cut from the same mold. When he arrived home one day when she was seven years old, she had built a replica of the site's tower crane from an erector set he had bought the day before for fifty cents at a garage sale.

He grew up in a time when *woke* meant no longer asleep. So, when Stephanie, in her final year of high school, told him of her desire to follow in his and her grandfather's footsteps, he tried to put his foot down and talk her out of it.

"It's not the kind of work a woman does," he repeatedly said. He also feared for her safety, given that the neighborhoods they worked in, often at odd hours, were some of the roughest and most dangerous in New York City. But his objections fell on deaf ears, and he was forced to struggle with a simple truth: construction was in her DNA.

Every day, Stephanie went from school to the site and helped with all kinds of basic tasks. One day when the crew was only a week into a new project, she discovered an engineering design flaw that had eluded everyone else. It would have cost Titan Fitzgerald tens of thousands of dollars in materials and time—and possibly, for some on the crew, their jobs.

The discovery blew a powerful gust of wind in her construction dream's sails, and Titan Fitzgerald wasn't about to let her get away. When she was accepted to New York's City Tech, they paid her first year's tuition—and it was money well spent.

She excelled, earning a bachelor's degree in construction management and engineering technology while doing apprenticeships with rebar and structural steel detailers and working with various machinery.

All the while, aware of the dangers lurking in some of the neighborhoods where she would be working, she studied Krav Maga, an Israeli form of self-defense, and one of the deadliest forms of martial arts to exist.

So, it's no wonder she not only became the youngest person—and the youngest female—to earn the title of construction foreman at Titan Fitzgerald but also became the youngest foreman in all of New York City.

When she landed the promotion, it was her father's proudest moment. And given that three months prior she had also earned her black belt, he pitied any jerk foolish enough to mess with his daughter.

After Ray viewed the black man's corpse, he questioned Stephanie and members of her crew. Right away, he recognized that Stephanie was smart.

Not just street smart, but book smart. And articulate, respectful, funny at times, and protective of her fellow workers—all qualities he admires.

But later, as he drives away from the crime scene, more intimate thoughts surface.

Her face . . . Attractive in a rough-around-the-edges kind of way. The imperfections here and there. A scar across her right ear, the result of a support cable that snapped and nearly tore it clean off. *Her smile* . . . Soft and disarming. *Her body* . . . Athletic and well proportioned. But he keeps circling back to *the confident no-bullshit way she carries herself.*

Several days later, he makes it a point to stop by the site with a few more questions.

Stephanie smiles when she spots his arrival and comes over. "Detective . . ."

"Call me Ray," he says, and smiles back.

They talk for five or so minutes before she has to deal with other pressing matters. But after Ray leaves, he can't forget her, even as he's buried in other cases.

Three weeks pass before *something about her* tightens its grip, and he asks her out.

It's hands down the best first date, and before long, they are an item. Everyone they socialize with, whether they are friends of Stephanie's or Ray's, is left with the same impression: they're great together.

It's easy to see why. Without thought and with little effort, they're a natural fit: a relationship defined by common interests, positive attitudes, ease of conversation, and more importantly, trust, honesty, and genuine love and appreciation for each other.

Even Stephanie's father, with his paternal protection instincts on red alert, ends up liking Ray. He loves to see his daughter happy, and tells friends and family, "They deserve each other."

Sure, they have the occasional fight. But they know how to. And how to reconcile—which then reminds them how perfectly their naked bodies fit together. It all comes easy—when they take the time.

But again, lack of time becomes an issue. Once they became an item, both promised never to allow work to get between them. But despite their best intentions, over the next several years, as the novelty of their relationship fades while their professional plates overflow, old habits and patterns reemerge, leaving them without the energy to fight the inevitable regression toward the mean.

They stick it out for eight years, but the foundation buckles, and they throw in the towel.

Both are devastated by the divorce. But as gut-wrenching as it is for Ray, it pales in comparison to the sledgehammer that hits him over the head six months later—a blow that strips him of the job he cherishes and the pension he deserves.

Still, despite it all, Ray and Stephanie love each other. So, when Stephanie opens the door for a second chance, they promise to make it work, and Ray goes all in, arranging a lavish romantic getaway.

Stephanie's father urges caution when his daughter brings up the trip and the possibility of their getting back together. "I know this man," he says to her. "And I know you. And I love you both."

He recounts the old fable of the scorpion that asks the frog to carry it on its back across the river and promises not to sting him because they would both drown. But halfway across the river, the scorpion stings the frog anyway, telling the dying frog that he couldn't help it—it's his nature.

"So, who's the scorpion and who's the frog?" Stephanie asks.

Her father laughs. "Unless you can figure that out and are ready and willing to accept it, don't go."

The next day, she assures her father she's both.

FOUR

Don't fuck it up.

Ray promised to make it work. And he doesn't break promises. Not in his wildest dreams did he ever imagine Stephanie would ever give him—them—another shot, let alone right after he lost his job and his pension. Once those were taken from him, he didn't have any dreams left at all.

Ray picks up some extra dough working private security gigs. And when Joe Wallace, his best friend, brother in arms, and former partner at the Bronx's Forty-First, put the word out, cops from all over the country kicked in to help keep Ray afloat for a while.

But in Ray's mind, the chance to propose to Stephanie again is worth whatever it costs, and Joe assures him Costa Rica—where Joe had proposed to his wife, Mary—is the place for Ray to lock in a yes.

"As long you don't fuck it up," Joe says.

"No chance," Ray assures him, and within days, he has the whole trip planned—or so he thinks.

Dawn's first rays peek over the horizon and bathe the secluded cove along the Costa Rican coast. Ocean ripples caress the shore, infusing salty notes into the dreamy, fragrant scent of Reina de la Noche, or Queen of the Night, that hangs in the balmy air.

Ray and Stephanie stroll barefoot, hand in hand, she wrapped in a flowing, sleek sarong, while he wears an open white casual button-down and NYPD shorts.

A homecoming feeling sweeps over Ray.

It feels like the first time I ever held her hand, he thinks. *Perfect.*

And their conversation still flows easily and naturally as they share intimate details of their time apart. The mutual trust to divulge such intimacies without judgment is one of the things they love about each other. And though it goes unsaid, each thank God the other didn't sleep with anyone else during the year they were apart.

They stroll and talk for over an hour, lost in the beauty of the surroundings and the comfort of being together—a sweet dream after a yearlong nightmare. And the look on Stephanie's face when, up ahead, she sees a guide awaiting them with two majestic horses . . . Unforgettable.

On their first date, Stephanie told Ray she hoped to own a horse someday, how she loved to ride ever since riding a pony at a local fair in Astoria when she was six. How, from that day on, her father set aside money from each paycheck so he could take her across the RFK Bridge to Randalls Island for lessons at the New York City Riding Academy. But how she hadn't ridden in several years, given her schedule. How much she missed it.

A perfect start to a perfect day, Ray thinks, confident. *Don't fuck it up.*

Between the lush rainforest and cheerful songs of the keel-billed toucans and scarlet macaws, their half-hour-long horseback ride seems to pass in a heartbeat. And the magnificent destination rivals the journey.

Steam rises off the thermal hot spring's vivid, teal-blue water while lavender and rose incense burn on stones framing the outer wall. Beyond, the view of a lush valley and coffee plantation is hypnotic and serene. And while Ray and Stephanie cuddle and soak in the healing waters, he serenades her with an off-key but charming version of Harry Warren's and Al Dubin's timeless classic, "I Only Have Eyes for You." They'd always loved the golden oldies.

Yet, even while wooing the love of his life, in stark contradiction to the song's message, Ray's eyes sharpen as they scan the dense jungle. A former marine and New York City cop to the bone, he's not a guy who relaxes easily. It's in his DNA.

Still, he says, "Sounds great," when after lunch Stephanie tells him how much she'd love to go to a nature reserve—another chance for a full one-eighty escape from city life and to be in the jungle among towering trees and beautiful plants and flowers and to see hundreds of wild animals, exotic birds, and insects in their natural habitat.

And therein lies the problem for Ray: it's *their* natural habitat.

Eight years in the Marine Corps—four of which were as a member of the elite branch of the United States Special Operations Command known as the Marine Raiders—peg Ray among the most skilled fighters on the planet.

The Marine Raiders were made famous by their World War II predecessors, whose divisions carried out some of that conflict's most dangerous amphibious and guerrilla operations. The actions of these elite fighters laid the foundation for the training and tactics of today's Special Forces.

But there was a vibe in jungles and forests that Ray found uniquely threatening. These are places where his and his unit's survival demanded that each soldier's critical high-alert senses operated at peak performance, often for twenty-four or more hours straight.

Nothing could be truer than when Ray and his unit had been on a nighttime tree-jumping training mission. "It's one of the toughest and scariest you'll be on," the commanding officer said moments before they dove out the back of the C-17 into the pitch black and parachuted deep into the rainforest along the Amazon River, where each then used a rope to rappel down from the forest canopy.

Unfortunately, when they hit the canopy, enemy troops were lying in wait—troops of black howler monkeys. Considered the loudest animal on earth, their howls can carry for over three miles, and they attack if they feel trapped or threatened.

Within seconds, it was monkey madness and a precursor for what lurked below: Pumas. Jaguars. Deadly poison dart frogs. Bullet ants. Foot-long Peruvian giant yellow-leg centipedes with a pair of modified legs that can penetrate human flesh and muscle, then inject a heinous toxic brew. And if those weren't horrifying enough, there was always the venomous Brazilian wandering spider and the dreaded fer-de-lance—one of the world's deadliest and most vicious pit vipers.

The experience left a lasting mark on Ray, what he calls PTJD, post-traumatic jungle disorder.

"It's one thing to be up against other human beings," he would say on the rare occasions he talks about it. "But it's a whole other bag when you trespass the home of lethal wild animals and insects that are far more perfectly adapted to it. And though we're not in their natural food chain, if they feel threatened, most often you never see them coming."

It's a scar he's never told Stephanie about.

They're about a mile into the nature reserve when their armed guide motions them to stop and be quiet.

The man points upward. Soaring high above, with a seven-foot wing-span, deep gray feathers, white underside, and black plumage around its neck, is a majestic harpy eagle.

"They are the largest of all eagles," the guide whispers. "Highly skilled predators. We call them flying wolves or jaguars of the canopy. And their talons . . ." From under his shirt, he pulls out a five-inch-long talon that hangs around his neck. "Bigger than grizzly bears'," he says. "And precision-made to crunch bone and rip apart flesh."

They watch with rapt attention, in awe of the eagle's stealthy agility through the forest at speeds up to fifty miles an hour, when in the blink of an eye, it dive-bombs, snatches a sloth out of a tree, and disappears above the canopy—its entire mission over in three seconds. The sloth never saw it coming.

For Stephanie, the deeper in they go, the more exhilarating—for Ray, the more nerve-racking. The latest downpour, the third in the last half hour, ushers in intense, rain-swept scents of everything from the myriad of exotic plants and vegetation to the drenched soil and decaying

wood. "Breathe," the guide says, and he takes a deep breath as they journey on. "It's the aroma of life."

Stephanie deeply inhales and ambles beside the guide to admire a
cluster of spiderwebs glistening like diamonds. But Ray, the unease in his
eyes mirrored in his measured steps, drops and rolls when a ten-inch-tall
squirrel monkey, hanging by its tail from a branch, snatches the NYPD
cap off his head, only to have it screech and fling the cap back in his face.

Ray's a guy more comfortable in a concrete jungle than a real one.

Several hours later it's smooth sailing as the captain pilots their catamaran
past their hotel—a luxurious hillside oasis overlooking the Pacific—the
magic-hour sky, a psychedelic explosion of vivid, breathtaking colors.
Ray's plans are back on track, and serenity finally settles in on his face
and in his eyes.

Stephanie lies in his arms—their faces happy, a lightweight Borucan
quilt draped over them. *Now we're talking*, Ray thinks. But while she marvels at the hotel's stunning setting, Ray slides his cell out from under his
thigh and taps into the NYPD website—not a guy who can fully detach.

When they're back in their suite, Ray realizes how much he has
missed her touch and taste, the perfume of her hair, the feel of her body
against his.

What an incredible day, he reflects as he buttons his shirt and Stephanie slips an elegant dress over her tastefully sexy lingerie. And from the
clothes strewn about their ocean-view suite and chaotically messy bed-
ding, it's not hard to imagine what kind of crazy hot sex happened here.
It defines another quality Ray loves about Stephanie: she's as confident
and comfortable in her own skin as he is in his.

Tonight's going to be better than perfect, he assures himself as he heads
into the living room and calls the maître d' to confirm his special dinner
requests, especially the one for which he shelled out a hefty up-front
tip. The one that requires the barista to separately brew Stephanie's favorite coffee blend: half Costa Rica 95, a quarter Indian Cauvery, and
a quarter Vietnamese Robusta. Ray knows just how it's done. While
they were married, he mixed the beans himself and brewed them for her

every morning. It was one thing he always got right, and he still dreams of one day opening a coffee bar featuring his homemade blends and the half a dozen or so that his mom taught him.

Twenty minutes later, dressed to the nines, they get on the elevator.

In awe of how beautiful she looks, Ray steals another head-to-toe glance. And as the doors close, he silently vows, *This time I'm getting it all right*—unaware he's about to plunge down an invisible dark shaft toward Wilbur Bailey.

FIVE

Wilbur Bailey has long been a tree-hugging, Patagonian sand frog–saving, Nissan Leaf–driving, New Green Deal–supporting kind of guy. Which makes it hard to understand how he ended up working for Amco Oil. Therein lies the human truth: we have far less control over our lives than we like to think. It's a truth that Wilbur knows all too well. A truth steeped and hardened by a series of devastating winds of change that blew his meticulously planned life way off course.

Fresh off the thirty-eighth birthday party his wife threw for him the night before, Wilbur stood atop a hill and gazed at the 250 colossal turbines spread across his sixty-thousand-acre wind farm—master of all he surveyed.

How lucky I am, he repeated to himself, an effort to fully grasp the realization that he was living his version of the American dream: not only was he married to his high school sweetheart, he was the cofounder of Zephyr, a California company on the cutting edge of wind power.

To top it all off, he and his wife had decided to have a baby, and they were less than a year away from being able to buy a cozy dream house somewhere in Marin County with a stunning view of the Golden Gate Bridge. Things couldn't be better.

But just two months later, the rug was pulled out from under them.

Zephyr was driven into Chapter 11 bankruptcy when Wilbur's best friend and business partner was charged by the Department of Justice with fraud and misappropriation of funds.

It didn't take long for Zephyr's investors to run for the hills, and within a matter of weeks, Chapter 11 morphed into Chapter 7 and put everyone in the company on the unemployment line.

Worse, the stench of scandal snared Wilbur in its web, making it impossible for him to find another suitable job, especially in a tough economy.

By forty, crushed under the weight of debt and out of options, he filed for personal bankruptcy, and he and his wife were forced to move back in with his mother, who lived in a small rural community outside Eugene, Oregon.

Several weeks later, out went rug number two when his mom died of a heart attack.

How unbefitting it is when tragedy piles onto insult and indignity, he brooded.

But it didn't end there. Less than a year later, a week before his forty-first birthday, Azrael, the Angel of Death, arrived to pull rug number three. His wife suffered a ruptured aneurysm attributed to a rare form of cancer.

An ambulance rushed her to the hospital, where surgeons stopped the bleeding.

"There's a good chance she'll be able to go home in about three weeks," the lead surgeon said to Wilbur. "But given her type of cancer, it's tough to say how long she has left. I'm sorry."

It's a testament to Wilbur's mental endurance that he was still standing after the multiple knockout blows and mounting medical bill jabs.

It can't get worse, right? he silently asked the heavens as he left the hospital and walked through the parking lot back to his car—lost in the pain and darkness of seeing his wife suffer so horribly.

"Wilbur?" a woman's voice called out.

Startled, he wheeled around to see Janice, an old college acquain-
tance. "My God, it's been . . ."

A glum smile crossed her lips, and she nodded at the hospital. "My
daughter is being treated here."

Over a glass of Veggie Vitality at a nearby Jamba, Wilbur and Janice
commiserated on the trials and tribulations they had been through since
last seeing each other in college. But he had no idea that when they went
their separate ways, Janice made a call to her cousin, who then called a
job recruiter he knew well.

The calls led to a job interview for Wilbur, one in which his geo-
logical, technological, and financial analysis skills could be put to use.

From the start, the offer from Amco Oil included full medical ben-
efits for him and his wife, an offer he knew he must seriously consider
even though the prospect of working for the company singed every fiber
of his being and accepting the position would require them to move to
Houston, Texas.

It all boiled down to desperation, he rationalized. The job enabled
him to take the best care of his wife, and that's all that mattered. But if
life's tragic lessons taught him one thing, it was that desperation plays
by the rules for the first half. After that, all bets are off.

His wife valiantly battled and hung in there for just shy of a year.
When she finally let go, Wilbur didn't know if he could go on.

The job kept a roof over his head and food on the table, but he
spent his days in the darkness of lonely solitude amid gloomy ruminating thoughts, toiling in the belly of the beast, the devil's workshop.

And there was work still to be done.

It's a perfect spring day. Not a cloud in the sky.

Hard to believe it's been five months since she died, Wilbur silently
laments, sitting in his yard.

Tick tock. Tick tock. Tick tock.

He flips halfway through an old-school composition notebook
boldly labeled VOLUME FIVE and tapes an article titled "FOUR TIME-
TESTED TACTICS TO TACKLE CHRONOPHOBIA" onto the next open page,

opposite another article titled "SIX CONFLICTING SIGNS YOU HAVE COGNITIVE DISSONANCE."

Wilbur and his wife always loved this time of year, when they would walk and ride their bikes through Marin County's hills and valleys, where millions of flowers delivered an olfactory and kaleidoscopic blast. And the springtime air was crisp but with hints of the impending summer winds.

Though the emotional pain of her death has begun to recede, spending his forty-second birthday alone last week was dreadful. He drilled into his mind the "EIGHT FOOLPROOF WAYS TO DITCH DEVASTATION" and plans to take a walk next week through the Houston Botanic Garden, hoping it might renew his spirit.

But instead, when the next week arrives, he finds himself inside a cold and barren room, deep within Texas Medical Center's Imaging and Radiology unit gripped with fear while he lies prone, strapped to the narrow exam table as it slides into the CT scan tunnel.

A crushing onslaught of thoughts floods into Wilbur's brain from all sides, though none seem to matter. In his gut, he knows this killer is here to snatch his final rug.

A half hour later, his doctor, Alan Lobel, with numerous CT scans lit up on the wall behind him, delivers the devastating news. And with his fears confirmed, Wilbur goes from terrified to broken and sobs uncontrollably.

Wilbur hides the cancer diagnosis from his few friends and colleagues and spends most of his time in search of a meaning for his life and lost in thoughts of dying.

Tick tock. Tick tock. Tick tock.

A couple of days after the diagnosis, as he sits alone on a park bench staring at the lone duck on the lake, it strikes him that he doesn't have a bucket list. Even if he did, he wonders if he would care about it.

Round and round . . .

. . . Until a mischievous seven-year-old screams nearby, scaring a squirrel up a tree, while his mother, not far behind him, has her head buried in her cell phone as she swipes away.

Irritated by the intrusion, Wilbur wheels around and shoots the kid a heavy dose of stink eye.

"Stupid kid," he mutters.

But his irritation rises to shock and anger when the kid scoops up a handful of rocks and hurls them at the squirrel. And if that's not bad enough, his shock and anger soars to flat-out indignation when his mother—after she watches him sling another handful—smiles at him and goes back to her phone.

"Hurting animals . . . One of three prepubescent signs your kid's a serial killer," Wilbur says, loud enough to make sure she hears him.

"Really?" she says, disdain in her voice palpable. She struts over to her son, takes him by the arm, and turns to Wilbur as she guides him away. "I'll make sure he starts with you. Nutjob."

Aghast, Wilbur watches them go but soon retreats to the dark cave of his mind and the lone duck on the lake. Five seconds later, a deep, gravelly Texas voice rings out from behind him.

"You're right about the animal thing, Wilbur."

Startled, Wilbur's eyes dart about their sockets as he tries to pin down the voice. If not for the mention of his name, he'd wonder if it's the kid's father, there to kick his ass.

But the second Phil sits down next to him, Wilbur's head slumps. "Oh Christ."

Phil turns and stares at him. "I'm not sure what that means, Mr. Bailey."

"You don't scare me, Agent Dancourt. You can't. Not anymore."

"And what about Mika Salko?" Phil says. "You no longer afraid of him either?" The question gives Wilbur pause. "You should be. He's a threat, not only to you but to this country. You know that."

Wilbur sighs. "What do you want from me?"

"I want what you *should* want—to do the right thing. Help us put Salko away. And I believe you've got the courage and moral fortitude to do it. It's why we chose you. Why *I* chose you."

The comment strikes a chord, and Wilbur draws in a deep breath. "You're right, I should. I do."

Phil leans back, sensing he's as close as he's ever been to having Wilbur in his grasp.

"We'll need copies of confidential files and emails, US and foreign bank and accounting records . . . the thousands of secret correspondences that detail what goes unreported. From where it comes to where it goes. Everything."

Wilbur turns and looks at him. But his eyes are distant. Detached. Somewhere far from here. A slight smile crosses his lips, and his face softens.

"Gimme two weeks," he tells Phil, unaware he's on a life-and-death ride aboard an unseen, out-of-control runaway train barreling down invisible rails toward Raymond Dawson.

SIX

Phil's unable to pin it down, but something about the abrupt shift in Wilbur's demeanor at the park leaves him uneasy. Something beyond the stranglehold a terminal diagnosis can have on a person's psyche. This was something different. This was something beyond a lack of fear. Something reminiscent of the feeling he had the first time he met Mika Salko.

Most Americans diligently and honestly fill out their tax returns after they dredge the pond for every penny of write-offs and deductions. Why not, if the law allows it. And they shudder at the thought of receiving a notice from the IRS that informs them they'd like to have a chat. Anyone who has ever received one has the same reaction—*Oh shit!*

Once the IRS is in seize mode, you might as well roll all your shit up in a rug and leave it at the curb for pickup. And, as Phil said, it's nothing compared to what eventually happens if you try to fuck them. A cavalry of heavily armed IRS revenue agents will bust through your door while you're taking your morning piss. All those on the receiving end of this also have the same reaction—*Oh fuck!*

But Phil can attest that Mika Salko is not like everyone else.

Mika Salko couldn't care less.

Everything about him—from his clothes and the set of his jaw to his attitude and his cologne—reeks of *Don't fuck with me*. To drive the point home, Amco Oil keeps a separate company bank account overseas for the sole purpose of paying off the customary multimillion-dollar fines that keep the IRS off its back for another year.

Best of all, Amco writes the fines off as a business expense. God bless the IRS!

It's also not Amco's first tap dance through the IRS audit minefield. Salko's second-in-command—Alex Zuyev, whom Salko met at Yale—oversees an army of accountants and lawyers, who for the sixth time in five years have created an endless labyrinth that makes IRS heads spin—with Zuyev often boasting that the leaky toilet on the second floor gives him more of a headache.

Despite Zuyev's bravado, or perhaps because of it, Phil senses he's a weak link. And he's not the only one to think so.

From the day Salko met Zuyev at a Yale Bulldogs game . . .

"Holy shit," Zuyev said to himself when three rows in front of him, he saw a stunning Russian model he knew.

She first arrived in the States a year ago. A family friend asked him to look out for her in New York City and help her settle in. Zuyev happily obliged, and it wasn't long before he made several advances. She thought he was a nice guy but always claimed she was already seeing someone. He still texts her from time to time to see how she's doing.

"Holy shit," he said again when she kissed the guy sitting next to her: Mika Salko.

As an aspiring lawyer and financial whiz, Zuyev knew who Mika Salko was. Seemed like everyone on campus did. And he was smart enough to know that a ride on Salko's coattails could gain him entry into the über-exclusive upper echelon. So when, at the end of the game, the crowd started to file out, Zuyev bid his time and sidled up to them on the stairs, feigning in Russian what a nice surprise it was to run into her.

Before long he and Salko realized they had similar backgrounds. Zuyev was also the product of immigrant parents with deep ties to Mother Russia. And though his family didn't play in the same financial ballpark as Salko's, they were at least in the same league—with a lavish Central Park West condo spanning the building's top two floors.

Right out of the gate, Zuyev looked up to him. Countless times he vied for an invitation to parties on the Salko family yacht, *Gold Mine*, or to one of Mika's weekend getaways to Vegas on a private jet or in a leased Ferrari. And Zuyev savored the endless supply of models who didn't make Salko's cut but still hung around and happily settled for him as his best friend.

But silently Salko didn't hold Zuyev in the same high regard. What he dug most about him is also what he loathed most about him—that Zuyev looked up to him, not out of admiration but out of deep-seated insecurity, an insecurity Salko saw as a chronic character flaw.

Despite Zuyev's legal and financial prowess, Salko struggled to over-look this aspect of his character when he later considered him for the position of Amco's president and chief operating officer. But in the end, Salko figured this loathsome trait also made Zuyev the perfect yes-man he could trust to watch his back.

None of Salko's or Zuyev's past bullshit matters to Phil, though, as he speeds past Amco's chiseled stone monument sign and makes his way across its vast campus to Salko's office, where he and Zuyev await his ar-rival. Two weeks had passed with no word from Wilbur. And now they can't find him. Time to go all in.

Salko's office is quintessential CEO: huge, and richly appointed with designer furniture, accessories, and expensive fine art. In the corner, a mock-up of the Rio Bravo refinery is extraordinary in its detail. Above it, a digital map displays Amco's active oil wells—each portrayed by a classic red oil well icon, below which the number of barrels pumped continually climbs like the number of smoking deaths.

Across the way, among the photos on the armoire is a prominent one of Salko with Vladimir Putin. There used to be another which included his wife, an attractive Jewish girl from New Jersey. But she divorced him after accusing him of having an affair. Salko denied it, not because he wasn't having one, but because he was having several, and no longer cared what she thought. She packed up ten suitcases of shoes and clothes and blew out of there, back to Jersey, with another seven full of cash.

The office door opens and in struts Phil in his navy IRS-CI windbreaker.

He stops and wheels around to Logan, the thirty-year-old brick-house Amco security guard on his tail.

"Not on the first date," Phil says. "Back the fuck up."

Logan glares at him, but with a nod from Salko, he complies.

"This is bullshit," Salko says.

"So is this," Phil says, and holds up a copy of Amco's latest tax return. He flips a few pages to a highlighted line item—TOTAL TAX DUE: $0.00—and hands it to Salko.

"It's an error," Salko says after a cursory look, and hands it to Zuyev.

"Not exactly," Phil says. "The whole return's a fake and was traced to Wilbur Bailey's computer."

Salko's brow furrows. "Who's Wilbur Bailey?"

"Works for you. You don't know him?"

"We have several thousand employees. Sorry if I don't know them all by name."

"He's in R and D," Zuyev says. "Came over from Zephyr when they went under."

Salko shoots him a look. "Zephyr? They made windmills. What the fuck is he doing here?"

"Think you call it Environmental Impact and Investment Analysis," Phil says.

"Our tax for the quarter was one hundred large. I signed off on it," Salko says as he takes a seat at his desk.

"And it was paid," Zuyev says.

"Not exactly," Phil says, and hands each of them a second set of documents. "Wire confirmations—also compliments of Mr. Bailey."

Salko and Zuyev leaf through the pages. Each of the fifty wires is for $2 million sent to fifty different shell companies with the acronym IRS.

"Do a lot of business with Idle River Steam in the Balkans?" Phil asks.

Salko tosses the documents in the trash. "Never heard of them."

"Neither have we. How 'bout India Rubber and Steel?"

Salko's and Zuyev's blank stares make it clear they've never heard of them either.

"Seems Wilbur Bailey took a page from your playbook. The hundred mil of your money—or should I say, *our* money—was routed to fifty offshore shell companies, which along with Mr. Bailey, are in the wind."

Twenty minutes later, the security door into Amco's Research and Development Division opens, and in flood a dozen heavily armed, tactically dressed, IRS-CI police, followed by Phil, Salko, and Zuyev.

Stunned assistants in the maze of cubicles and executives in glass-walled offices stop what they are doing and look on as Phil and his team beeline for the one office with its blinds drawn and door closed.

Phil holds his badge up to the employees. "Special Agent Phillip Dancourt—IRS."

The lead officer knocks on the door. "Wilbur Bailey! Federal Agents! Open the door and come out with your hands in the air."

After ten seconds with no response, sound, or any sign of movement, Phil nods to him and he slides a thin metal filament into the door's lock, steps back, and . . . *BANG!*

Except for the five laptops hardwired to each other on the desk and to a server on the floor, it's a typical executive office, though devoid of any personal touches beyond the ponytail palm sitting on the armoire in a biodegradable fiber pot.

The officers bag and tag what they need while Phil rifles through Wilbur's desk, which he finds empty save for an envelope in the top center drawer.

He pulls out the enclosed document and stares at it in disbelief. Under the Amco Oil letterhead, it reads "From the desk of Wilbur Bailey," and across the page, in big handwritten letters above a smiley face, is the word *ADIOS!*

SEVEN

How could I have not seen this coming? pounds through Phil's head. *No one to blame but myself.*

Never has he had such difficulty connecting the dots. Never had he so badly misread and underestimated a target confidential informant. Never had a case he oversaw had such broad personal and political ramifications. Never had a case caused him to question his judgment. Never had he sat on a gut feeling before.

I knew something wasn't right that day at the park. Damn.

Never had a case caused him as much agita.

The urge to suck in an unfiltered Camel grips his neck as he strides into his office and plops into his chair.

"Thank God," he mutters as he reaches into the bottom desk drawer, grabs a fresh Banana Nut Bread cartridge from the box, loads it in the vape's chamber, and fires.

Phil's your classic hard-pounding, beef-eating, chain-smoking, Crown Victoria–driving kind of guy. Upon first meeting, you might think he's a good ole boy, unsophisticated and boisterous, especially after a few beers.

But that presumption would be a mistake. Underneath the good-ole-boy exterior is a caring, thoughtful, and intelligent guy with

an unshakable loyalty to his family, friends, and others who have posi-
tively impacted his life.

Born and raised in a blue-collar Houston suburb, Phil was always a
bit brawny beyond his years. His mom and dad raised him well—she a
secretary at a Houston real estate firm, and he a beloved local mechanic.

"He's a good man" is the compliment his parents often receive about
Phil from other long-standing members at their local Evangelical Baptist
Church, where they still never miss a Sunday—often praying for Jesus
to free their son from the shackles of nicotine.

Nor could they have been prouder than when he was accepted to
Baylor. Phil, however, chose Texas A&M for their petroleum engineering program, with an eye toward a career in oil and gas—despite having
no real passion for either. Little did he know how fateful the decision
would be right out of the gate.

The eighteen buses, loaded with a thousand freshmen students, or "fish"
as they're known in Aggie lore, motored out of the Texas A&M campus
and set out on the one-hundred-mile drive to the Lakeview Methodist
Conference Center—a 1,300-acre recreational retreat in the Piney Woods
region of East Texas where, for the past seventy years, Aggie fish gather for
their first Aggie tradition: a three-day orientation known as Fish Camp.

He couldn't see her face when he stepped off the shuttle bus, but
still, his eyes were drawn to her among the hundreds of other freshmen
who were already there. Her long dark brown hair and olive-toned skin.
Her great legs.

But when she turns around and looks at no one in particular . . .

Man . . . She is beautiful.

The crook in her nose. Her full lips and those big brown eyes. It
was as if she was the first girl he'd ever seen, and the hundreds of other
freshmen were invisible. Sure, he had dated other girls he thought were
pretty and sexy. But her . . .

Way out of my league.

Phil was locked in a grip of emotions unlike any he'd ever felt before.

Man . . . She is beautiful.

Once everyone was seated inside the conference center, one of the upperclassmen counselors welcomed the class to their first day of life in Aggieland and proclaimed they were now officially a part of the Texas A&M family.

"Focus, Phil," he reminded himself.

But no matter how hard he tried, his eyes kept drifting back to her, several rows ahead, and his mind was standing room only with a myriad of thoughts about what she might be like.

Man . . . She is beautiful.

Focus, Phil.

An hour later, when the counselor concluded his speech, he and a handful of other upperclassmen broke the class up, first into groups of a hundred and twenty, and eventually into groups of ten to fifteen.

Over the next couple of days, Phil saw her maybe half a dozen times, but each time, it didn't seem like the right time to approach. Or maybe it was nerves. Every time he saw her, his heart started to pound.

The three days flew by, and as his bus pulled out of the conference center, he thought he'd never see her again. That he would never even know her name. But an hour and fifty minutes later, back on the Texas A&M campus, Phil disembarked and stopped cold when he saw her come out of the bus two back from his. His heart felt like it was going to pound its way out of his chest, and he knew it was now or never. He grabbed his duffel bag from the cargo bay and hustled over.

"Hi. Let me help you with that," he said and slid her carry-on out from her bus's bay and pulled up the arm.

"Thank you," she said.

"I'm Phil. I wanted to say hello to you every day at Fish Camp, but ahh . . ."

She could see Phil was nervous, but from her radiant smile, and the glint in those big, beautiful brown eyes, it was clear she, too, felt the spark.

"I saw you there too," she said, her Colombian accent slight, with a distinct Orinoquía region edge. She extended her hand. "Lorena Mitchell. Nice to meet you."

What are the odds?

Later that night, Chimy's, a raucous Aggie favorite, was packed as usual. But Phil and Lorena were at the bar absorbed in each other, laughing while they shared one of Chimy's famous chimichangas and sipped on margaritas.

"I'm going to be a prosecutor," Lorena confidently said. "With a major in criminal justice."

Phil's eyes lit up. "Me too," he said.

First thing in the morning, Phil submitted the required forms and switched his major to criminal justice: a surefire way, he thought, for them to study and spend more time together. And it worked.

Before they knew it, they were spending more time together than apart. And that first time she came over to his place for dinner . . .

The moment he opened the door, the sweet aroma of ripe bananas, cinnamon, and toasted walnuts enveloped him like a warm quilt.

"Hope you like banana nut bread," she said. "Made it myself."

"If it tastes half as good as it smells . . ." Phil said and kissed her. "I hope *you* like grilled ribeye," he said as they headed inside, confident his one culinary skill was sure to impress her.

"Yum," she said. "Love it. Especially the spinalis." Phil hesitated, a dead giveaway he had no idea what that was. "You know," she said, "the juicy, tender part just above the eye of the primal—with the fantastic marbling."

"Yeah," Phil said, and smiled. "The spinalis."

Lorena laughed. "Sorry, I couldn't resist," she said. "Growing up, I spent many summers and vacations in Colombia with my grandfather, a fifth-generation cattle rancher."

Still, she was impressed when Phil cooked the steaks perfectly. But most of all, she loved the thought and effort he put in to make their dinner fun and romantic.

And Phil couldn't deny what he later told his mom: "Her banana nut bread is all git-out."

The relationship quickly blossomed into love. Phil thrived on her passion, her tenacity, and her determination—qualities instilled in her by her parents. He often joked, though, that it was her eye for the perfect cut of beef and guarded, family-secret steak rub that sealed the deal.

But what snuck up on him, what he didn't anticipate, was how much he loved his criminal justice courses, and his grades reflected it. The university career fair turned him on to federal jobs—most notably one at Houston's IRS headquarters, where his exceptional ability with numbers could be put to good use.

Phil graduated in the top 5 percent of their class, and when the IRS offered him the job later that day, he jumped at the opportunity. And if that wasn't impressive enough, Lorena graduated in the top 2 percent and was accepted into Texas's number one ranked law school—the South Texas College of Law in Houston.

By the time her final semester began, she had five offers from Houston's most prestigious law firms, and she settled on Watkins, Smith, Garcia, and Jones LLP, an international firm with deep Texas roots, where she specialized in oil and gas law.

They tied the knot shortly thereafter, and their life together could not have gotten off to a more perfect start: in love; two well-paying, burgeoning careers; a cool converted loft in Houston with skyline views; and a new, top-of-the-line charcoal grill and offset smoker on their rooftop deck, compliments of Lorena's grandfather.

The best part arrived a couple of years later—a beautiful baby girl they named Emmi.

It took some juggling, with busy schedules that got steadily busier, but they made it work. Because *they* worked. And their worlds were on cruise control.

So they thought.

The years flew by, and Emmi flourished. And for her seventh birthday, Phil, Lorena, Emmi, and their good friends, another couple whose daughter is Emmi's best friend, took off on a weeklong trip to Florida, a trip they planned for over a year.

The first three days at Disney World were a blast, and they made the drive from Orlando to Miami in under four hours and checked into a beachside hotel around 7:00 p.m. After dinner, Lorena ran off to visit her old college roommate, who had moved there shortly after graduation.

"I'll be back in an hour or two," she said, and kissed Phil goodbye.

But less than six miles from the hotel, on a lazy boulevard, Lorena's path intersected head-on with a kid blissed out on weed and heroin.

What are the odds?

A month or so later, Phil eighty-sixed the unfiltered Camels for a banana-nut-bread-flavored e-cig. For his parents, it was an answered prayer. For Phil, a tether to a promised life together. A tether to keep him from falling off the cliff and into the black hole punched through the fabric of his and Emmi's lives.

Being a single parent is never easy. Even more so when it's thrust on you in the blink of an eye. But Phil dug in deep, and with help from friends and family, he remained steadfast in his determination to provide Emmi with the best possible childhood.

All the while, he built up his stats and ascended the IRS ranks to become one of the top special agents in their Criminal Investigation Division—each a step onto, or further down, a tortuous road of truths and deceptions to the intersection of Dawson and Bailey.

EIGHT

The first hit of Banana Nut Bread brings immediate relief, and Phil settles in behind his desk for the monumental task at hand. With Wilbur flush with millions, finding him will be like trying to find half a needle in a global-sized haystack—the odds are slim to none.

But Phil can't deny finding him is now personal, and he sucks the cartridge dry while scanning footage of Wilbur taken from a camera inside Dr. Lobel's office. Two more vape cartridges are spent as Phil sifts through hundreds of notes and transcripts archived from the first time he and Wilbur spoke to the moment of the raid—scouring anything that might provide a clue to Wilbur's current whereabouts.

"He say anything about taking a trip or his own life?" Phil asks the nice couple in their sixties who live across the street from Wilbur. It was Phil's fifth investigative interview of the day.

Both nervously shake their heads and look at Wilbur's house. Unmarked sedans out front bear the Department of the Treasury seal, and crime scene tape stretches across the front door. Inside the garage, crime investigators dust Wilbur's Nissan Leaf for prints.

"Anyone see him here recently? Paid with cash." Phil says to the dry cleaner's anxious owner and employees as they stare at Wilbur's newly printed IRS wanted poster. Next to his photo is a litany of crimes ranging from tax fraud, wire fraud, and grand theft to conspiracy to defraud the United States government. Down below, in bold print: REWARD $5,000,000.

But one by one, the owner and employees shake their heads—another dead end, as are the day's next twenty interviews. No one has seen Wilbur recently or has any clue where he might be.

Exhausted, Phil's eyes reflect the fog of war that blankets his mind, and he takes a seat on the same bench where he last met up with Wilbur, contemplating his next move. At this late hour, the park is desolate save for the lone duck on the lake, visible in the lamplight. He's captivated by its movements; so effortless, as if it didn't have a care in the world—a paradigm he longs for but knows will never be.

It's just shy of midnight when his boss's text pings his phone: "MY OFFICE 8 AM," it demands.

Everyone knows that shit only rolls one way. With Wilbur off the radar and Phil's boss John Callahan's shot as the state's finance chief on the line, the mountain of shit barreling Phil's way gains momentum.

Callahan has long been a political animal, careful over the years to slather extra suck-up sauce on Texas's governor, Roy Hargrove. He knows people who've known Hargrove going back to his early days as a prosecutor, and as his popularity rose, so did the length of his coattails—coattails on which Callahan intends to hitch a ride. And Hargrove's bought into his hard-nosed approach.

Outside of three or four early missteps, most everything throughout Hargrove's gubernatorial term has gone according to plan, which is reflected in his high job approval numbers. And between the state's changing age demographic and the influx of New Yorkers and Californians, the TV talking heads and so-called pundits are already proclaiming the upcoming election to be a cakewalk for him.

But COVID-related shutdowns, illegal border crossings, and rising crime rates are taking a toll. According to recent polls, the gap between Hargrove and his Republican challenger—a woman from Plano—has narrowed to percentage points within the margin of error.

It's a tough pill to swallow for a guy whose sights are set on the White House, a guy who ran on being tough on crime—and not just murders, rapes, and robberies, but also tax cheats.

"After all," he says to a gaggle of reporters at his latest campaign stop, "the victims of tax cheats are not merely Texans but every hardworking American citizen. God bless Texas. And may God continue to bless the United States of America."

With climate change at the forefront of the world's consciousness, Callahan knows a scandal involving Amco Oil could snowball into global headlines. And he's not about to let a good crisis go to waste—or take him down. He's IRS to the bone, and the red ink that flows through his veins throbs with the IRS motto hanging on the wall behind his desk: WE'RE NOT HAPPY TILL YOU'RE NOT HAPPY. And at 8:00 a.m., in his fifth-floor floor corner office, where he glares at Phil, he's not happy.

"What do you mean you don't know where he is?"

"As in, 'I'm not aware of his whereabouts,'" Phil says flippantly.

"Don't fuck me with smart-ass bullshit, Phil. It's a fucking disaster. *Your* fucking disaster!" Callahan says, infuriated.

"I'll find him."

"Damn right you will. 'Cause if this goes further south, the media will have a field day. And there'll be an internal investigation, which we both don't need. Understand?"

Phil nods and starts for the door.

"Phil . . ."

When he turns back to face him, Callahan drops the hammer. "You find Bailey by Friday, close the case, and this office is yours when I'm gone. Finally get your wish to get off the field."

"Thank you, sir."

"No thanks yet. 'Cause if he's not back here by Friday, neither are you."

As Phil walks down the corridor, Callahan's ultimatum cuts to his core. Familiar dark thoughts barge in unannounced, as if they are old friends.

He's lost count of how many times, especially in the last few years, he's told himself it was time to get out.

Maybe Callahan's threat is a sign from above, he mulls over—a green light to finally cast the risks aside and take the leap of faith he covets.

If only I had faith, he laments. Not average, garden-variety faith. But real faith. Blind faith. *The kind Lorena had.* The kind that brings peace in knowing everything will be okay despite the realities right before your eyes that relentlessly dictate otherwise.

Round and round . . .

"I'd be lying if I told you the pressure to close the case didn't feel like a ghost pepper suppository," Phil says to the trainees, keenly aware, as were Callahan and Hargrove, of the need for this case to close with a good headline. Keenly aware that a bad one, in today's cancel culture, is a career-ender.

"It was the perfect storm," he says, loading the fresh Banana Nut Bread cartridge into the chamber. "Election a week out, the race too close to call. A high-profile bust is just what Hargrove and Callahan needed. But more importantly, total abject failure is just what they didn't."

Phil floods his lungs with Banana Nut Bread and levers the cloud as he takes a seat on the stool. "So, after five years it all came down to one question: Where's Wilbur?"

NINE

"Good evening," Wilbur says as he ambles into the elevator dressed in an uninspiring pale gray canvas outfit with matching shoes and floppy hat and holding a large tan-colored cup.

Ray and Stephanie can't help but notice his drab outfit but refrain from cringing as their olfactory nerves are assaulted by the pungent, earthy cologne that wafts in after him—a funky cross between wet dirt and peat moss.

"Hey."

"Hello."

They both offer up an obligatory smile.

"You both look very nice," he says and settles in across from them.

"Thank you," Stephanie says.

"You too," Ray adds.

Wilbur fidgets with his cup. Despite his polite smile, it's clear he's picked up on Ray's insincerity. But as if by a switch, his smile disappears and his eyes narrow and fixate on Ray's shirt.

Ray's posture straightens, and after a once-over of his shirt, he finds nothing wrong. "What?" he asks.

The tart tone in Ray's voice snaps Wilbur out of his mini-trance,

and Stephanie, sensing the elevator might hit a patch of turbulence, en-
twines her arm with Ray's.

"Your, ahh . . . Never mind. It's none of my business," Wilbur says.

"What?"

"No, really, it's not any—"

"Say it," Ray says, cutting him off, his tone elevated to authoritarian.

Wilbur flippantly points at Ray's shirt. "Your shirt . . . A quarter of
the fibers are acrylic."

Ray and Stephanie share a surprised glance, unsure of this guy's
mental stability.

"Excuse me?" Ray says.

"It's one of six insanely harsh fabrics every man should avoid. The
synthetic resins . . ." Wilbur waves his hand past his nose as if he can
smell them. "They're polymers of acrylic acid. Can lead to erectile dys-
function, depletion of sperm robust enough to make the journey—and
that's if you don't get cancer."

Ray leans into Stephanie and whispers, "And it's the *fabric* he thinks
is insane."

She playfully nudges him with her elbow to knock it off as Wilbur
carries on.

"Resistant to everything from moths to crude oil. Even sunlight."

Ray shoots his hand up. "Enough, pal."

After a brief awkward pause, Wilbur indicates his outfit. "Hundred
percent hemp and bamboo. Zero toxicity, and I must say . . . quite light,
airy, and durable." He holds up his cup. "Made from recycled lawn clip-
pings and dung paste."

Ray, again, leans in and whispers to Stephanie. "I hope they have
dung paste on the menu tonight."

She clenches her jaw to stifle her laugh, when without warning, the
bottom of Wilbur's cup falls out, and all three of them are splattered
with dark green wheatgrass and kale sludge.

"Oh my gosh! I'm sorry. So sorry," Wilbur says, horrified.

Ray's ready to pounce. "I oughta bust your ass you stupid—"

Stephanie grips Ray's arm. "Ray! A new beginning, remember?"

Ray holds his tongue as the elevator stops, and he and Stephanie head out.

"Please . . . It was an accident. I'll take care . . ." Wilbur says, his voice trailing off as the doors slide shut.

TEN

What are the odds? Ray silently steams as he and Stephanie make their way to the restaurant. *What are the odds I'd end up in the elevator with that jerk?*

Tonight's not the first time Ray has pondered such a question. Not by a long shot. It's dogged him ever since the night of his fourth birthday—a night that forever changed his life. A night, after which, he forever questions . . .

What are the odds?

Birthday nights were the one night of the year that Ray's mom, Elanor, a talented and resolute schoolteacher, and his dad, Michael, a detective first grade in the Bronx's Forty-First Precinct, allowed him to stay up past nine—which was closing in, thanks to a triple homicide two hours earlier that had Mike running late.

It didn't matter, though. Tonight was all about Ray and taking him to Serendipity to feast on a couple of foot-long hot dogs and fries and indulge in their decadent Insanity Sundae with some Frozen Hot Chocolate Stars. Yum!

It was a hair shy of 7:30 p.m. when they spilled out of their apartment and hustled over to Eighth Avenue to catch a cab for the trip up and across town to East Sixtieth Street. From the looks on their faces, it was tough to tell who was more excited, Ray or his parents.

The city swarmed with the usual rush-hour hustle, bustle, and traffic.

At this hour, cabs are tough to come by. After ten minutes, Mike finally flagged one down, only to have some creep hop into it first.

"Hey, jackass!" Mike shouted, and the guy flipped him off as the cab screeched away.

If only you knew I was a cop, Mike steamed.

"Oughta be jail time for jerks," he said to Elanor. "Ease the city's congestion, for sure."

"Wasn't meant to be," she said with a smile, and a moment later Mike flagged down another.

They piled in, and before Mike had the door closed, the driver pulled away.

The crosstown traffic was a crawl at best, and it took a half hour to zigzag up and over to East Fifty-Sixth Street. And as soon as they crossed Park Avenue, an accident at the end of the block brought them to a standstill.

"Let's bail," Mike said.

He paid the cabbie, and they hoofed it the rest of the way.

"Such a beautiful night," Elanor said as they strolled up Third Avenue.

It was one of those rare crystalline nights when heaven's brightest stars pierced through the city lights and a calming crisp autumn wind brimmed with the aroma of cinnamon and roasted chestnuts.

"Mmm . . . Smell that?" Elanor said.

And the joy in young Ray's rosy cheeks and the excited anticipation in his eyes couldn't have been more innocent and carefree as he hopped and skipped along, hand in hand with his mom and dad.

Straight out of the Academy, Mike was assigned to the Bronx's Forty-First.

Make no mistake, being a cop is a dangerous—potentially deadly— job no matter the precinct. But with a father who, at the time, was Chief of Department, few could understand how joining the perilous Forty-First was at the top of his list.

During the seventies, eighties, and nineties, much of the Bronx, especially areas of the South Bronx, descended into a perilous hellscape when a virulent outbreak of arson burned out many of the buildings that lined its streets. And as a malignant crack and heroin epidemic took hold, so did a rapid escalation of heinous violent crime. It made it one of the toughest and most dangerous areas in the country, and residents warned the unsuspecting: Don't let the trees fool you.

On average, the Bronx recorded roughly eighty thousand major felonies a year, and it bled city cash. When public sentiment finally wore down to the bone, law enforcement cracked down.

Still, the gears of change grind slowly, especially in lower-income areas like Hunts Point, Port Morris, Mott Haven, and Fordham, to name a few. Many, especially its youth, see it as social injustice. It's one of the reasons why so many in poor neighborhoods end up entangled in a web of law enforcement akin to a nightmarish stay at Hotel California—they can check out anytime they want, but they can never leave.

And in a never-ending loop, the unjust system is unduly seen as an injustice perpetrated by cops simply because they're the first to show up and take away your freedom, or your life.

In those days, the Forty-First sat on Simpson Street, in the heart of the urban decay, and by the time the neighborhood's death and mayhem reached its insidious peak, it was known as Fort Apache, and it, too, was a crumbling, decaying, dilapidated structure just as dangerous on the inside.

"I'm sure," Mike told his father when asked whether this was the right move. The Forty-First was where he wanted to be. Where he thought he could do the most good. Where he believed he could truly make a tangible, calculable difference and offer a renewed sense of hope to those residents who still had faith that better days were ahead.

Elanor began her career teaching eighth-grade math at Brearley, an exclusive all-girls private school. Everyone at the school, especially her students, loved her. And she loved them. But something was missing. Somewhere in her heart, and deep down in her gut, there was an unfulfilled calling.

"I'm sure," Elanor told the school's brass at the end of her first year.

Despite the sizable off-the-books bonus they offered her to stay, she left Brearley School to teach at the South Bronx's Banana Kelly High School—the academic equivalent of a journey to the far side of the sun.

The school's students, if they showed up, needed to move mountains to have any shot at life's so-called equal opportunities—opportunities that rarely materialized. Principals and staff blew through like the wind. By the midnineties, Banana Kelly had one of the highest dropout rates in the city and was forced to build a dormitory to house the sweeping number of homeless students.

Choosing to teach here was a gutsy, dangerous move, especially for a white woman who lived down South on Forty-Eighth Street between Ninth and Tenth Avenues—a section of Manhattan known as Hell's Kitchen, which was a tough enough place on its own.

One morning, after her hour-long, graffiti-strewn bus and subway commute, Elanor savored her last sip of coffee and went into the school's storage closet for a new box of chalk, only to find a student's stabbed and battered body.

Mike was assigned the case, and though there were no surveillance cameras, or students willing to talk, it didn't take long for him to catch the killer—or for him and Elanor to fall in love.

What are the odds?

ELEVEN

They were less than a block away from Serendipity when Mike spotted a guy holding up the pizza joint across the street.

No words were needed between him and Elanor. She was familiar with the look in his eyes and hustled Ray into the pharmacy behind them and warned other pedestrians nearby to do the same.

Mike darted across the street, his gun drawn, and he confronted the late-teenage perp as he barreled out the door.

"Police! Drop the gun!"

Pedestrians scattered, and with the jig up, the guy complied.

"Face down, on the ground now, hands behind your back," Mike ordered. Again, the guy complied, and Mike knelt on him and patted him down.

Several looky-loos in front of Mike suddenly screamed and ran, one of them yelling, "Gun!"

Mike looked behind him, and it was as if time stopped.

A terrified eight-year-old came out from behind the trash bin by the curb, his trembling hands gripped around a gun.

"Take it easy, kid," Mike said, holding up his hand.

BANG!

The bullet severed Mike's spine and ruptured his thoracic aorta, and in an instant, his life ended and Ray's and his mom's were indelibly changed.

Poof. Just like that.

The kid and his older brother . . . in the wind.

Mike's funeral came with all the pomp and circumstance reserved for royalty, which in the cop world, Mike was—from his early days as a novice beat cop who scored a record number of arrests to his rapid march to become one of NYPD's most decorated detectives.

Cops and firefighters from all five boroughs and Long Island converged on the city to pay tribute. Countless others who'd served with Mike in the Marines or knew him growing up or in college came in from out of state. The funeral procession was a mile long. And as the cortege made its way down New York City's streets, the imagery and sound of the sole trumpeter playing "Taps" and sixty bagpipes playing "Amazing Grace" behind a horse-drawn, flag-draped coffin was unforgettable.

"It wasn't Mike's nature to stand idly by when others needed help," his captain said in his eulogy. "No matter if he was on or off duty. No matter if his own life was on the line." He looked at young Ray and his mother in the front row. "We will forever be proud of your father, your husband, our brother."

The eulogies that followed were no less heart-wrenching. Especially those from other cops who had served with Mike in the Marines. One mentioned how, from an early age, Mike "heard the call"—a catchphrase that stuck with young Ray and is still used today about officers who join the force and those killed in the line of duty.

With each passing year, the Question bounced around Ray's head with greater speed and intensity, ensnaring him in an endless loop.

What are the odds?

What call did he hear?

From whom?

From where?

Would my father be alive if not for the call?

Would my father be alive if not for my birthday?
Would my father be alive if he hadn't been running late?
Would he be alive if that guy hadn't jumped into the first cab?
If the accident hadn't blocked the street?
If we hadn't walked the rest of the way?
Is it possible for a cop to be in the wrong place at the wrong time?
Isn't that the job?
Round and round . . .

In a bizarre twist, a year after Mike was killed, the Forty-First Pre-cinct moved from Simpson Street to Longwood Avenue, up the street from Longwood Preparatory Academy—formerly known as Banana Kelly High School.

Ray never spoke about the difficulties he and his mom endured with-out his father. He soon realized how blessed he was to have a mother as strong and loving as his. A woman who believed her son's life was bigger and more important than her own and who allowed nothing to stop her from providing him with the best possible upbringing.

Somehow, between the second job she took doing the books for a local coffee importer, and the love and generosity of their second family—the force of the Forty-First—all ends were met.

Ray did his part too. At age six he helped local shopkeepers stock their shelves and throw out the trash. By eight, he swept the sidewalks out front and shoveled the slush as winter closed in—anything to make a buck and help make his mom's life a little easier. And he saved some for toys and such so he could pay for them himself. And he never let up.

By age fourteen, he worked two, sometimes three, jobs at a time. But the one that had the greatest impact on him was at Spagnoli's Hard-ware on West Forty-Eighth Street, near Pier 88 on the Hudson River.

Founded by Angelo Spagnoli's father, Salvatore, who everyone knew as Sally, Spagnoli's Hardware had served the neighborhood going on eighty years. Ray offered to work there for free, not because Angelo was suffering from the early stages of Parkinson's, but because he and Sally, God rest his soul, had been close with his dad—given the neighborhood had its share of violent crime. Angelo, of course, refused and made it Ray's highest-paying job.

One day, Ray ran back to the stockroom to grab another box, when he came upon a black teenager who had jimmied the back door open and was stuffing tools down his pants. They locked eyes for a moment, and after sizing Ray up, the kid smirked and stuffed another wrench into his waist.

He never saw the shovel Ray cracked into his thigh, but what stopped him cold when he looked up was the gold shield hung around Ray's neck, still draped with a black band. He knew enough to know that messing with the kid of a cop killed in the line of duty could bring a whole host of troubles. It scared every tool out of his pants, and he ran off.

Ray never told Angelo and apologized for taking so long. It was Ray's nature to handle it this way.

Angelo never let on that he knew what had happened. He loved Ray's rock-solid personal integrity—another trait instilled in him by his mother—and it earned him the nickname Angel.

TWELVE

By the time Ray hit high school, he, too, heard the call and understood. So, it was no surprise when he followed in his father's footsteps and joined the Marine Corps.

From the day he arrived, the commanding officers recognized he was going to be one of the best of the best and set him on a path to becoming a member of the elite Marine Raiders, where—after a stint at Camp Lejeune, North Carolina, for advanced training—he and Joe were assigned to the same fourteen-man Marine Special Operations team of the Second Marine Raider Battalion and deployed to Afghanistan.

Ray and Joe became friends right out of the gate. In many ways, they had similar backgrounds. Joe also grew up in New York City, in a rental unit on the top floor of a five-story walk-up on East Thirty-Second Street in Murray Hill.

His father worked for the New York City Transit Authority on a subway rail maintenance crew. His mother was a teller at a local Bank of America branch. And like Ray's parents, they worked hard at home to set and keep Joe on the straight and narrow.

Ray and Joe also shared numerous traits: similar senses of humor, compassion for others, belief in loyalty to friends and family, and a lack of patience for bullshit—not trash-talking, locker-room bullshit, but the kind that spews from liars, frauds, backstabbers, and those who blow in the wind to deceive or hide their true intentions.

Still, despite the common threads, there was no denying that Joe's early years were a bit more freewheeling than Ray's. And with no woman in their unit, Joe often regaled them with stories of *his* good ole days growing up in New York City.

"Grossed me out when my mom would lick her finger and wipe a smudge off my face," Joe said to the unit, sitting around the cave on a food break. "Even worse when my grandmother did it. But Katie Donahue . . . the hottest girl in high school. When she sloshed her tongue around my mouth . . . Houston, we have liftoff. OORAH!"

There were also stories about the days he and his buddies played hooky and caught the subway to Yankee Stadium for the rare weekday day game, and others when they snuck into Times Square's triple-X video stores and live-girl peekaboos. OORAH!

The deeper they pushed into Kandahar, the more outrageous the stories. Especially wild were the tales about the nights at New York's infamous nightclubs and the frat-house-worthy escapades at the summer beach house he and his friends rented on the Jersey shore—all told in vivid detail. OORAH!

And, of course, there was his favorite story about the fateful day, in between his first two tours, when he met Mary, his future wife, at the Church of Saint Catherine of Siena.

"We're at this baby's baptism, and I take one look at her," Joe said and chuckled. "Ceremony's about to start, and I double-time it into the confessional and confess to a litany of carnal sins I hoped to soon commit." OORAH!

Once he and Mary started dating, though, Joe's penchant for wild escapades crashed and burned. Luckily for him, she fell for him too—despite the objections of her parents, and her being opposite from him in fundamental ways: Joe a streetwise, cut-to-the-chase New York cop, Mary a worldly and reserved Upper East Side–raised art gallery curator.

Sure, Ray knew Joe's stories were garnished with a fistful of locker-room trash talk. But it didn't matter. What did was that Joe, like Ray, had rock-solid personal integrity when it mattered most—when lives were on the line.

Plus, his stories brought relief in situations where it was hard to believe being amused was possible—especially for those in the team who, before serving in the corps, had never traveled far from the small towns they'd grown up in.

Their special operations team saw the best of humanity and the worst. One night in Afghanistan's Helmand Province, an hour into a special recon mission, they came upon a cinder-block structure surrounded by IEDs. But it was nothing compared to what was inside, where a small group of remaining Taliban true believers meted out their draconian punishments on three women who they deemed had defied Taliban dictates.

They cut one woman's fingers off because she adorned them with nail polish. They cut the second woman's ears and nose off because she stood on her balcony without wearing a burqa, believing a woman's face is a source of corruption to any man other than her husband or a blood relative.

Ray and his team were able to save the third right before they were about to set her on fire for striking the abusive husband who repeatedly beat her. Along the way, they killed every Taliban member they came across inside the structure, but not before Ray took a .44 slug in his lower back.

Luckily, the slug bypassed his vitals, and as soon as his fourth tour ended, he continued along his father's path and became a cop.

Joe wasn't far behind.

Despite how wild his late teens and early twenties were, if today was the first time you met Joe, it wouldn't take long to recognize certain key qualities he shares with Ray: the way he carries himself; his mannerisms; his congenial but firm attitude; the air of something calculating, something intimidating.

It all distills into one thing: pure cop. And as soon as Joe earned his gold shield, he and Ray became partners.

Still, with each new case, the Question invaded Ray's mind—especially when it involved murders absent a link between victim and assailant, murders whose odds of occurrence are so low they're incalculable.

What are the odds a woman from out of state, on her way to a meeting in the Bronx, tears a hole in her stocking on a corner trash can and enters a store to buy a new pair at the exact moment a deranged lunatic pulls out a meat cleaver and hacks her to death?

What are the odds a three-year-old, while her mommy reads her a bedtime story, sits up in bed at the exact second a stray bullet ricochets off a rock, blasts through the wall, and shatters her skull?

What are the odds that, out of the hundreds of people hustling on the sidewalk, you're the one hit in the head by the two-by-four a deranged ex-con tosses off the roof of a building, thirty stories up?

When the odds of an occurrence are so astronomical, is it irrational to not write it off as chance or coincidence?

Ray tried to process his thoughts as he knelt beside the young girl's body, the splintered two-by-four a few feet from her mangled head.

Over and over, he played out in his mind how she got out of a cab, started walking down the street, smiling, laughing, talking on her cell without a care in the world—oblivious to the fact that in another four and a half seconds, her life would end.

Poof. Just like that.

Was everything she and the other victims did throughout their lives, however long or short, random? Or were they unknowingly on a prede- termined, silent, unseen path to a head-on collision at the intersection of Wrong Place and Wrong Time?

Whether each victim's demise was orchestrated by karma, destiny, fate, or simply bad luck, they all have one thing in common—the odds of their occurrence are off the charts. And while this infinite thought loop might have paralyzed most, it made Ray a better cop. One of the greats. One to be proud of. The kind of cop rookies hear about when they enter the academy. The kind that becomes the youngest at the Forty-First to make detective first grade.

Still, he never considered that his path to greatness would one day lead to a sweltering August night after which the Question would no longer dog him but haunt him. A night that would, again, forever change his life and the lives of one family. A night that pounded the nail into his professional coffin.

THIRTEEN

"From the gentleman at the bar," the waiter says to Ray and Stephanie, and he sets a small envelope on the table and presents the laser-engraved label on the gold-plated bottle of Dom Perignon White Gold.

Within a half hour, the elevator fiasco seems far in the rearview. The ambiance in the lavish, upscale, candlelit setting is warm and inviting with elegant furnishings, seasonal arrangements, and sparkling place settings. Formally dressed waiters quietly move about, attending to the well-dressed guests while, at a secluded table on the patio, nestled among the lushly landscaped courtyard and balmy breeze, Ray and Stephanie share their first glass of Barolo, their faces happy and relaxed. Beyond, a full moon sparkles off the ocean. Everything speaks of romance.

And the dinner—to say Ray has gone all out is an understatement. He's thought of it all, from the wine and grilled lobster tails with caviar and creamy risotto to Stephanie's favorite dessert—crème brûlée and strawberries topped with maple syrup—and, of course, her favorite coffee blend.

At the bar, Wilbur—in a clean canvas outfit, sans the floppy hat—sheepishly smiles when Ray and Stephanie look over.

Without his hat, the clear look at Wilbur's face sends a surge of adrenaline through Ray's veins, and his eyes sharpen.

Where have I seen this guy before tonight?

It doesn't take long. Disquieted by Ray's intensity, Wilbur stands and leaves.

"Your dinner this evening has also been taken care of," the waiter says. He uncorks the bottle, fills their flutes, and sets the bottle in the table-side ice bucket. "Bon appétit."

"See, Ray . . . People can surprise you," Stephanie says.

"That's why I carry a gun," Ray says as he scans the wine menu. *Jesus,* he thinks to himself when he finds the White Gold—it's $2,865.

Stephanie pulls the card from the envelope and reads it aloud. "My deepest apology. Randolph."

Ray shifts in his chair at the mention of the uncommon name. "Be right back. Gonna hit the men's room."

Her antennae up, Stephanie's eyes search as she watches him disappear inside, and her father's voice rings in her ears: *I know this man.*

The smooth stone walls, beveled glass mirrors, elegant and sleek fixtures, and hand-painted inlaid tile floor define the bathroom's modern, tropical aesthetic. The first three louvered, Spanish cedar stall doors are open, but the last one, by the far wall, is locked with an Out of Service sign hanging on it.

Inside the stall, shooting up, is a menacing-looking, crazy-eyed, tatted-out, raw-boned kitchen staffer in his thirties named Diego—not a guy any restaurant patron would want one sweaty, drug-trembling headshake away from their food.

Strands of his straggly hair are matted to his face. The rest hangs beneath a partially torn net, and his utility apron is covered with food stains. To steady the shakes, he presses his rubber-booted feet against the back of the stall door and drains the needle into his arm when the bathroom door swings open.

Ray glances inside the first three stalls and under the door of the fourth, and with the bathroom seemingly empty, he pulls out his cell.

At this hour, the Bronx's Forty-First still buzzes with police activity.

"So, you whip your sister to death with a water hose over a bag of

Cheetos," Joe says to the gruff dirtbag across from him in the interrogation room.

"And a Mello Yello," the guy says, agitated. "How many damn times I got to say it? Bitch was hoggin'."

Joe's heard enough. He heads back to his desk to scour dozens of crime scene photos for a common thread between three armed home invasions in the last two weeks and another dozen in the aftermath of a gangbanger who, earlier in the day, tried to recreate the Saint Valentine's Day Massacre on several opposing gang member's sisters—one of them just nine years old.

During their time as Raiders and as partners at the Forty-First, there's one thing Ray and Joe never questioned, never thought about: whether they had each other's backs. Both are endowed with an unshakable faith that each would do whatever it took to save the other's life and the lives of strangers in need, even when it could cost them their own.

Two months after they made detective, that faith was put to the test less than twenty-four hours into a new case—an abhorrent assault of a paraplegic young man who was beaten and left for dead by some two-bit scumbag out to steal the thick copper wire from the engine that powered his wheelchair.

They had been working several leads, the last of which led them to Port Morris, a heavily industrial area just south of Hunts Point dominated by mid to late nineteenth-century manufacturing and warehouse buildings. Half of the neighborhood residents lived below the federal poverty line.

By midnight Ray and Joe realized the lead was a dead end, but as they headed back to their car, they observed several local kids, no more than twelve or thirteen years old, smoking weed and tagging traffic signs and other city-owned maintenance equipment—*too young*, they both knew, *to be roaming these streets alone at this hour, let alone committing crimes while doing so.*

Ray called out, and when the kids saw him and Joe heading their way, they took off down the street, and Ray and Joe hightailed it after them. But as they closed in further down the block, the kids rounded the corner and darted into a decrepit abandoned building—a move that escalated the chase from dangerous to outright hairy.

Sure, it would have been safer and easier for Ray and Joe to write them off as kids being stupid. And tagging is a low-level crime that was well below their detective pay grade. But it was more than that for Ray and Joe. Taking the easy way out was not in either's playbook, especially when it involved kids on the cusp of messing up their whole lives. The critical time to catch them was now—still young enough to be impacted and have a chance at a better life.

Their guts told them there was a reason the kids had chosen this building to run into, most likely the safety of others they knew were inside.

Joe called for backup, and in they went.

Down pitch-black hallways and up stairwells, all rank with the foul stench of piss, puke, and mold. Save for their footfalls and random creaks of floorboards and warped doors, the silence was entrenched deep enough to hear the proverbial church mouse—until they reached the fourth floor.

It was all clear as they came out of the stairwell, but three steps in, Ray and Joe's nostrils flared with the smell of sweet, cheap cologne. Seconds later, as if they had stepped on a hornet's nest, kids, ranging in age from nine to their midtwenties, swarmed in and out of doorways and holes in the walls.

One ten-year-old girl shot out of the wall like a moray eel and sank her teeth into Ray's calf. Another, a kid about nineteen or twenty, nailed Joe in the back with a bat, gripping him in breathtaking pain and dropping him to his knees, sending his gun to the floor. The kid dragged him inside a room and slammed the door.

Ray separated the young girl from his calf with the butt end of his gun, which cost her the upper and lower rows of her front teeth, and without hesitation, he grabbed Joe's gun, bashed through the door, and blew away the guy with the bat, saving Joe's life.

But when Ray handed Joe his gun back and knelt to help him up, there was a muzzle flash from inside the closet behind him. A 9 mm slug tore into Ray's back near his right shoulder, and with Ray's body slumped over him, Joe reached around and blew away the thirty-eight-year-old ringleader hiding inside.

It turned out to be a huge bust. Hidden in the walls, under floorboards, inside closets and sewage lines, police found cash and stolen goods valued at over three hundred grand. And Ray, thank God, survived without a hitch and was out of the hospital and back at work in a matter of weeks—a bit more of a celebrity for his bravery and heroism.

When all was said and done, they broke through to a handful of the kids and set them on a different life path—a path Ray and Joe could only pray they stayed on.

Joe smiles when he sees the caller's ID, and he tosses the last crime scene photo back onto his desk and makes sure no one is in earshot. "Knew you'd never make it home before calling," he says.

"Hey, Joe."

"What's on your mind, Ray?"

"The guy all over the fed wires today . . . What's his name?"

"You're kidding me, right?

"C'mon, I'm on the clock," Ray says, while inside the stall, Diego's meth-fueled eye flickers through the tiny crack between the door and the frame as he hangs on Ray's every word.

"You owe me, asshole," Joe says, resigned, and he pecks at his keyboard. "Bailey, Wilbur Bailey. IRS tag out of Houston."

"Wilbur?" Ray asks, incredulously.

"Whaddya want, Ray?"

"Whaddya got?"

"What I got is no longer your business," Joe says.

"It might be, so stop bustin' my balls."

Joe can't help but chuckle, and again pecks at the keyboard. "Steph know you're making this call, or you hidin' out in the bathroom?"

Ray chuckles. "If I'm right, Wilbur just sent us champagne."

"The good stuff?"

"Some pricey shit called White Gold."

"Dom Perignon. A client of Mary's had it at a dinner party. Said she found it 'naive yet intimidating.'"

"I find it I'll rip your tongue out if I ever hear *you* say something like that."

Joe laughs. "Forgot who I was talking to," he says, and pulls up a copy of Wilbur's IRS wanted poster. "Damn, this *is* your lucky day."

A second later, Ray's phone pings.

"Bingo," he says aloud the moment he sees Wilbur's face, but he's taken aback by the size of the reward and jumps back on the line. "Jesus . . . Five million bucks for this guy?"

Inside the stall, Diego's eyes bulge and he kisses the syringe and presses his ear over the crack in the door. Still, he can't decipher Joe's muffled voice, but whatever it is that Joe tells Ray, it catches Ray off guard and gives him a different, and unexpected, perspective.

"You're kidding me," Ray says. "Does he know?"

"No. And I'm warning you, Ray," Joe says. "Unless you wanna see your pretty face on one of those, stay out of it. Feds'll fry your ass if you stick your dick in some international bullshit."

"Hand to God, I'm out. Just make sure Houston spells my name right."

Ray ends the call and does a touchdown dance out of the bathroom. "July Fourth just got a whole lot luckier."

FOURTEEN

Back in Houston, it's a typical summer night save for Citgo's annual Fourth of July Freedom over Texas festival. Fireworks light up the stagnant air, still thick with humidity. A mile and a half away, Phil's Crown Victoria cruises down the interstate past Minute Maid Park, where the Astros, already bruised from a nine-game losing streak, are getting pounded by the Yankees.

With nothing but dead ends after a long day, the corners of Phil's brain are taking a pounding of their own as he motors through downtown to a comfortable Houston suburb, taking a modicum of solace from Tony Bennett's velvety, hypnotic version of "Fly Me to the Moon" radiating from the speakers.

Phil softly sings the last *I love you* before he cuts the engine and heads up the walk of the modest townhouse, a six of Bud in hand.

As if on cue, the front door opens and his daughter, now twenty-four, greets him with her big, beautiful smile. Nothing brings Phil a greater sense of calm and peace than Emmi's smile—a gift her mom bestowed on her.

"Hey, Dad."

"God left you here for a reason you don't want to miss a minute of," Phil's father said to him a week after Lorena's funeral.

It was advice Phil heeded, and he buckled down with a fierce determination to become a steadfast cornerstone that blanketed Emmi
in safety, anchored her with a solid foundation, provided her with a
keen understanding of right and wrong, and empowered her with a
not-even-the-sky's-the-limit attitude.

Before long, he became the big cliché: the proud dad whose daughter was his greatest achievement. And why not? All his efforts to be a
great dad paid off.

Emmi blossomed into a smart, honest, fun-loving, and compassionate person—someone others love to be around. The kind of person her
mother would be proud of. Lorena's influence on her was undeniable—
Emmi's a natural in the kitchen and the classroom.

"Dear Ms. Dancourt: On behalf of the University of Texas at
Austin, I am pleased to offer our congratulations," the acceptance
letter began in praise of Emmi's top 5 percent finish in high school,
which guaranteed her admission. And her subsequent master of science in nursing paved the way to Houston Memorial Hospital's ICU,
where she's still a critical care nurse—loved by patients, their families,
and colleagues alike.

She also inherited her mother's eye for great men—at least, according to Phil. He admired and was comforted by her nature to go steady
with one guy for long periods rather than playing the field—and he
thanked God that, so far, they were all nice, decent guys.

"C'mon, it's our last chance for a fun night out before finals," her best
friend said when, at the last minute, Emmi wavered on whether to go
to the party. She gave it one last thought and figured it was their senior
year, she knew her stuff . . .

"Okay, I'm in," she said.

One hour later at the party, merely nice-and-decent stepped aside
when up walked the One.

"Hi, I'm Matt," the good-looking young man said to her.

The rest is history.

When Phil met Matt several weeks later, he was thrilled. He could tell Matt was a great guy and that they had similar backgrounds in the things that matter: hard work, persistence, honesty . . .

These core values, combined with a bachelor of science degree in supply chain management, landed Matt an entry-level management training position in the Houston branch of one of the country's largest retailers—with a starting salary of fifty grand.

With his nose to the grindstone, and well liked by his colleagues, Matt was recognized by management as a real comer. One year later, the CEO personally approved his promotion to a supervisory position with a staff of seventeen, a six-figure salary, and an annual budget nearing a billion dollars—the youngest at the company to be given such a promotion. More importantly, he and Emmi decided to live together and pool their money to rent their cozy two-story townhouse, with an option to buy.

Six months later, after he first swore Phil to secrecy, Matt went old school and asked for his blessing to marry Emmi. Thanks to the promotion, he was well on his way to saving enough money to buy a Tiffany ring—a ring he knew, the moment he saw it, was the one meant for her.

Phil didn't hesitate and gave his blessing.

Matt was on cloud nine. Everything was on cruise control—so he thought.

The very next day, news broke that the CEO was stepping down amid accusations of inappropriate sexual behavior at a retail convention in Vegas seventeen years ago. And despite his vehement denial of the two-handed ass grab because one of his hands was in a cast at the time, the company's stock nosedived 15 percent—a precursor of things to come.

The onslaught continued the following morning before the opening bell when the company's latest quarterly earnings revealed that Amazon, the digital great white shark of retail, had ferociously gnawed away at its market share and revenue—the Wall Street equivalent of a Costco-sized barrel of chum which fueled the stock's free fall as other sharks swarmed to feed.

Six weeks later, a new CEO was announced, and within an hour of her arrival, a notice was sent out from the company's New York City headquarters: Three hundred stores nationwide would be shuttered, and several layers of middle management phased out.

By the end of the month, Matt was given two weeks' severance and a place on the unemployment line. And despite his great credentials, the stench of being one of the retailer's fungibles has made it tough for him to land another job at the same level.

"Hi, honey. Sorry I'm late."

"I'll take late over bailing again," Emmi gently ribs him. "I made pasta with my new secret sauce."

No sooner is Phil about to head inside when his cell rings, and he sighs when he sees the ID, leaving him no choice but to take the call. "Dancourt."

Callahan's voice growls from the phone. "Hey, Phil, it's your unlucky day."

The look on Phil's face says it all. Emmi's smile fades as she heads back inside, and Matt appears at the door. "Too bad . . . This pasta's better than a ribeye."

Phil hands him the six-pack. "If it's half as good as her mother used to make, you're a lucky guy."

Emmi reappears at the door with a Tupperware-full.

"Sorry, honey. I love you," Phil says. She hands him the pasta. "Thanks. First home-cooked meal I've had in weeks."

FIFTEEN

A lucky break was Phil's initial thought when he got the call. But as he drives away, Callahan's reference to it being his *unlucky* day irks him and reminds him of a time soon after Emmi was born.

"It's a plan that provides steady growth with minimal to moderate risk," the broker said.

Phil and Lorena looked at each other. *Sounds good to me* are the unspoken words between them, and they cut the check for their entire savings.

Year after year, the account showed solid returns. Until it didn't.

The market took a dive, and as the saying goes, stocks take the stairs going up, and the elevator going down. They watched their savings vaporize for as long as they could until panic set in and they sold for a huge loss.

"An unlucky break," they were told, and rationalized that they were young, had good jobs, and would eventually make it back. Except Lorena didn't make it back. The debts piled on. And on his government salary, Phil has since lived one paycheck away from financial disaster.

One night, after he put Emmi to sleep and racked his brains out over the bills, the words of an evangelist on the radio caught his attention.

"You might be in poverty, but don't let poverty be in you," the evangelist said.

The declaration spoke to Phil's core, and for the first time, it hit him how their financial struggles had changed him in ways he hadn't anticipated. How it had ensnared him in fear, a fear unlike any other—especially of being homeless or having to rely on friends or family. How, without blind faith's defenses, it festered into a rabid Pavlovian dog whose embedded razor-sharp teeth restrain him, to this day, from spending on little else beyond necessities and minor luxuries.

Perhaps that's a good thing, he ponders while he scarfs down the pasta and packs a bag. *Or maybe the gambling adage is true—scared money never wins.*

Round and round . . .

But when it comes to executing a raid that goes south or leaves him and his unit empty-handed, Phil knows one thing for sure: scared and unlucky beats blind faith and dead. Still, it's been a while since he's felt a case sliding deeper than this one into the IRS tax code rabbit hole—a hole that runs deep.

Just below the surface of upright citizens is a large group of tax filers who fudge expenses and boldly skirt the law, often in the belief that they already pay more taxes than they should.

Further down is an elite class of the rich and powerful who think they are insulated and untouchable or have lost sight of how far down the rabbit hole they are. These are the fat cats the IRS covets, the high-profile scores that flood the headlines designed to bring satisfaction to the law-abiding and instill fear in those who aren't.

Case in point: the headlines devoted to the IRS's then-latest high-profile whipping boy—attorney (or rather, former attorney) Michael Avenatti. Almost overnight he had gone from having a porn star client to a media darling who many expected to be the one to take out future Supreme Court justice Brett Kavanaugh and then-president Donald Trump. The admiring media gushed as he proudly announced his presidential run to the DNC's Ethics Council.

The result? A lifetime of fortune and fame was decimated in less than fifteen minutes, stymied by numerous felony charges. And while Avenatti was on the stand inside a Los Angeles courthouse at his disciplinary hearing before the state bar, the court took a break, and IRS special agents took him down on a bail violation. And after he attempted to extort $25 million from Nike and pled guilty to embezzling millions more from clients, he was sentenced to fourteen years in federal prison for defrauding them, and for obstructing IRS efforts to collect millions in unpaid payroll taxes from his coffee business. And let's not forget the $11 million in restitution he has to pay back.

Avenatti's not alone in the high-profile sandbox. Wesley Snipes ring a bell? How about country legend Willie Nelson? And who can forget America's favorite madam, Heidi Fleiss, who had the happy ending of money laundering and running a prostitution ring—mostly for Hollywood elites. And, of course, there's baseball great Pete Rose.

Any baseball fan who's old enough remembers the shit pile that gambling brought into Rose's life. But few recall the six months he spent behind bars for failing to report the income he earned from memorabilia and signing autographs. Sure, his actions got him in the jam. But once there, who can blame him if he, perhaps, used the money to pay off gambling debts that might otherwise have left him with detached kneecaps—or worse.

Further down still, you'll find kind, loving people like the notorious "Queen of Mean," hotelier Leona Helmsley. According to one former employee, she once said something to the effect of "Only little people pay taxes."

Unfortunately, then–US attorney Rudy Giuliani let her know that it's not only little people who go to federal prison and put her away for conspiracy to defraud the United States along with three counts of tax evasion, three counts of filing false personal tax returns, sixteen counts of assisting in the filing of false corporate and partnership tax returns, and ten counts of mail fraud. In a fitting ending, Helmsley was ordered to report to prison on April 15th.

You'll also find guys like former Tyco CEO Dennis Kozlowski. Put

aside his and his wife's lavish lifestyle and the multimillion-dollar parties they threw. The IRS nailed him for not paying taxes on a dozen
priceless paintings. He settled the tax bill, but soon after was carted off
to prison for stealing more than half a billion dollars from Tyco. You
can't make this stuff up. It's what happens the deeper you delve down
the rabbit hole.

Eventually, you arrive at the depths reserved for the most coveted
and most feared. Folks who think the IRS and its code can kiss their ass.
Folks who have a total disregard for the law and have shown no limit
on how far they will go to remain free of it.

Down here, you might run into folks like Al Capone, who the IRS
finally nailed on tax evasion and sentenced to eleven years. And of course
the Teflon Don, John Gotti, who was nabbed on tax fraud, among a
few other, more heinous, crimes.

Down here is where Phil hopes to nail Mika Salko and make him
bleed with a good headline.

"When the odds are impossible, never discount the value of luck," Phil
says as he ambles before the agent trainees and runs his hand through
what's left of his hair. "Most often, that's what ends up determining success or failure. Or whether you live or die. And good or bad, when luck
intervenes, there's not a damn thing you can do about it."

He takes a seat on the stool and loads a new cartridge into the vape's
chamber, telling the trainees, "Would've taken weeks to secure the international paperwork. It wasn't like Bailey was an imminent national security
threat. But with the impending gubernatorial election, waiting wasn't an
option for Callahan. And losing my job wasn't an option for me."

With a pull of the trigger, he fires another blast of Banana Nut
Bread into his lungs.

SIXTEEN

"Hi there," Ray says as he hustles to the maître d'.

"Mr. Dawson, how can I help you?" he says with a warm smile, remembering Ray's gracious tip for the secluded table.

"The guy who sent us champagne," Ray says, another folded ten-spot clutched in his fingers. "What room is he in? We'd love to thank him."

"I'm sorry, Mr. Dawson, I can't give out that information. Perhaps leave a note at the front desk or with me, and I'll make sure he receives it. I hope you understand."

Ray smiles and pockets the bill. "Of course."

Stephanie studies Ray's face as he makes his way back to the table. "Feel better?" she says.

"Much. Thanks."

"What was that about?"

"Asked for his room number to send him a thank you. And apologize."

As if he anticipated the skeptical look on her face, Ray outstretches his arms and smiles his winning smile. "See, babe . . . People can surprise you." He raises his flute in a toast, and she follows with hers. "Anyone can lose the one they love. But only a schmuck would do it twice." She chuckles, and his eyes twinkle. "To me finally getting it, and for the second chance to prove I'm not a schmuck but the two-time luckiest guy in the world."

Stephanie smiles a big, happy smile, and they clink glasses and take sips, and Ray raises his flute again. "And to Wilbur."

"Who?" she asks.

Realizing the slipup, Ray glances at the card. "I mean Randolph," he says and flips the card back on the table. "Wilbur, Randolph—same thing."

But as soon as Stephanie brushes it off and they clink and take another sip, Ray glances over her shoulder, and through a lobby window across the courtyard, he spots Wilbur, his carry-on beside him, at the hotel's front desk checking out.

"I, too, would like to propose a toast," Stephanie says, and raises her flute.

Ray winces and grabs his stomach. "Hold that thought."

"You okay?"

"Traveling . . . Always does a number," Ray says, and heads back to the men's room.

Again, her father's voice rings in her head: *Unless you can figure that out* . . . Still, she doesn't press and peruses her phone while Ray hustles past the kitchen. But as he ducks around the corner, he catches sight of Diego staring at him from behind a rack of dirty dishes. The sharpness in Diego's glassy eyes leaves an imprint while he maps out his next move. And with Stephanie's focus elsewhere, Ray darts to the far side and shadows a waiter out of the restaurant.

A moment later, he barrels out of the hotel's main entrance just in time to spot Wilbur pulling out of the main drive in a cab and speeding off. Seconds later, out of the corner of his eye, he sees Diego hustle out a side door and jump into a blue Chevy van, which peels out after the cab.

I got a bad feeling about this. Ray's gut churns.

The moment of truth has arrived, and Ray hesitates, looking from the hotel back to the road. Stephanie? Or Wilbur and five million bucks? It's as if he knows he is about to make a terrible mistake.

SEVENTEEN

A million thoughts scamper about Ray's brain as the cab motors out of the main drive. His text to Stephanie simply reads "XO R," but no matter how hard he tries, he can't shake how selfish, callous, and mind-bogglingly stupid he is to have left her at the table—a heinous act on any night, let alone on the one he long dreamed of but thought would never happen.

One thought in particular—his silent vow at the elevator—pounds away at his temples: *This time I'm getting it all right.* How ridiculous it sounds now.

But isn't it right to go after a wanted man who could also be in grave danger?

Isn't it right to do what I'm trained to do?

What I was born to do.

Isn't it all right?

Round and round . . .

Further ahead, Wilbur's cab cruises along, while inside, oblivious to the blue van trailing a short distance behind, Wilbur sits stoic, his eyes fixed out his window on the rainforest flickering past in the full moon's light.

It reminds him of happier times—the nights with a full moon when he and his wife would go to their favorite park and sit on the hill with a bottle of pinot grigio and watch the fanciful dance of moon shadows. But tonight, as he stares out the cab's window, the dance of the moon shadows seems chaotic, their movements disorderly and unpredictable.

When the cab rounds the bend, it veers to the side of the road, and Wilbur gets out with his carry-on. He doesn't give much thought to the approaching van until it screeches to a stop beside them.

Diego and his cohort, José—another twitchy, tatted-out thug—jump out, flashlights and AR-15s locked and loaded.

A short distance behind, Ray's cab approaches the bend. With each passing second, his heightened adrenaline tightens its grip. He cherishes the exhilarating moment, which takes him back to his days in the NYPD; the moment when he senses he's closing in, and pure cop thoughts crystallize into one objective.

"Let's go—punch it!" he says, and snaps a twenty-dollar bill up to the driver, who snatches it without taking his eyes off the road. But when they speed out of the bend and see Diego and José turn their way, the driver slams on the brakes.

Ray slams into the partition with a thud.

"Here's good," he says, and when the driver guns it in reverse and pulls a one-eighty, he tumbles out the door and barrel-rolls into the trees as the cab disappears back the way it came.

"¿Cinco millónes de dólares por esto?" *Five million dollars for this?* José says to Diego with a nervous laugh, flicking his AR-15 toward Wilbur.

Diego shakes the coating of pasty meth sweat off his face. "Sólo en América." *Only in America.* But no sooner do the words and spittle fly from his mouth than branches snap and rustle up the road.

Diego and José scramble for cover in front of the cab, and through its front and back windows, they unload a barrage of bullets along the tree line. But as soon as they're done, branches snap and rustle on the other side of the road, and they blast another volley in that direction.

In the melee, Wilbur scurries into the forest.

This time, when the gunfire ends, silence fills the air.

Diego beams his light back and forth along the tree line. Seeing no movement or signs of life, he motions José to head up the road and check it out, and he bounds into the forest in pursuit of Wilbur.

José loads a new clip, but his eyes say it all. He'd rather eat rusty nails than head up the road, though he figures it's better than what Diego will do to him if he takes off and leaves him here.

So he thinks.

Sweat pours down his face with each timid step, unaware that Ray is behind him, rummaging through their van, where he finds the Smith & Wesson .38 Special José had hidden under the driver's seat next to a Papa John's soda cup full of bullets.

"Perfect," Ray whispers, giving the gun a quick once-over. He's as proficient with a .38 as he is with a Glock. From the day he joined the force, he was rarely without his .38 strapped to his ankle.

Ray loads six bullets in the cylinder's chambers and stuffs a seventh in his sock for good luck—a reminder of an NYPD operation that would have gone fatally south if not for the seventh bullet he kept in a sleeve on his .38's ankle holster. But as he rights himself, his elbow hits the door, and it squeaks.

José, trembling, wheels around and sprays the open door with bullets as he makes his way back toward the van.

"Drop the gun," Ray calls out, repeating it in Spanish. "Suelta el arma."

José stops cold and then wheels back around and canvasses the tree line with his light, unsure where the voice came from. "No bueno, señor," José says, and aimlessly sprays the trees with bullets.

As soon as the barrage ends, Ray leans out from behind a tree. "No," he says. "*This* is no bueno, asshole."

BANG!

A .38 slug rips into José's thigh and sends him reeling. Still, he manages to hobble for cover in front of the van and again opens fire, unaware that while he hobbled to the van, Ray had bolted to the other side of the road.

"This may sting a bit," Ray softly says, and he empties the .38's chambers into the van's gas tank.

KABOOM!

Back at the hotel, a soft, knowing smile crosses Stephanie's lips—her eyes fixed out the suite's bedroom window on the glow of the distant fireball, her packed suitcase on the bed before her.

What a waste, Ray thinks to himself as he stands over José's burned and mangled body, the Chevy logo from the grill embedded in his forehead. He tucks the spent .38 in the back of his waistband, grabs José's AR-15 and flashlight, and heads over to the cab.

"You okay?" he asks the cabbie, supine on the front seat covered in shards of glass, metal, and fabric.

With a nod and a smile, the cabbie rights himself, and as if nothing happened, he shifts into drive and pulls away.

EIGHTEEN

Deep in the forest, the full moon's beams slither through the canopy.

Wilbur, winded and sweaty, trudges through the foliage with his carry-on. He can't help but notice that the dance of the shadows now seems downright hostile, their movements aggressive and foreboding.

Following broken branches and twigs, Diego closes in and indiscriminately unloads a hail of bullets in Wilbur's direction.

The foliage only feet from Wilbur shreds, and he drops to his knees and belly-crawls around a towering ceiba tree and over to an old, rotted stump with a red cloth nailed to its side, below which he retrieves a hand shovel buried under a pile of leaves.

Twelve seconds later, Wilbur unearths the large Ziploc full of wrapped stacks of hundred-dollar bills, but three seconds after that, Diego blows off another barrage, exploding the bag from Wilbur's hands.

Amid shredded leaves, branches, and bark, tens of thousands of dollars' worth of C-note confetti rain down around Wilbur—save for two intact stacks tucked between the tree's buttress roots.

Cowering, Wilbur slowly crawls toward the tree but freezes when a distant blast from another AR reverberates through the forest.

"José?" Diego calls out.

"José can't make it," Ray says. "He's burnt out."

Wilbur snaps his ear toward the familiar voice.

Diego sprays the forest with bullets in the direction of Ray's voice, but no sooner does he empty his clip than a flashlight's beam lights up his back, and he wheels around to find Ray no more than five feet in front of him.

Sweat drips from his hair, and his eyes burn with fear as he tosses his spent AR-15 aside, pulls a twelve-inch butcher's knife from his waist-band, and raises it, ready to strike.

"That's a 'no bueno,'" Ray says, and blows him away.

"Wilbur, it's me, Ray Dawson," he calls out. "I wanna thank you for the champagne and apologize for my behavior."

Wilbur takes off and cocks his head, startled at the mention of his real name.

"And killing me and those men is the best way to do that?" Wilbur calls behind him, quickening his pace. But three seconds later, his face illuminates, and he jolts to a stop, breathless.

Ray is no more than five feet in front of him.

No two men in sports coats and slacks having a conversation in the middle of a Costa Rican rainforest at night could look more out of place and absurd.

"It's more personal than a card," Ray says. "And I'm not here to kill you."

"What do you want?"

"Same as everyone. Lower taxes, cheaper gas," Ray says, and holds up his NYPD badge. "And five million bucks, once I turn your ass over to the feds."

Wilbur eyes the badge, confused by its New York City insignia and the word RETIRED, where the shield number used to be. "NYPD? Retired?"

"Too young, right?"

"Not what I expected," Wilbur says, and his gaze snaps upward. "Viper! Look out!" he shouts.

Ray drops, rolls, and sprays what's left in his clip into the tree, only to realize the snake is no more than a twisted band of vines. Worse—when he whips around, Wilbur's gone.

Seconds later there's a noise: *Zzzzzzzzzzzz.*

By the time Ray makes it to the old zip line, Wilbur, his carry-on hooked to the handlebars, is already across the ravine.

"Oldest trick in the book, Ray," Wilbur says. He turns and disappears down a forest path.

Ray can't help but chuckle as he grabs the retraction rope, yanks the handlebars back, and sets off. But when he is halfway across, Wilbur reappears at the landing platform and smacks the emergency stop button.

The cable jerks to a halt.

Ray dangles sixty feet over the ravine. Within seconds, his hands and arms burn and vibrate from the strain. He tries to swing his legs up and around the cable for relief, but each attempt comes up an inch short.

"In truth, it's not, Ray," Wilbur says.

"Not what, Wilbur?"

"The oldest trick in the book. Not even close. The left shoulder tap when you're on the right . . . Goes back to 10,000 BC. 'Check's in the mail' . . . 9000."

"You must get laid a lot with facts like those," Ray says while his mind churns for a way out.

Wilbur's eyes flash with sadness. "There was only one woman who mattered."

"You're married? Hard to believe."

"Was. She died of cancer. All the garbage we put in the air, the sea, the soil . . ." He taps his chest. "It all ends up here."

"That why you stole the money? Start your own dung paste factory? Make the world a greener place?"

Wilbur brushes off the slight with a damp smile. "Things aren't always what they seem, Ray."

"Yeah? You seem like a pain in the ass, so sometimes they are." Ray's veins bulge as he struggles to hang on. And the last thing he needs to hear is the Jessie J, Ariana Grande, and Nicki Minaj "Bang Bang" ringtone he's reserved for Stephanie. "Oh, Christ. Hear that, jerk-off? That's the sound of *me* losing the only woman who matters."

It takes every ounce of Ray's strength to hang on while he digs his phone out of his pocket. And the second he does, a rivet pops off the axle, the handlebars lurch downward, the phone slips from his hand, and he watches in horror as it plummets into the ravine.

The last "bang-bang" booms before it shatters on the rocks.

Ray hangs there, stunned.

"If she loves you, she'll understand it's just your nature," Wilbur says.

"Yeah? Well, my nature just saved your ass, so why don't you shut the fuck up."

"There's nothing you or anyone else on earth can do to save me."

"There it is. You and every other dirtbag oughta try finding Jesus before you break the law." Ray tries again in vain to thrust his legs up and around the cable.

"You this crass with your wife?"

"She's not my wife anymore, but I was gonna ask her again. Then you crossed my path." Ray huffs and thinks aloud, "What are the odds?"

There's a tinge of compassion in Wilbur's eyes as he watches Ray dangle and sway. "Goodbye, Ray," he says and disappears back down the forest path.

"Wilbur! Wilbur!"

NINETEEN

Save for the zip line's creaky axle, the forest is deathly quiet. "Okay, Ray, You stepped in it this time. Think," he says, and closes his eyes. His thoughts take him back ten years to the day.

"You'll be ridin' along with Staten Island's 121st Overdose and Gang Squad," the lieutenant told Ray and Joe.

Cops from all five boroughs were deep in coordinated efforts to track down those who were behind a vicious interborough drug organization responsible for 40 percent of the fentanyl that snaked its way onto the street.

On an unrelated drug bust, a confidential informant had tipped Ray and Joe off that Sal's Auto Salvage in Staten Island was encasing large amounts of drug cash in crushed vehicles which, through a series of middlemen, were then exported to China as recycled materials instead of waste.

It was the break they'd all been looking for, and with the massive amount of money at stake, they knew the heavily armed narcotraffickers weren't going to take kindly to a surprise visit.

The next batch of cash-laden crushed vehicles was due to go out in three days, during which time Ray, Joe, and the dozen other officers surveilled the facility and surrounding area twenty-four seven, both on the ground and through aerial photos taken from choppers high above.

Every aspect of the facility's layout was noted and studied, from the auto parts store and front office along Richmond Terrace to the cages behind it that housed the four pit bulls that patrolled the grounds after hours.

Beyond, in the center of the yard was a two-story-high, 150-foot-long row of stacked square and rectangular compartments filled with countless categorized auto parts. Across the top, running the entire length, car doors of all sizes and colors hung on hooks like beef carcasses at a meat processing plant.

Around the perimeter was the lot of old and disabled vehicles awaiting their fate and the various stations where they'd be drained of fluids and stripped of their interiors, after which the claws of massive engine biters would rip out the engines and a second forklift would place the pressed, vacuum-sealed vinyl bags of cash into the cavities and carry them to the crusher.

From there, the crushed, cash-filled vehicles were stored in a large shed until several unmarked eighteen-wheelers would arrive to take them to the Port of New York and New Jersey.

And on the third day . . .

Storm clouds darkened the sky, and the wind picked up, rattling the tarp-covered chain-link fence that ran along the east side of the yard behind which Ray, Joe, and the other cops waited for the final go-ahead. Further to the northeast, an angry, jagged lightning bolt struck the Bayonne Bridge, illuminating the Kill Van Kull tidal strait and, beyond, the Bayonne, New Jersey, shoreline. The ground rumbled with the crack of thunder.

When Ray got word in his earpiece that the storm was tracking north and would bypass them, he raised his index finger and twirled it, letting the team know it was all systems go. And at precisely thirty minutes before closing time, when the dogs were released, the cop next to Ray and Joe knelt by the fence, made a half-inch slit in the tarp with a box cutter, and inserted the six-millimeter-thin camera cable. Using the joystick on the handheld control and LCD monitor, he made a tactical inspection of the area.

Ray pulled his Glock and double-checked to make sure his .38 was secure in its ankle holster.

"Good to go," the cop next to him said, withdrawing the camera cable. And with a bolt cutter, he cut a four-by-four-foot section out of the bottom of the fences, slit the tarp, and the team streamed in.

As they moved deeper into the yard, the lack of any employee in sight gave Ray his first indication something wasn't right. The lack of noise gave him a second hint. The third came as they neared the long two-story row of auto parts: several compartments that had been filled with parts in yesterday's surveillance photos were now empty.

Fearing they might be sitting ducks, Ray put his hand up, stopping the group. But when Joe turned to him, the back of his leg hit a tripwire, setting off automatic rifles hidden in the darkness of the empty compartments, each of which had been modified with an electronic trigger.

Turns out the narcotraffickers had gotten a tip that Ray and Joe had gotten a tip. They rigged the whole joint.

Bullets flew every which way, and the team scattered for cover wherever they could find it. But in the melee, a bullet ricocheted off a pile of scrap and hit a seventh bullet Ray had in a sleeve on his .38's ankle holster. The force sent him flying into Joe and they both went down— their faces less than an inch away from another tripwire that they later learned was attached to an acid bomb.

What are the odds?

The raid was a bust, but by the grace of God, every cop made it out unharmed, and the bullet on Ray's ankle holster has been his lucky seventh bullet ever since.

Still hanging on, Ray's eyes snap open, and after several thrusts of his knees to his chest, he snags the seventh bullet he stuck in his sock and pops it into his mouth.

"You still got it, Ray," he garbles, and pulls the .38 from his waistband.

The last time he chambered a bullet with his teeth while oscillating was on a target practice training exercise—parachuting in over a target the size of a tire.

It's one thing when a small target is moving. It's another when it's not, but you are, he thought at the time.

Well into his second wind, now is another time. And as the rivet's flange begins to squeal, he wrangles the bullet into the .38's chamber, gets a bead on the cable behind the axle, and *BANG!*

It's a direct hit, and the cable shreds but for one strand.

"You're kidding me!" He groans in utter disbelief and tosses the gun.

But as if on cue—*TWANG!*—the strand snaps, and he Tarzans into the brush and rocks on the slope of the ravine's far side.

Wilbur can't help but wonder if the gunshot signifies Ray's demise as he waits at the edge of the pitch-black dirt access road and flags down his cab—as if a man in dirty, torn, twig-infested clothes with a carry-on at his side waiting for a cab on a pitch-black dirt access road is nothing out of the ordinary.

"Good evening," he says and settles in.

The nervous cab driver acknowledges him with a nod and U-turns back the way he came.

If only to ease his conscience, Wilbur swivels and looks out the back window for any sign of Ray, hoping he might stumble into view, but the distance fades into blackness.

"Sorry, Ray," he whispers, thinking aloud, and the moment he turns back around . . .

THWAP!

Dotted with cuts and bruises, Ray lands on the cab's front window and clings onto the hood when the driver slams on the brakes.

"Hey, Wilbur," he says, his tone maniacal. He slides off the hood and hops into the back seat beside him. "Thought you were home free, didn't you, nature boy?"

Shocked and bewildered, Wilbur takes a moment to collect his thoughts. "You know there are nine proven ways to ascertain someone's nature?"

"No, but I know five ways to beat you to a pulp."

"See?" Wilbur says, his finger pointed at Ray. "Temper. Lack of patience. They're numbers three and six, and both indicate a propensity for violence."

Ray clocks him in the jaw and knocks him out cold.

"Right hook. Number one." He turns to the driver. "Let's go."

The driver guns it, and they head back to the hotel.

TWENTY

On the lonely ride back to the hotel, the searing burn in Ray's stomach is fueled by thoughts of Stephanie, casting aside the Mount Everest pile of shit he's now left in his wake. No need to call ahead. He can feel that she's already gone.

What a schmuck, he broods.

Beside him, Wilbur ruminates on how the rest of his life, however brief and painful, will be spent in a non-eco-friendly six-by-nine-by-twelve-foot cement cage.

Ray has the driver avoid the hotel's main entrance and drop them off by the side door he saw Diego come out of. A half hour passes before another staffer comes out, and Ray pulls Wilbur inside and onto a service elevator.

Soon after that, they're both showered and in fresh clothes, and Wilbur sits cuffed to the bedpost.

"Why'd you retire?" Wilbur asks.

Ray pulls a yellow Post-it note off the mirror and takes a last look at the *XO S* before he tucks it into his wallet and stuffs his remaining belongings into his duffel.

"To no longer have to deal with people like you."

"I'm serious. You seem like you'd love being a cop."

The comment hits home. "I do—did."

"So, why retire?"

Frank Sinatra's silky-smooth "Summer Wind" begins to play in Ray's head as his thoughts drift back six months to the vivid memory of a fateful day.

The crime scene was grotesque, even for a cop.

It was the wee hours of the early morning, and Ray scoured the scene for the twelfth time. It was the third murder and rape in as many weeks. And as he stood over the bloodstain, its outline still visible despite the cleanup crew's efforts, the scene's soul whispered to him the full stench of its brutality, its terror, its rage—an audacious, brazen crime with the violated corpse left in a shallow grave in the historic Hunts Point Slave Burial Ground.

The horrific scene rumbled in memories of another crime that was committed last summer.

It was one of those nights when the heat and humidity executed their blistering assault on anything in their path. The kind of night when, for most in the city's lower-income neighborhoods, the only relief was found under the spray shooting from a loosened fire hydrant cap or sitting on the stoop or fire escape fanning themselves and their kids with a torn-off top of a Trix or Cocoa Puffs box.

The sheer audacity and cruelty of the crime never left Ray. Nor will anyone ever be able to explain why the thirty-one-year-old freak who committed it cut off his ears, nose, and nipples ten minutes before he went on his killing and dismembering rampage, then cut off his penis and stabbed himself until he died.

When it comes to violent crime scenes, these early morning hours are when Ray was at his best. At his sharpest. His most focused.

There was a serenity, he told anyone who asked, that came over him while the masses slept—when the city's air was at its quietest and a crime scene was free of the distractions of other units, whose work is done.

It was within this brief window, before the static din roared in as the city came alive, that a crime scene's soul told its tale. And anytime Ray got the chance, he preached to rookie detectives how the first ten canvasses of a crime scene turned only the conspicuous stones. It was thereafter that the hidden gems that cleared someone or caged them for life were often found.

He'd long thought the city's oppressive heat and humidity had skin in the violent game. Nothing compares to its vile heavy funk magnified by the mass of humanity ebbing and flowing through the city's gauntlet of skyscrapers while drowning in a polluted sea of honking horns, fumes, sirens, whatever. When the heat and humidity struck, the result was fierce, dogged, and merciless. While it brought the cement, bricks, and asphalt to tears, it gnawed at New Yorkers' souls. Even the pigeons and rats would go mad.

But on this night, in the wee hours of the early morning, it was different. On this night, a frigid bone chill stung the air. On this night, the crime scene's whispers were indistinct.

It was a hair shy of 3:00 a.m. when Ray, exhausted, clamped his coat around his neck and headed back to his sedan while, overhead, a low-flying police chopper thumped past on its way across the river to Rikers.

As he made his way across town to the Bruckner Expressway, the gentle sway of Sinatra's cashmere voice crooning "Summer Wind" emanated from the speakers and ushered in a wave of calm and warmth. Ray's eyes finally relaxed, unfazed by the intermittent pounding and clanking triggered by countless potholes.

Thoughts of his father breezed in. Not a day went by when Ray didn't feel his father's presence on these streets. Nor was Ray ever prouder than when older, long-standing residents would tell him they knew his dad, and that he was a good man.

Thanks to people like his father, and others like him, of all races and genders, the Bronx has come a long way since the burned-out buildings and drug-infested, crime-ridden streets of the seventies and eighties.

In pockets like Hunts Point, though, if the trees do fool you into

dropping your guard, there are plenty of other reminders that it's still a
tough part of town: from gang graffiti on bodegas and housing project
walls to handmade signs hung on lampposts that read DON'T SHOOT.
CHILDREN AT PLAY.

It was all green lights to the Bruckner Expressway, and Ray headed
up the ramp to head south to the Major Deegan and eventually to the
Third Avenue Bridge back to Manhattan. But a mile ahead, a fuel spill
forced him off the expressway and deep into the South Bronx neighborhood of Mott Haven.

Together with Hunts Point, these two neighborhoods account for
two of the top three most dangerous neighborhoods in New York City.

Famous for its murder rate, Mott Haven is often touted as an out-
door shooting range. Averaging a crime rate 400 percent higher than
the national average, residents know to be on guard during the day and
to stay inside when it gets dark. Nearby nonresidents know to avoid
the area altogether. Your chances of being a victim of a violent crime in
Mott Haven are one in thirty-two, only to be outdone by Hunts Point,
where it's one in twenty-two.

At this hour, the streets of Mott Haven were desolate, save for the
homeless, passed-out addicts, gangbangers up to no good, and a few pedestrians heading home from graveyard shifts. On many of the streets,
the asphalt was so worn that huge patches of the original red brick laid
in the early 1900s were exposed.

As Ray cruised down Westchester Avenue, he was too worn out to
be irritated by the lit orange detour sign and A-frame barricades that
blocked the street at the next intersection.

The arrow directed him to the right, onto East 156th Street, and
he made his way across town to Third Avenue and hung a left for the
one-mile ride down to the bridge. But as he cruised through the intersection a few blocks later, out of the corner of his eye, he spotted an older
man in a janitorial staff uniform being mugged by a stocky dark-skinned
guy in a wool cap and a lime-green bandanna masking his face.

The colors pegged him as a member of the Trinitarios, a violent
Dominican-American prison and street gang on the rise.

Adrenaline tore through Ray's veins. He slammed on the brakes, called for backup, went lights-and-siren, and peeled over. It took less than a heartbeat for the guy to bolt, and after Ray checked on the older man, he took off after him shouting, "Police!"

Backup did their best to track Ray as he chased the guy down the garbage-strewn street, past a group of homeless heroin addicts sucking down Big Gulps, then over a boarded-up graffiti-covered fence. Rats the size of Subway foot-longs scattered as Ray chased him across the rubbish-filled vacant lot and back over the fence on the opposite side.

Closing in on him, it became clear the guy was a teenage kid—well past old enough to be a killer, especially when he's a Trinitario.

Several blocks later, the kid ducked down a dark, narrow alley in between two run-down three-story apartment buildings—one above an old deli, the other above a boarded-up discount sofa store.

A wary Ray followed him in, and as the gap between them narrowed, there was enough ambient light for him to see the kid wheel around and take a shooter's stance.

Ray fired, and the kid, way out of his league, tumbled backward and dropped.

But then another shot rang out from above.

It missed Ray's head by an inch, and he got off a shot at another lime-green-bedecked banger on the roof and retreated out of the alley as backup arrived.

The chase netted several collars, and while the crime scene investigators began their long task ahead, in the alley, Ray stared at seventeen-year-old Isia Serante—the dead gangbangers name—as the coroner tagged and bagged him. *What a waste*, he thought to himself, and the questions began their stampede through in his head.

Would Isia be alive if I hadn't pulled a double shift?

Would Isia be alive if I had left the crime scene a minute earlier?

A minute later?

If the lights had not all been green?

If the expressway had not been shut down?

If I had taken a different street?

If there had been no detour?
Round and round . . .

"Wow . . . That had to be tough, but . . . sounds justified," Wilbur says.

Ray stuffs his last item into the duffel and zips it up. "They never found the kid's gun."

"Still . . . justified."

"Not according to the news, or to Black Lives Matter and every other civil rights group." The rawness of the emotional wound is still evident in Ray's voice. In today's cancel culture, with its anti-cop drivel, Ray's lineage did little to help him. If anything, it provided the politicized news media an opportunity to create a synchronized media blitz that featured Ray as merely a product of a family and a flawed system defined by white privilege, toxic masculinity, and police brutality against blacks, Hispanics, and other minorities—each sensationalized story handcrafted to foment greater outrage and get higher TV ratings.

It takes a moment, but the realization hits Wilbur. "Wait a minute. You're the . . . They forced you out."

"Way to go, Einstein," Ray says.

Wilbur lets it sink in. "Too bad you're a middle-aged white guy. Made it easy."

Ray can't help but smile, and he slides Wilbur's carry-on over, pulls out one of the stacks of hundreds, peels off a grand, and stuffs it in his pocket. "For the flights."

"There's ten million more for you if we call it a day. I'm sure it beats whatever your pension would have been. I don't need it all anyway."

The magnitude of the offer gives Ray pause. He doesn't accept it, but he doesn't immediately reject it either.

"Ten million?"

"Make it twenty. Do something special for Stephanie. Win her back."

Ray mulls it over for another moment. "Pay it to the piper."

Wilbur's head and shoulders slump. "Don't forget housekeeping."

"Oh yeah. Good call." Ray sets another two bills on the nightstand and tucks the rest back in the carry-on when something else inside catches his attention, and he pulls out an old-school composition note-book boldly labeled VOLUME ONE.

Wilbur squirms. "Raymond, please . . . It's personal."

Ray flips through the pages. On each is a numbered, handwritten list of Dos, Don'ts, How-Tos, Ways to Know, Things No One Will Tell You, and so on. He chuckles at a few of the titles: "FIVE SIGNS THAT RASH COULD BE FATAL," "SEVEN WAYS CATS DON'T GET IT," "SIX WAYS TO RUIN BRUNCH," and "MANSCAPING: SEXY OR WHAT THE FUCK IS THAT? (NINE SHORT CUTS TO AVOID)."

"Where are the ten ways how not to be a putz?" Ray asks.

"Right after the twenty on how not to be a schmuck."

Ray claps the notebook shut, sticks it back in the carry-on, and pulls out Wilbur's passport. The name reads Randolph Thurston Turner, with a Vermont address.

"Amazing the quality you can obtain online today," Wilbur says.

"The best name you could think of to replace Wilbur was Randolph?"

"It's my middle name."

"You're kidding."

"No, why?" he asks, unsure of the problem.

"And for middle, you went with Thurston?"

"It was my grandfather's name."

"You're kidding," Ray says again with greater incredulity.

"No, why?" Wilbur asks, dumbfounded.

"Never mind," Ray says, and tosses it back in the carry-on.

TWENTY-ONE

The clock on the terminal wall ticks to 1:30 a.m. Despite the hour, a considerable crowd hustles and bustles through the airport amid a cavalry of armed *policía* on patrol, all in dark navy Policía SVA uniforms.

Over at the security checkpoint, an SVA officer studies the images on the X-ray screen and sends Ray and Wilbur's baskets through.

But when they reach for them, a burly female officer named Segura snatches them away, saying, "Follow me, please."

They trail her to an inspection table, where Wilbur, stiff and unblinking, eyes her every move as she sifts through his carry-on, disturbing his meticulous packing job.

His distress doesn't go unnoticed.

"There a problem?" she asks with a snap as she rifles through his clothes.

"No, no problem. It's just that, uh . . . Unrolled underwear . . . It's not one of the eight most effective ways to pack a carry-on."

Her eyes linger on him given the ludicrous nature of the comment, but she brushes him off, tosses his stuff back in the carry-on, and moves on to Ray's duffel.

"We can't miss our flight. It's the last one out," Ray says.

"I understand, sir. But we are taking extra precautions tonight. There was an audacious shooting earlier."

"Yeah, heard about it."

"The shooter may have been an American."

Wilbur looks at Ray. "Gives the rest of us a bad name."

Ray bites his tongue, and when Segura opens his duffel, she's taken aback when she sees his NYPD badge and picks it up.

"I'd love to stick around and help you catch the bad guys, but"—he smiles and points at his badge—"I'm retired."

Wilbur snorts, and Segura places the badge back in the duffel and pulls out three small Ziploc bags of coffee beans—one labeled Cauvery/India, another Robusta/Vietnam, and the third, Costa Rica 95.

"Umm," she says after she sniffs the Cauvery.

Ray's eyes brighten. "Hints of citrus, right?"

She nods and does the same with the other two bags. "Could use a cup now," she says and gives a bean from each bag a swab test. "Enjoy your flight."

"What is it with you and those beans?" Wilbur asks as Ray hustles him through the terminal.

As they stride to the last gate at the far end, the PA blares. "This is the final boarding call for Spirit flight fifty-three to Houston, Texas, leaving out of gate number ten." They hand the gate agent their tickets without a second to spare—while out the window, Phil and other passengers deplane, making their way down the mobile airstairs from a Delta jet.

Phil's flight made it to Costa Rica in less than the standard three-and-a-half hours but still landed ten minutes late. *Not bad*, Phil thought considering the half-hour departure delay because of a faulty first-class toilet.

Happy, albeit tired, to be on terra firma, he scuttles along with the herd across the tarmac and into a covered passageway leading to the terminal. But as he makes his way down, out one of the passageway's large windows, he notices two guys on the tarmac, hustling toward a Spirit jet.

At first, it's meaningless. But when Wilbur trips and goes down, Phil does a double take, and to the chagrin of other passengers, he muscles his way to the window.

"Motherfucker!"

Ray helps Wilbur get up. And as if by a sixth sense, he catches sight of Phil staring at them from the passageway window.

On any given day, he would have blown it off, but something about the intensity of Phil's stare and rigid body language leaves its mark as he and Wilbur bound up the airstairs, the last ones to get on the plane. And under the weighty glare of the other impatient passengers, they march down the aisle to their seats in the third-to-last row.

Ray tosses his duffel in the overhead bin, but Wilbur sets his carry-on on the aisle floor.

"What now?" Ray whispers, irritated.

Wilbur opens the carry-on and takes out his dye-free recycled polyester fanny pack, from which he retrieves a spray vial and spritzes their seats. "Five, four, three, two . . ." A universe of tiny incandescent specs appears on the seats.

"See those?" he says. "Millions of germs, bacteria, and viruses that can potentially kill you. Including the Corrrooonaaaa."

Ray holds his hand up to Wilbur's face, his fingers outstretched. "See these . . . Five things that can *definitely* kill you. Sit down."

Ray grabs Wilbur's collar when he goes for the aisle seat. "Don't even . . ."

"Fine," Wilbur says, resigned, and he maneuvers into the middle seat. "But if they're overbooked, let's take the money."

With the end in sight, Ray settles in, when something out the window catches his attention, and he leans over for a better look. It's Phil inside the terminal with the gate agent, animatedly pointing at their plane, but it's clear she's not accommodating when he throws his hands up and stomps away.

Wilbur follows Ray's gaze. "What? They catch the shooter?"

TWENTY-TWO

"Holy mother! What are the odds?" Phil says as he ambles before the trainees, tethered to a Banana Nut Bread contrail.

Catching sight of Wilbur Bailey on the tarmac was the kind of lucky break Phil would never have thought possible. Not a life-or-death lucky break, but the kind of monumental stroke of good luck that he rarely feels and hasn't felt in a long time. The kind that brings a swift end to what could otherwise be a long, drawn-out, risky venture in a foreign country. The kind that will not only save his job but put another notch in his closed-case belt and pave the way for him to take his rightful place in the fifth-floor corner office.

"Texas two-step," Phil says to the bartender at the Holiday Inn bar, grateful the joint was still open after he dropped his stuff off in the room. Ruminating on his lucky break gives him a second wind as he nurses the shot of whiskey and a beer.

With each sip, the magnitude of the break grows, and he thinks back to the last time he got this lucky on a case—it was his first, right after his promotion to deputy agent in charge.

A guy from Austin had embezzled a boatload of cash which he laundered through phony charities set up in foreign countries, where the cash was converted into cryptocurrency. From there it traveled around the world through various international transfer apps and was funneled in increments back to what appeared to be a legitimate US charity for the homeless. To pull off the elaborate scam, eight of the charity's beneficiaries were part of the charade and lived as homeless people for over two years.

But one of them, antsy with his newfound wealth, began layering cash payments through a guy he knew who knew another guy who knew another guy who knew another guy's mistress. And after each siphoned off their cut, the cash was routed and rerouted through several temporary accounts at large and small banks, after which he used his remaining boatload to buy a fully loaded boat and a grandiose house with a dock in a tony Miami neighborhood on one of the canals.

At first, Phil's investigation was on the fast track to nowhere, until one day, a boat full of coeds on spring break was cruising by and snapped photos of Mr. Homeless basking in some Pornhub-worthy carnal nasty with his girlfriend on the bow of his. Within ten minutes, the pics, adorned with inspired slogans, went viral. If not for that, everyone involved in the scam would have been home free.

"I didn't know who Ray Dawson was when I spotted him at the airport with Bailey, or if they were working together," Phil tells the trainees. "The truth is I didn't care. I was just thrilled I'd be going home. I phoned Callahan and told him it was in the bag—Wilbur Bailey would be landing in Houston at 7:00 a.m."

The Banana Nut Bread vapor cloud billows as it erupts from his lungs.

"Or so I thought."

TWENTY-THREE

It's a beautiful night to fly. The captain announced his anticipation of a smooth ride and encouraged everyone to sit back, relax, and enjoy the flight.

An hour into the flight, there's not been so much as a ripple of turbulence as they cruise over northern Honduras. From here, the flight path takes them over Belize and the southeastern tip of Mexico, and then it's a straight shot over the Gulf of Mexico into Houston.

Inside the cabin, it's quiet save for the hum of the engines and overhead A/C spouts. Most of the passengers are asleep, while others read, watch movies, or are busy on laptops and tablets. One young woman stares out her window, lost in thought, while in the seat behind her, a young kid on his first flight has his eyes glued to the flight map video display of the plane's location, altitude, ground speed, time in the air, and time till they land.

But back in the third-to-last row . . .

"I'm just saying . . ." Wilbur says to Ray, his voice hushed.

Ray's eyes snap open, and he pops his seat upright. "You gonna leave me the heck alone?"

Wilbur stares straight ahead and slides the tips of his index finger and thumb across his lips. But no sooner does Ray recline and settle back in and close his eyes than . . .

"With that attitude, you're gonna die alone, you know that?" Wilbur says. "Take it from someone in the know. Loneliness is no fun. It's a dark chasm with no bridge. A venom with no antidote. It's like you're the only fish in a fishbowl in the middle of the ocean—locked in the grip of routine futility where unfettered emotions roam unchecked and fester." His head droops, and his tone turns more earnest. "It strips away your confidence, your dignity, and eventually your soul—your head-stone the only trace you were here."

Ray's eyes again pop open, and his seat uprights. "Who are you, Dr. Phil now?"

"I'm just saying there are eleven surefire ways to win Stephanie back."

Ray squirms in his seat. *Here we go again.* "Why don't you tell me something useful, like one surefire way to get you to shut up."

"Short fuse . . . That's the third most self-destructive behavior."

"*My* behavior is self-destructive?" Ray says, fending off the insatiable urge to knock him out cold again. "No. Self-destructive is stealing money from a boss with Russian mob ties, defrauding the US government, com-mitting wire fraud, money laundering, traveling on a phony passport, and living your life by the one hundred most effective ways to be a fool."

Wilbur turns to Ray, his eyebrows raised. "Russian mob? Mika?"

"That's right, dingbat."

After that sinks in, Wilbur sits back and smiles. "Wow. Icing on the cake."

"Glad you think being chopped up or spending the rest of your life in prison is icing 'cause both are likely in your future."

The fight drains from Wilbur's face. "I have no future." He grabs his fanny pack and pulls out an envelope from Alan Lobel, MD, at the Texas Medical Center, and hands it to Ray. The lab report inside de-tails that Wilbur Bailey has stage IV pancreatic cancer. "Six months, at best," Wilbur says.

Ray looks at him, searching. "This why you took the money?"

Wilbur nods. "I thought I could put it to better use. Help the en-vironment. And the animals. Awful what we do to animals because we think we're superior."

Ray's eyes mellow, and his demeanor softens—until he bursts out laughing.

"That funny to you?" Wilbur says, taken aback.

Ray stops laughing. "No," he says, and reveals what he had heard from Joe in the hotel bathroom. "But the fact that your doctor, Lobel, is a mole for the IRS, and you're in perfect health, is." Ray smiles. "May not be the oldest ruse in the book, but one of the most successful."

Wilbur, dumbfounded, tries to comprehend.

"Christ, Wilbur, even my dog gets it. They took a kill shot. Lobel owed over half a mil in back taxes, and the IRS ate it in return for the fake diagnosis. But instead of clearing your conscience, like most on death row, and helping the IRS nail Salko, you go full-tilt Bernie Madoff." Ray tosses the lab report into Wilbur's lap. "How's that icing taste?" he says and reclines, settles back in, and shuts his eyes.

Wilbur turns pale and starts to hyperventilate. "Motherfucker!" he blurts out loud.

Startled passengers nearby jerk awake and shoot looks his way.

Seconds later, Donna, the senior flight attendant, appears at their seats and kneels beside them. "Gentlemen, is everything okay?"

Wilbur lowers his head and nods. Ray glances at her name tag. "Couldn't be better, Donna. Thank you."

"Okay, but please keep it down. Other passengers are trying to sleep. And . . . watch the language."

"We're sorry," Ray whispers, and casts Wilbur a disapproving glance. "Could I trouble you for a pillow?" he asks Donna before turning to Wilbur. "Pillow?"

"Filtered mountain spring water, please," Wilbur mutters to her, his head still down.

Donna heads to the back galley and returns with both. "The pillow's five dollars, but I'll let it slide if you both promise to behave."

"Cross my heart," Ray says. Donna starts back up the aisle, and Ray reclines, sticks the pillow behind his head, puts on headphones, and closes his eyes. "Night, Wilbur."

Wilbur drains his water and takes several deep breaths to calm himself, when across the aisle on the tray of the sleeping passenger, he spots a pen lying on the open magazine's crossword puzzle.

"I'm gonna be sick," he says as he clutches the lab report, stands, and shimmies past. Without missing a step, he snatches the pen, heads to the bathroom, and once inside, he locks the door and paces around in a tiny circle like a caged animal.

"Fuck. Fuck. Fuck. Fuck. Fuck."

Staring at himself in the mirror, he comes to terms with what he's about to do.

TWENTY-FOUR

"Excuse me," Wilbur says to Donna. "My name is Randolph Turner. I'm in 22D."

"I know," she says, her face expressionless.

"I don't want to cause a panic, but the man next to me . . . Raymond, I think his name is. He's a psychotic ex-cop. Suicidal. Maybe on drugs."

She eyes him, unsure where this is going.

"As soon as we took off," Wilbur says, "he launched into this rant about how his wife left him, and he was fired and lost his pension, and . . . this fell out of his pocket." He holds up a torn-off quarter of the lab report, points out the cancer diagnosis, and flips it over to a hand-written note. "He's not going out alone."

Donna's face reflects the gravity of the note's key details: *My dog told me . . . There's no hope . . . a bomb . . . Go out with a bang, my father always said . . . Steph, love you always. Everyone else, bite me! . . . Forever Yours, Raymond Dawson.*

"Sit there, and don't move," she says, indicating the flight attendant's seats, and she heads into the cockpit.

Within thirty seconds, the cabin is secure, the seat belt indicators illuminate, the alert chimes, and the captain's voice fills the air. "Folks, this is the captain. Due to a security threat, we're making an unscheduled stop in Honduras. Everyone, please remain seated for the duration of the flight."

The plane lurches into a steep descent. Those passengers who didn't wake during the announcement do so now—including Ray, who jolts up and whips around toward the bathrooms. A young mother and her small child come out of one, and he unbuckles and heads back to check the other.

"Sir, you need to take your seat immediately," snaps the male flight attendant in the rear galley. But despite the command and the green 'vacant' indicator on the bathroom door, Ray peeks inside and hustles back up the aisle, scanning each row.

"There's always one," an angry passenger says as he breezes past.

Halfway up, Donna stops him cold. "Mr. Dawson, get back in your seat."

"I'm looking for my nephew, Wilbur. I mean, Rudolph. No, I mean—"

"Enough," Donna says. "Sit down. Now."

A beefy guy comes up behind her. "Sir, I can assure you he hasn't left the plane."

"Why don't you mind your own business," Ray says. "I'm a cop."

The guy flashes his air marshal badge. "You mean an ex-cop."

Ray furrows his forehead, caught off guard by the marshal's awareness. "Once a cop . . ." Ray says as he heads back to his seat.

"Yeah, right," the marshal says and makes it clear Ray's now in the middle.

Twenty minutes later the Spirit jet touches down on a remote runway—a former mainstay for drug traffickers until ten years ago when it was seized and used for military training before its conversion to a municipal support facility for the local agriculture business.

The bright yellow jet looks incongruous as it decelerates past crop dusters, single-engines, and old military aircraft and stops at the end of the runway, where a dark van awaits.

Donna opens the door, and five armed Honduran police in tactical uniforms rush in and beeline down the aisle past the anxious passengers. But none of them are more shocked than Ray when they stop in front of him, the air marshal standing at their side.

"On your feet and turn around," the squad's captain says in English with a thick Spanish accent.

Ray looks at him in disbelief. "You're kidding me, right?"

"Up now and turn around."

Ray complies, and they cuff him, grab his duffel bag, and escort him up the aisle to enthusiastic passenger applause. And as Ray and the officers near the front door, Wilbur peeks around the partition and waves bye-bye.

"Dead! You hear me, Wilbur? Dead!" Ray shouts as they hustle him out, toss him in the van, and slam the door shut.

TWENTY-FIVE

"To say Callahan was a little bugged is like saying Kim Jong Un is a little soft on human rights," Phil says to the group of IRS trainees. He takes another swig while the group laughs.

Phil doesn't like Callahan. Never has. Sure, he puts up with him and respects his position of authority. But on a gut level, Phil thinks Callahan's actions invariably reek of ulterior motives—personal and professional—coupled with an extraordinary commitment to self-promotion and self-preservation, at any cost.

"I wanted to tell him to kiss my ass. But when debt has your balls in a vise, and you're one paycheck away from disaster, you swallow your pride, keep your mouth shut, and do what you're told."

Sucking in a pull of Banana Nut Bread, Phil's thoughts drift back to the moment he learned the Spirit jet carrying Wilbur Bailey had landed in Honduras, and how, for reasons he can't explain, memories of Lorena flooded in.

She was already on his mind when he left the Holiday Inn bar and went back to his room to grab his stuff and catch the next hotel shuttle back to the airport.

Ever since the day Lorena died, hotel bars and rooms, especially those far away, depress him. He knows it sounds corny, but before the accident, he looked forward to cases that took him out of town because he loved the feeling of missing her and the anticipation of going home. Home always meant Lorena.

Still, *it's funny*, he thinks, how when he got the call about Wilbur Bailey's plane, the first memory that popped into his mind was his and Lorena's love of grilled steak. How it made no difference whether it was a filet, New York, or their favorite—thick, juicy ribeyes with sautéed onions and mushrooms and a dollop of seasoned steak butter.

It was more than just eating a good cut of meat. It was a Sunday night ritual they performed together from beginning to end—from the preparation of the meat to popping the first can of Bud and sucking down that first cold, crisp gulp. From firing up the new hickory and oak to preparing the sides, salad, and dessert. From the sizzle of the meat when it first hit the rack, to the aroma that smoked off to the heavens. And yeah . . . that first bite together. The comfort and joy of love. Of being home.

The thoughts linger as Phil heads out of the room, and he turns more introspective. He still looks forward to that grilled steak and cooks it perfectly, but it never tastes as good. It doesn't taste at all. Nor does the Caesar salad or the sautéed onions and mushrooms. None of it. No matter the extra dollop of steak butter or extra garlic cloves. Or endless shakes of salt. No matter his effort and desire to recreate the taste, the feeling, it all proves futile. Not even bacon can paddle a pulse. *Bacon, for Chrissake!*

Several minutes later, staring out the shuttle bus window, he realizes it was his and his wife's habitual behavior, their rituals, that brought him comfort, that made life taste great. And though the performance of the rituals is the same and always will be, for the first time he accepts that without her, everything else won't—and never will again.

The finality of the admission drives his thoughts further out, deeper.

Man . . . She was beautiful.

Am I lost?

Did Lorena's death cause me to feel this way? I mean, other things I had long enjoyed before her no longer feel worth doing or as enjoyable without her.

Or did the natural, relentless progression of Father Time make me lose interest in these things?

And why is it Father Time and Mother Nature?

Which is more powerful?

Do either realize how sexist they sound today?

Should Time and Nature be fired? Canceled? Jailed? Impeached at the very least?

Am I breaking PC law if I tell the woman on the third floor she looks nice?

Can I be canceled merely for thinking it?

When did we go from "Sticks and stones will break my bones" to "What the fuck did you just say?"

How did all this happen?

Please . . . I need to find my way home.

Man . . . She was beautiful.

Round and round . . .

From somewhere in the back rows of the FLETC lecture hall, the shout of a female trainee breaks Phil's reverie. "Where's Wilbur?"

TWENTY-SIX

Maybe it's the raw fear in his eyes. Maybe it's the predawn dark of night. Either way, with a deflated airplane flotation device around his neck and another around his carry-on, Wilbur doesn't see the chain-link fence as he hauls ass through the tall grassy field along the airport's perimeter.

The jolt when he runs into it stops him cold, and the recoil flings him onto his butt, dazed and terrified an alarm is sure to scream and trigger floodlights.

But neither happens, and he pulls himself together, plows through a series of back, neck, hip flexor, and shoulder stretches, and over the fence he and his carry-on go.

Thirty seconds later, the sound of rushing water hits his ears, growing in intensity with each step. And in another minute, he spills out of the tall grass onto a riverbank.

His eyes drift downriver as a fiercely churning current rushes by. The rage and power of it give him pause. He's never been a good swimmer, and at age ten, after he saw *Jaws* at a friend's house, he avoided being in the water at all costs.

For over a year, he wouldn't even take a bath, let alone go for a swim. But on a deeper level, being in the water carries the risk of drowning. The risk of not being able to breathe. Here, too, the wind played a role.

A therapist told him his fear of the water was rooted in his fear of death, which was rooted in his fear of being unable to breathe, which was rooted in his falling off the playground climber when he was six and couldn't breathe. "You knocked your wind out," his father had told him. It left a mark.

To this day, the fear of not being able to breathe still grips him. On his list of "THE FIVE WORST WAYS TO DIE," burning in a fire and drowning are numbers one and two. Number three is drowning while trying to save yourself from burning.

Wilbur sometimes thinks about those who in protest set themselves on fire or commit suicide by walking or plunging into the ocean, a lake, or a river—driven by what must be some form of mental illness or a deranged devotion to some cause. Still, he can't help but respect and appreciate the sheer will, determination, and courage it takes for them to knowingly cut off their ability to breathe.

It's a fear Wilbur vowed he would one day overcome, though he can't recall the last time he made the effort. But here at the water's edge, confronted with the now or never, he yanks the flotation devices' rip cords, and with a final deep breath, he steps into the water and—*whoosh!*—he and his carry-on are swept away.

"You're making a big mistake, pal," Ray says, his face red, rife with anger and frustration.

It's more than a bit of a stretch to call the small airport's main building a terminal, given it's one large cinder-block building with a handful of windows and a corrugated steel utility roof. Inside, the air is dank and heavy with mildew and acrid fumes of gasoline, pesticides, and a host of other toxic chemicals.

Tucked in the back of the building, in a room designated the security room, the officers mill about the antiquated surveillance apparatus, furniture, phones, and other equipment, all of which reflect the airport's physical decline and low-level security. It's also why, instead of in a holding cell, Ray sits cuffed to a chair in the corner, the contents of his pockets and duffel bag scattered across a nearby table.

The captain sidles up and backhands him across the face. "Cómo se dice . . . bullshit!" he says.

Another officer enters the room and strides over. "A passenger is missing—a Randolph Thurston Turner. And this was in the plane's bathroom garbage." He hands the captain the rumpled remaining three-quarters of Wilbur's lab report, and when he aligns it with the quarter on which Wilbur wrote the note, they complete Wilbur's name.

"Cómo se dice 'I told you so, asshole,'" Ray says. "Wilbur Bailey is a wanted criminal. You need to set up a perimeter. Bring in dogs and air support. And check the passengers and crew—see if any are missing phones." The captain glares at him, but Ray can see uncertainty in his eyes. "I can help you. You don't know this guy. His behavior, his habits . . . So, get me out of this damn chair."

For Mika Salko, life is much more pleasant.

Just as he does every sunrise, he heads out with the *Wall Street Journal* and his tablet to his usual chair at the table along the edge of the terrace off his kitchen, where his house staff serves him his organic kasha and fried egg Butterbrot.

The terrace is one of the main reasons he bought the twelve-thousand-square-foot, six-bedroom, eight-bathroom Piney Point Village estate. The other is its position, set back on a private road that affords him the privacy he wants, the security he needs, and the natural splendor of the ten acres on which it sits along the Buffalo Bayou.

But what he loves most is sitting in that chair along the edge of the terrace and watching and listening to the birds that bathe and feed along the bayou and among the majestic old oak trees and hundred-foot-tall sycamores with their massive trunks and large sharply toothed bright green leaves. It brings him a peace and serenity he finds nowhere else.

This sunrise, however, Salko's a bit uneasy, his focus is on the CNBC anchor reporting the breaking news on his tablet.

After Wilbur Bailey went AWOL, Salko contacted several close confidants and asked if they could poke around and let him know if they heard anything regarding his whereabouts. One of those calls paid off—an old girlfriend at Yale who now works for a deputy attorney general in Washington, DC, and is plugged in all over the town. She tipped him off when Bailey was due to arrive at George Bush Intercontinental Airport.

Salko let her know his gratitude would be expressed in a hefty donation when she made her run for Congress. Of course, he left out how her assistance would enable him to have members of his private security lying in wait for Wilbur at the airport, ready to deliver justice in a more decisive way than the feds.

"Several premarket movers took a hit when the Houston-bound jet made an emergency landing at a small airstrip in Honduras, but later rebounded after the bomb threat was ruled a hoax," the TV anchor reports.

A thumbnail photo of Ray appears on the screen. "Former New York police detective Raymond Dawson, the alleged perpetrator of the hoax, was restrained by Honduran authorities and escorted off the plane. You may recall, Mr. Dawson was forced to resign after he shot and killed fifteen-year-old Isia Serante in an alley next to the family's Bronx home."

Within minutes, it's the lead story on every morning broadcast and news station. In New York City, across the Harlem River from Yankee Stadium, on Frederick Douglass Boulevard near 155th Street, the early morning crowd waits along the bodega's counter for their usual grab-and-go. But all eyes are glued to *Good Morning America* on the small overhead TV.

Among them are Stephanie and three of her crew, waiting for their order as host Robin Roberts continues her report with Ray's thumbnail still on the screen. "This video, shot by a passenger on the plane, captures those final moments."

The image on the TV changes to choppy phone video footage of the Honduran police escorting Ray off the plane to passenger applause. After he shouts, "Dead! You hear me, Wilbur? Dead!" the image freezes on Wilbur peeking around the partition and a thumbnail of his IRS wanted poster appears next to Ray's. "The man Dawson is threatening in this video is this man, Wilbur Bailey, one of the IRS's ten most wanted fugitives."

"The dung paste guy," Stephanie blurts out as she stares in disbelief at the screen.

Norma, the elderly proprietor behind the counter, sets the four bacon, egg, and cheese sandwiches and coffees on the counter in front of her. She looks from the TV pic of Ray back to Stephanie. "What is it you see in that man, darlin'?"

TWENTY-SEVEN

The makeshift security room's ancient fax machine spits out a low-quality copy of Wilbur Bailey's IRS wanted poster, and one of the Honduran officers grabs it and hands it to the captain.

"Sólo en América," the captain mumbles when he sees the reward.

Ten minutes earlier, at Ray's request, the captain had ordered a check of the passengers and crew to see if any were missing phones. Of the five people who couldn't locate their cells, Ray zeroes in on the flight attendant, Donna, and a ping triangulation confirms his hunch.

With a cell crooked in his shoulder to his ear, Ray jots the phone's pinging coordinates on his palm as they come in from the cell's surveillance engineer, and he joins the captain and others around a table, a large map spread out before them.

The captain plants his index finger on a dot in the northeast corner of Honduras near its border with Guatemala. "This is us," he says to Ray.

"Odds are he's somewhere in here," Ray says and draws a circle around the dot. "Her phone pinged twice." He glances at his palm. "First here, twenty minutes ago." He draws another circle. "And here, ten minutes later." He draws a third and marks an X over the spot where the three circles overlap. "Then it went silent."

"Because it's underwater," the captain says, and after a final gut check, he offers Ray a 9 mm and a pair of cuffs, their eyes conveying solidarity.

Ray takes both and grabs his badge, passport, and wallet as they file out. Two seconds later he pops back in, grabs his baggies of beans, and darts back out.

The early morning sun is already intense as the motorized police raft carves its way down the river. It's been two and a half hours since Wilbur slipped away. Still no sign of him. But with less than a quarter of a mile to go before they reach the Guatemalan border, one of the officers spots the flotation devices lying on the side of a tire-track dirt road that rises from the water's edge.

A hundred yards in, they come upon a modest-sized cornfield with a hand-painted sign that reads *Granja Orgánica*—Organic Farm.

A bullet train of adrenaline rockets through Ray's veins. He motions for everyone to stop, then climbs a nearby tree and dials Donna's number.

Deep in the cornfield, Wilbur, in dry canvas pajamas, lies fast asleep, his wet clothes draped like a scarecrow on the stalks above. From his hearty snore and incoherent mumbles, it's clear he's immersed in a dream when, next to his head, Donna's cell lights up. But with the sound off, he snores away.

Still, as Ray gazes over the field, he senses he's out there. "Wilbur, it's me, Ray. I'm not angry. I just wanna talk!" he calls out, his hands cupped around his mouth.

Wilbur's eyes snap open mid-snore and he pops up, clears the cobwebs, and snatches his clothes, rustling the stalks.

"Bingo," Ray says.

He jumps off the limb, and he and the officers take off across the field.

Wilbur, his carry-on clutched to his chest, scurries every which way—a mouse caged in a mirror maze of endless rows of corn. But as he rounds into the next row, he's met with a gust of wind.

It's as if it's the first time he's ever felt the wind, and he jolts to a stop and closes his eyes. Calmness washes over him while flowing manes of corn silk feather his face—a moment he wishes would last forever. But it vanishes as quickly as it blew in, and with a final deep breath, he opens his eyes, and his body stiffens—Ray is no more than five feet in front of him.

"Christ! How do you do that?"

"It's a gift," Ray says.

Ray's innate ability to hunt someone down is tough to define and can't be taught. Sure, anyone can learn various methods and techniques. But to be one of the greats, you either have it or you don't.

Ray has it—an intangible God-given X factor residing deep in the recesses of his subconscious. Always there. Hovering. Waiting for its silent call to duty to track prey regardless of whether he's in an urban jungle, where there are no footprints in the mud or broken twigs to lead the way, or in a Costa Rican rainforest or Honduran cornfield. Even at age four, the details he provided—details no four-year-old should ever have to remember—enabled NYPD detectives to track down the armed creep and his eight-year-old brother who killed his father.

"There's a better way, Ray," Wilbur says.

"Lemme guess. Number four of the eight better ways: Shoot Wilbur."

The sarcastic dig is easy for Wilbur to brush off. The tat-covered Hispanic twentysomething that appears further up the row behind Ray with a sawed-off shotgun in one hand and a machete in the other is not.

"Look out!" Wilbur shouts.

Ray doesn't budge. "Sorry, Wilbur . . . Not this time."

But as soon as the shotgun-machete-wielding thug charges toward them, gunfire erupts throughout the field, and a bullet tears through the thug's spine and drops him in his tracks.

Ray hits the deck, taking Wilbur down with him, and he tries to figure out what's happening. But he's at a loss, and as the gunfire intensifies, he crawls over to the guy, tosses his shotgun aside, and confirms he's dead, his focus momentarily drawn to the "17" inked over his entire face—only to look back and see that Wilbur's gone. "Shit!"

Ray grabs the guy's machete and takes off, weaving his way through the cornfield back toward the road they came in on, pausing along the way when he comes upon the bodies of the police captain, another officer, and several dead thugs with similar "17" tattoos.

As he nears the cornfield's edge, the gunfire ends, and the air vibrates with the rumble of a muscle car engine, and he double-times it the rest of the way. But by the time Ray reaches the road, the last two tat-covered thugs pile into a Pontiac GTO and speed away.

Ray looks around, bewildered. There's no sign of Wilbur, only the bloody bodies of two more thugs and the remaining three officers. But when a faint noise blows in off the river, he darts back into the field.

A moment later, a maroon Ford Fiesta motors in, stops beside the cornfield carnage, and out steps Phil—his weapon drawn, his face flush with the realization he's in deeper shit than he bargained for when he, too, hears a faint noise crack in the wind, and he hustles back to his car.

At the riverbank, Wilbur, frantic, pounds the choke on the police raft's motor and musters up all his strength for another yank of the pull cord.

It finally kicks over, and he shoves off and throttles up just seconds before the maroon Fiesta skids up, leaving Phil with nothing more than a fleeting glimpse as the raft disappears around a bend.

"Motherfucker!"

Within an hour, CNN is the first to break the news.

"All six members of the Honduran police unit were killed in the ambush by the heavily armed members of Central America's most violent gang, MF-17, who have strong ties to Mexico's notorious Cartel del Norte." A thumbnail of the cartel's logo appears on the screen: a red, white, and green patch with the initials CDN. "A local source with knowledge of the massacre, who spoke exclusively with us on the condition of anonymity, said it appeared the criminal gang had rescued Dawson and Bailey, who had escaped from the Honduran police and hid in the cornfield. US authorities fear the two men are now on the run under CDN protection."

Wilbur cruises down the river. "Sorry, Ray . . . Not this time," he declares, his arms thrust high in victory, and he savors the moment with a long deep breath. *Peace be with you*, the wind's delicate notes whisper in his ears, its voice calm and still. He throttles down and ponders how amazing it is that life can turn on a dime.

But no sooner does he kick his feet up and settle into his newfound freedom for the second time than the raft rounds into another bend and picks up speed. At first, the mild acceleration goes unnoticed. But as it comes out of the bend, swells rise over submerged boulders, and the raft slides into a churning gauntlet.

As much as Wilbur never liked being in the water, he's never liked being on it either—for fear he might end up in it. He snatches his carry-on, flings open the zipper, and yanks out another old-school composition notebook boldly labeled VOLUME TWO.

He rifles through the pages, past "EARWAX OR TUMOR? FOUR HIDDEN SIGNS," "IS SHE A BITCH? TWO WAYS TO TELL," and "IS HE AN ASSHOLE? FORTY-SIX WAYS TO TELL" and slaps it shut, stuffs it back in the carry-on, and pulls out VOLUME THREE.

With precision, he cuts straight to the list he's looking for: "TEN NO-NOS WHEN WHITE-WATER RAFTING."

1. NEVER TRAVEL WITHOUT A PADDLE.

The initial surge rocks the raft while he scrambles in search of a paddle but finds none, and he goes from zero to panic in under a second, only to be hit with . . .

2. DON'T PANIC.

The next vicious lurch sends him flying off the seat, and he jams the notebook back in his carry-on and hangs on for dear life as the angry swells and unpredictable boiling eddies strike with extreme force.

"Oh God. Oh God. Oh God."

Though it seems to last forever, the raft somehow manages to avoid the jagged rocks and is spit out on the other side. Delirious, Wilbur jumps to his feet and raises his arms in a gesture of praise—oblivious to the machete that pokes five slits through the bottom of the raft.

"Thank you, Lord," Wilbur cries out to the heavens. "From here on in, I promise I'll—" His eyes snap downward as the first jolt of frigid water hits his feet. The fear of drowning tightens its grip with each futile attempt to tap dance over each slit and stem the tide.

"Fuck. Fuck. Fuck. Fuck. Fuck."

Terrified and lucky. It's how Wilbur feels when the sinking raft begins to drift toward the riverbank, and his spirit renews the moment the raft runs aground.

Lucky break, he muses while he rummages for sticks, leaves, dirt . . . Anything he can grab to cloak the raft. But when he scoops up another batch and wheels around, Ray, soaking wet, is no more than five feet in front of him.

"If not this time, Wilbur, when?"

Stunned and bewildered, Wilbur sighs and hangs his head in defeat.

"Told you. It's a gift."

TWENTY-EIGHT

"What is it with you and those beans?" Wilbur says as they stumble out of the forest onto the two-lane road, cuffed together and Ray wearing grossly ill-fitting canvas clothes—his wet ones draped over Wilbur's carry-on.

Ray stuffs the scrunched-up baggy of beans into his pocket. "What is it with you and oil?"

The question catches Wilbur off guard. But his face softens as a gust of wind blows through and the leaves rustle and sing in orchestral harmony. "Wind, Ray. It changed humanity; the first to know that to start a fire, you need to blow on it. The world was discovered thanks to the wind. And its impact on all forms of life, from plant regeneration to wildfires to its effect on climate . . . It's a force so far beyond what any of us on earth can deliver."

It's no surprise that Wilbur developed a passion for clean energy such as wind. Most, if not all, of his progressive values were shaped during his childhood. His grandparents, on both sides, were academics at the University of Oregon, and all were ardent supporters of environmental and climate change issues. Their influence on Wilbur's parents, who met while attending Berkeley, was readily apparent. But it's the wind that, in one way or another, has been a force in Wilbur's life since the day he was born.

His dad fired up their Volvo station wagon and sped off to the hospital as a storm out of the north roared through. The wind was howling at a steady forty miles per hour, with gusts topping sixty.

It was tough enough for Wilbur's dad to maintain control of the Volvo, let alone with his very pregnant wife screaming and baby Wilbur ready to make his big debut.

As luck would have it, his dad spotted a cop, who took over from there and escorted them to the hospital, where at 3:00 a.m. the resident doctors, many of whom were on their fourth watch, welcomed Wilbur into the world at six pounds two ounces.

And after that, the wind never stopped playing a role in his life.

By age five, he was fascinated by how wind helped make his wishes come true—whether by blowing white dandelion puffs into the breeze or blowing out his birthday candles. When his wish for a new bicycle came true, his fascination became an obsession. He pedaled that bike as fast as his legs would go and sought out every downhill slope so he could coast for a while and feel the wind. It was his truth, and it set him free.

To this day, among other influential, deep-seated childhood memories, beyond having the wind knocked out of him on the playground, his most vivid recollection is the fresh, clean floral scent in the breeze after it passed through the laundry his mother hung out back to dry.

Close behind are the melodies of the wind chimes that hung on the patio outside his bedroom and lullabied him to sleep. And, of course, there was Co-op, their dog. Oh, how little Wilbur loved to play with Co-op and see the joy on his face when he ran or hung his head out the car window to feel the wind rush over his face and flap his jowls around.

A few days after Wilbur turned twelve, Co-op died at the ripe old age of sixteen and a half. For weeks Wilbur went to the pet cemetery, not only to sit by Co-op's grave for a while, but to walk among the array of pinwheels, whirligigs, and whirlybirds that adorned many of the headstones—all the while keeping an eye out for any dandelions.

Coupled with Wilbur's growing passion for wind was a keen mathematical prowess. By the time he hit high school, his ability for calculation was well beyond kids several years his senior, and it was then that his affinity for lists began: lists on notebooks, on his backpack, on his sneakers—anywhere he could write.

Soon there were lists everywhere, including a long one reminding him which list to read depending on the circumstances. There was also an ever-growing list of lists he'd read elsewhere, which he cut and pasted into notebooks.

Several doctors suggested he had obsessive-compulsive disorder or might be compensating for a form of early memory loss. One urged electroshock therapy.

"I don't have a problem. I just like to be organized and prepared," Wilbur said decisively. And he never looked back.

High school, though, also brought new challenges and new concerns. Each year, Wilbur became distraught when the Santa Ana winds signaled the beginning of wildfire season. But he became outright irate when some moron—yes, moron—flicked a lit cigarette out the car window or set off fireworks and triggered a massive blaze.

Little did he know, though, that at the start of his senior year, his passion for the wind would play a greater role in his personal life—far beyond what he could have imagined.

A new girl recently moved to the area after her mother landed a job as a meteorologist on the local news. The moment she walked into the classroom, Wilbur knew.

He wasn't sure what he knew, but he knew. And the rest is history.

They both went on to attend Berkeley, where Wilbur earned a master's in energy and resources with an emphasis on engineering, geophysics, and geoscience, and she a master's in ethnic studies with an emphasis on social science and cultural studies.

By the time he graduated, his mind was set—he would dedicate his professional life to doing everything he could to help the environment and every living organism that depended on it.

This truth, his truth, was in his DNA. And as far as he was concerned, nothing is truer than the air we breathe and the power of the wind. A power that dates to the four winds of the Bible—at times beneficial, at times fierce and destructive.

"You ever stop to think about how the wind plays more of a role in your life than any other aspect of the weather?" Wilbur says as he and Ray continue down the two-lane road.

"You mean like the hot air coming out of you?" Ray says. "I promise I will if you shut up."

"You're not alone," Wilbur says. "Most never do, yet we always know when it's there. No one looks out the window and hopes the sun won't mess up their hair or blow away the patio furniture. Nor do they think about how their umbrella is of little good on a windy day or how winters would be a bit more bearable if not for the windchill factor."

"Or how wind shear is what pilots often fear the most," Ray says.

Wilbur's eyes light up, and he smiles. "Yes, Raymond, very good. And wind shear's nothing compared to the average hurricane, which releases the equivalent of roughly two hundred times the total electrical generating capacity on the planet. Far greater for tornadoes, with wind speeds that can reach two to three hundred miles per hour."

"Yeah?" Ray says. "Well, if you really wanna change mankind, maybe one of you geniuses should find a way to harness knowing right from wrong."

"Touché. But every year, in the US alone, wind power keeps over sixty million tons of greenhouse gases from going into the atmosphere and conserves over twenty billion gallons of water."

"Good to know," Ray says.

"It's our planet's most sustainable natural resource, especially for generating electricity. Sure, there are countless obstacles: protests over turbine placement, risk-to-wildlife assessments, endless regulations and government permits, a dizzying array of infrastructure needed to transport the power from the turbines to the people . . . And it takes a whole wind farm, not a turbine or two."

"So, wind power is the reason you went into oil," Ray scoffs. "There's always something you can pin on why people do what they do. But you and oil? . . . Doesn't track. Nor does stealing the money, even if you were dying."

Wilbur hesitates. "Desperation. A windmill company I founded went under about five years ago."

His thoughts drift back to a cold, rainy, gray day—Zephyr's final day.

Zephyr.

It's Greek for the west winds, which signal early spring and summer breezes.

For Wilbur, its meaning was much grander. It signified the realization of a lifelong dream that blossomed into 250 colossal wind turbines spread across sixty thousand acres.

But on a rainy, blustery day, Zephyr's last day, only one turbine remained on. And as Wilbur stood in the cherry picker and ascended the face of its 350-foot steel tower, the aerodynamic swoosh of the windmill's 175-foot blades, as they passed the tower, was breathtaking.

When he stopped before the massive turbine, it was tough to tell if the drops running down his face were rain or tears. And with one final word into his walkie-talkie, he gave the order to pull the plug.

As if a lethal cocktail of drugs used to carry out a death sentence had entered his veins, his chest heaved, and the massive blades ground to a stop.

"We were the talk of the town. The envy of the industry. Cocktail parties. Interviews on all the major networks. Invites to speak at the Ivy Leagues. Paid trips all over the world. A huge digital profile and countless press releases on how revolutionary we were," Wilbur says.

"Then one morning . . ." His face saddened. "A story broke. Unwise decisions my partner made behind my back—and *poof.* I lost a big part of myself that day. But soon after . . . my wife, Wilma, became ill, and I realized I hadn't lost anything so long as she was alive." He takes a deep breath. "I took the job at Amco to take the best care of her I could."

"Your wife's name was Wilma?" Ray asks in disbelief.

"Yes, why?"

"Wilbur, Wilma . . . What are the odds?"

"Odds of what?"

"Never mind."

Wilbur brushes it off. "When I got the cancer diagnosis, I was terrified. I mean, who wouldn't be? And after seeing what it did to Wilma . . ." He smiles, and his eyes soften. "The toughest part was going through it without her to lean on. Alone. Adrift in endless dark thoughts."

Ever since the first time Wilbur's parents took him to Bible study, it struck him how the first thing God saw that wasn't good was for man to be alone. It became Wilbur's greatest fear. The one that caused him the most anxiety. Not alone for a short time, but alone virtually all the time—around people, only peripherally, for short periods every so often.

"Everything looks and feels different when you're alone," he had said to the one coworker he opened up to after Wilma died. "It's like I'm the pelican in the wilderness. The owl in the desert. My highs, my lows— each one a tree that's fallen in the forest with no one there to hear it."

"Snap out of it, Wilbur. In a way, you're lucky," the guy said to him, and poured some powdered creamer into his coffee and gave it a stir. "You're now free to do whatever you want whenever you want."

Wilbur's grip on his coffee tightened. "Thank you. I hadn't thought about it that way," he said to him and smiled while in his mind he seethed. *You fucking scumbag.*

One day, on his way back to Houston from another environmental impact study near Rio Bravo, he was passing through San Antonio when his focus was drawn across the street to Lockehill Cemetery. *Perhaps Wilma's death is still raw,* he thought, unsure why he felt so compelled to pull in.

He meandered through the grounds, each tombstone telling its own short story. But when he stumbled upon one at the cemetery's northern end, a sense of why he had been drawn here crystallized.

Her name was Grace Llewellyn Smith. There is no engraved date of birth nor a date of death. Only the names of two men she had married. But it's Grace's epitaph that captivated Wilbur.

SLEEPS, BUT RESTS NOT
LOVED, BUT WAS LOVED NOT
TRIED TO PLEASE, BUT PLEASED NOT
DIED, AS SHE LIVED, ALONE

"As a man thinketh, so is he," Wilbur says to Ray with a chuckle as they plod down the two-lane road, hoping the next town isn't much farther away. "Heard it countless times at church as a boy, and I thought God took Wilma from me to drive the point home. Then one night, lying in bed, I couldn't stop laughing about *my* diagnosis. I thought—no, I believed—Wilma had done this to me. Her way of saying she wants to see me again." He chuckles again. "She always was a bit heavy-handed."

Ray smiles, sincere and warm. "Cheer up, Wilbur. Plenty of time for God to yank out a rib and make you a new Wilma."

Wilbur chuckles, when, as if by a switch, Ray's smile disappears and he yanks him off the road, down into the foliage, and removes the cuffs as an old box truck comes around the bend. "Anything stupid, and I go straight to number four."

Ray yanks him back onto the road and flags down the truck.

The grizzled Hispanic driver in his sixties reaches for the .45 under his seat but never takes his eyes off Ray as he climbs to his window and flashes a C-note.

TWENTY-NINE

"Reports of the Spirit jet's emergency landing sped through government ranks," Phil says to the group. "I had just settled in at a hotel near the airport when I got the call from Callahan. There was no time to think. I ran back to the airport and was lucky enough to catch a delayed charter for the short flight to Golosón Airport, in nearby La Ceiba, Honduras." A blue star appears, marking the spot on the electronic map displayed on the screen behind him. "I was already in the air when a satellite picked up signals from the flotation devices' emergency radio beacons."

Phil sits up straighter and sucks down a few gulps of water. "Had I not stopped twice to take a leak after we landed, I might have been killed at that cornfield. Never thought I'd thank God for an enlarged prostate," he says to hearty laughter. "One thing was clear, though. I wasn't going home anytime soon."

Still, as disconcerting as that thought of not going home soon had been, the bloody carnage at the Honduran cornfield had been worse, taking Phil back to a time and a place he never wanted to revisit.

The Miami-Dade paramedics phoned Phil soon after they arrived at the site of the car crash. He left Emmi with their friends and arrived at the nightmarish scene fifteen minutes later. There was blood everywhere—on the road, the lamppost, the twisted wreckage strewn about. Both vehicles looked like they had exploded.

"Mr. Dancourt, it'd be best if you step back and wait with me," the young Miami firefighter said.

Four more excruciating minutes passed before the jaws of life managed to cut away a large enough swath for them to pull out Lorena, her body a bloody, mangled mess. Her right leg was gone from the thigh down. No one could believe she still had a pulse as a chopper airlifted her to the University of Miami Hospital ICU, where she was put on life support.

There were ten or more doctors, nurses, and technicians on her team, each of whom provided her with loving care and did everything possible to save her life. But the writing was on their faces.

"The ICU is a place unlike any other," Phil said to the few friends he spoke to about it, and expressed how on one hand it's a facility where medical marvels and brilliant minds are on full display, and how on the other it's a cold, stark corridor through which the Four Horseman roam from one glass-enclosed room to another—their regular arrivals announced by an array of flashing multicolored warning lights and beeping alarms.

Hours later, overtaken by a sense of hopelessness, Phil prayed while her team raced, and on a cavalry of monitors, he watched Lorena's life slip away in vibrant HD color.

Still, his most vivid memory, though he's not sure why and has never told anyone, is standing at the window in the ICU's third-floor lobby and watching the planes, one after the other, roar overhead after taking off from Miami International.

He stood there for over an hour and imagined those on the planes were either heading home or off to a business meeting or somewhere exotic. But he also couldn't help but think how not one person on any of those planes knew they had just passed within a few hundred feet of people who were dying—or those like Lorena, who just had.

For the next couple of months, Phil battled to keep at bay an all-consuming sense of grief and disorientation. And the endless whispers, especially at church, of how Lorena had "passed away," "passed on," "passed." It seemed like every which way he turned, Lorena *passed*—a universal catchphrase no matter the religion, philosophical or spiritual belief, whatever . . . *She passed.*

The more he thought about it, the more it agitated him.

Didn't she walk according to the Bible? Through the valley with the shadow? No, we know better. She passed.

Passed to where? Heaven? The wild blue yonder? Off into the sunset?

And to whom? God Almighty? Satan? To anyone? To anything? Who knows.

Passed. Like a football. A thing of beauty. Tom Brady perfect. Maybe that's what we should say. She Tom Bradied, her soul soaring to Shangri-la in a perfect Hail Mary spiral.

Phil avoided church for a while. But in time, he realized that *passed* is less scary. Realized a pass is over to another place. Another place better than where we had been a mere heartbeat ago. Realized that we, as humans, believe. Must believe. Must have faith. In something. Something unseen. Must have hope. Hope in the intangible.

Or is it fear? A defense mechanism against the frightening frontier of the unknown that follows the lethal dose issued by whoever, or whatever, is the warden over our lives. Fear of the reality that when it's time, when your number is called, there is no stay. No delay. You are going to take the walk through the valley.

Faith? Or fear? Both require a belief in the unknown.

Round and round . . .

"No matter where you are, never drop your guard, and never forget that anyone facing years, or life, in a cage can turn into a killer," Phil says to the trainees. "Still, I assure you, the odds any of you will one day find yourself at the edge of an organic cornfield in Honduras after a massacre are less than the odds you'll win Powerball and Mega Millions twice in the same week."

The group laughs, and Phil cracks another bottle of water. "By the time I'd catch up, Bailey and Dawson were already well into Guatemala."

On the map, a yellow line traces Ray and Wilbur's route northward, and a blue star marks the spot.

"I had no clue what happened to Dawson, or what hell went down in that cornfield," he says and takes a sip. "Truth is I didn't care. I finally had Bailey in my sights and was closing in for the kill." He sucks in a lungful of Banana Nut Bread and exhales the vapor cloud. "So I thought."

THIRTY

Horrific images of the cornfield carnage thunderclap through Phil's brain as he motors his maroon Ford Fiesta down the two-lane road—one eye on the road and the open map that spans the passenger seat, the other on fleeting glimpses of the river through the trees and foliage.

Focus, Phil, he repeats to himself for the third time in the last half hour. But frustrated, he hammers his fist on the center console as the road curves away from the river. But no sooner does the pain surge through his wrist than a burst of sunlight reflects off something shiny by the riverbank, and he slams on the brakes.

The glare off the raft's motor intensifies the closer he gets. But given the effort to conceal it, he quickly surmises Wilbur is long gone. Without another flotation device, Phil doubts Wilbur's in the water and further down the river. And the endless miles of forest provide ample cover in every direction.

When Phil arrives at the raft, a jumble of footprints in the mud around it offers few clues, but he's taken by the several inches of water pooled toward the back. *Could be from splash,* he thinks.

Shoving the leaves and sticks aside, he leans in for a closer look and spots the five slits on the raft's floor. He pokes his finger into one and rubs it around its edges. *Definitely made with a blade.*

Phil's thoughts are a ball of confusion, but he's sure of one thing.

There's no reason for Bailey to have slit the raft on his own. Had he wanted to come ashore, he would have just done so. He stands and looks out at the river and the surrounding woods, gripped with the prospect that without an entire search party, it's over.

"Fuck!"

As he makes his way back to the car, he's not sure if he believes it's over or wishes it is. But the moment he steps out of the forest, something at the road's edge catches his eye. A closer look triggers a blast of adrenaline. Each is no more than four inches long and an inch wide—the unmistakable muddy wheel tracks from Wilbur's carry-on trailing the remnants of four muddy footprints.

Sitting on boxes in the old box truck's cube-shaped cargo area, Ray and Wilbur sway with the rhythm of the road and the truck's worn-out shocks. Bullet-sized holes in the walls and an eight-by-eight-inch cutout in the roof are their sole sources of fresh air and light—enough for Ray to grow increasingly uncomfortable with Wilbur's blank stare.

"Whatever you're thinking, Wilbur . . ."

Wilbur snaps out of his trance. "Was thinking about Wilma, how in many ways she was like you."

"Thinning hair. Rough beard," Ray says.

Wilbur chuckles. "Fearless. Her intoxicating, unapologetic sense of self. Everything I'm not. Proof that opposites attract. Even when she was sick . . . The courage. And the drugs were worse than the cancer. The most common side effect of one was death. Another had thirty-three confirmed deadly side effects and one which may cause kidney failure, though it had never been reported. Know why?"

Ray's stare provides his answer.

"Because no one survives the new or worsening genital fungus that precedes it."

"I could have gone without knowing," Ray says. "Sorry you lost her. Sounds like she was a good woman."

"A saint. Possessed, at least, eighty point six percent—maybe even point seven—of the ten most attractive things in a woman: vibrant, smart, dynamic . . . so perfectly comfortable and confident in her own skin, which I must say was soft and supple."

An almost imperceptible twitch fires through Ray's body. "Nice. But don't let me hear you say the word *supple* again. Certain words give me the heebie-jeebies."

"And *heebie* and *jeebie* don't?"

Sputum.

It's a nasty-sounding word with slangs that run the gamut from *loogie* and *phlomit* to *lung cheese, pavement oyster, Marlboro pudding,* and *land clam*—none of which have ever been craved with a nice cabernet or single malt.

It's also the word that launched Ray's vocabularic heebie-jeebie affliction during a frightening and odious experience on the subway with his mother when he was nine years old.

With the windchill, a polar vortex has New York gripped in single digits. Ray and his mom were headed downtown to Paragon Sports on Eighteenth Street and Broadway. A clearance sale was underway, and Ray needed a new winter coat.

At the next stop, a disheveled, obese man, drunk or high on God knows what, got on the train and took the seat across from them, wobbling from side to side, forward and back, but never taking his glassy eyes off young Ray.

Fortunately, their stop was next, but as they moved toward the door, the guy coughed up a golf-ball-sized, milky-green glob of lung cheese, and it landed on Ray's chest. He yelped and dry-heaved as his mother pulled him out of the car, and a doctor, who was in the car and saw it happen, came over and offered his hankie to Ray's mom, and he looked down at Ray and said, "Don't worry, young man. It's just a little sputum."

The moment the word hit Ray's ears, he tossed up bile-infused chunks of the peanut butter and jelly sandwich he ate before they left, and the vocabularic damage was done.

Ray and Wilbur cling to the side rails as the box truck rounds into a bend.

"What about you and Stephanie?" Wilbur asks. "How'd you meet?"

The question gives Ray pause. It's not something he's thought about for a while. "Nine years ago," he says. "At a murder." A smile crosses his lips as his thoughts drift back to that fateful day.

The call came in at 7:45 a.m. Construction workers found a dead homeless guy in an abandoned Bronx tenement set to be razed to make way for a new apartment complex.

It's the kind of call the media refers to as routine. But cops quickly learn that being lulled into thinking any situation is routine is not a mistake they want to make. Those that do often end up in flag-draped coffins before bagpipe processions and grieving left-behinds.

Even without mistakes, being a cop comes with enormous life-and-death risks most people are not mentally or physically equipped to bear, or willing to bear even if they are. Still, regardless of how aware a cop is to never drop his or her guard, being human allows for the ever-present risk of a first time for anything and a breath that could be their last.

When Ray arrived at the site less than ten minutes after the call came in, uniformed cops had already cleared the building and cordoned off the area with crime scene tape. With the site on lockdown, the construction crew milled about out front, and across the street a crowd of looky-loos had gathered.

Ray headed inside the building. The air in the dimly lit decrepit hallway was dank and musty, and his eyes saddened the closer he got to an old, beat-up shopping cart stuffed with disheveled random items sitting outside the room at the end. It's a shopping cart he was familiar with, and his sadness deepened as soon as he pushed the warped, paint-chipped wooden door open.

Staring at the man, a myriad of thoughts barreled through Ray's mind. But the most difficult one for him to digest was how and why a person went from being a handsome, powerful man and decorated army lieutenant to a toil-worn, grime-covered homeless drug addict in shabby, filthy, ill-fitting clothes lying on a cold and barren cement floor in a pool of his own blood and feces.

His name was Harold Wilkens.

He'd been living on the streets for a long time and was addicted to anything that would take him out of his head for a while.

Day and night, through summer's searing heat and winter's bone-chilling cold, Harold would wheel his scant belongings from street to street in that old, worn-out shopping cart, stopping only to pass out in a doorway or sit on a bus bench and eat whatever "gifts of food," as he called them, he believed had been bestowed upon him by the God of Trash.

Being military veterans was Harold and Ray's common bond, though Harold's service had been in Vietnam.

Underneath Harold's pain, anguish, booze, and drugs, Ray knew him to be a decent guy who never stole from anyone, and after the war, never hurt another human being. And Harold wasn't just any decorated army lieutenant. He was a war hero who saved the lives of his unit when, early one morning while on jungle patrol, a stray round of five-hundred-pound bombs and napalm forced them deep behind enemy lines.

"It's funny," he often joked to Ray, "how when the weapon of death comes from your side, they call it friendly fire."

Harold's most treasured possession, which he always kept in his pocket, was his Purple Heart. It was the one thing in his life he had left that he was proud to show off and often did—making it known you'd have to kill him to take it from him.

Ray gently felt his skin and confirmed Harold hadn't been dead for long. *What a waste*, he couldn't help but think as he looked at the empty worn velvet presentation box still clutched in Harold's hand.

Caught up in grim emotions, Ray was oblivious to the strung-out junkie slithering out from a screenless air duct above him, ready to plunge a fistful of hypodermic needles into his neck.

From out of nowhere, a Timberland boot shattered the junkie's arm and sent the needles flying. Despite the explosive jolt of adrenaline, Ray barely had enough time to leap aside and pull his gun before a second roundhouse kick slammed the junkie's face through the drywall.

The guy's gaunt, bony body slid out of the vent, an unconscious bloody mess, and Ray found his gun trained on thirty-year-old Stephanie Morego.

"You ought to be wearing a hard hat. It can be dangerous around here," she said, and offered Ray one and a hand to help him up.

Ray took both. And after he cuffed the guy and called for an ambulance, he patted him down. Stuffed in one of his dirty socks was Harold's Purple Heart.

"That what I think it is?" Stephanie asked.

Ray nodded, gave it a shine with his shirt, and pinned it on Harold's chest. "Semper fi, Harold. Safe travels."

"The rest is history," Ray says to Wilbur, and seconds later, the old box truck screeches to a stop, and they're both flung across the cargo bed and slam into the front wall.

THIRTY-ONE

"Oh, Christ," Ray says, motioning to Wilbur to keep quiet as he crawls over to a hole in the front wall. When he sees the maroon Ford Fiesta blocking the road, he knows this can't be good. But he's shocked and perplexed when he sees Phil step out of the foliage with his badge held high.

Phil presses a copy of Wilbur's IRS wanted poster on the driver's window and points from Wilbur's photo to the driver's eyes. "You see?"

The nervous driver shakes his head, but Phil, suspicious of his demeanor, motions for him to get out and open the cargo bay door.

The driver's hands shake as he unlocks the padlock, rotates the latch, and slides the door up. But he doesn't flinch when he sees a floor-to-ceiling wall of boxes.

Try as Phil might, none of the boxes in the bottom row move, so he hoists himself onto the back lip and checks those on top. Same result.

But no sooner does he take a deep breath than a faceful of Ray's fist explodes through the box below it, sending Phil flying off the lip and onto the pavement—out cold and his nose a bloody mess.

Ray scatters the boxes aside, hops off, and when he rifles through Phil's pockets and finds his IRS badge, Joe's voice rings in his ear—*They'll fry your ass if you stick your dick in some international bullshit.* Befuddled,

Ray slips the badge back into Phil's pocket, takes his car keys, and now knows one thing for sure: there's some international bullshit going on.

"Get down here and get his legs," he says to Wilbur and grabs Phil under his arms.

Wilbur, stupefied, stands there and smiles. "Assaulting an IRS agent . . . How's *that* icing taste, Ray?"

"Now, moron, before he comes to," Ray says.

Wilbur lowers his carry-on, slides off the lip, and after they hoist Phil onto the cargo bed, Ray pulls the door shut, locks the padlock, and stuffs another C-note in the driver's shirt pocket.

"I'd say your treatment of Agent Dancourt is consistent with your history of excessive force," Wilbur says.

It's the first word either of them has said in the five minutes they've been speeding down the road in Phil's maroon Ford Fiesta, Ray behind the wheel.

"I'm feeling a bit consistent now if you don't come clean," Ray says. "He the one who set you up?"

Wilbur sighs. "Devious little prick."

"What'd he want? Before you screwed him."

"What they always want. A rat to fill in the blanks."

"Fill 'em. I'll put in a good word."

"I can't. That's the irony. They've been auditing Amco for years, but the well always came up dry." He looks at Ray and smiles. "A little oil humor."

"Very little," Ray says, still skeptical.

"Everything's numbers, Ray. They can be massaged, manipulated . . . But when you drill down, they never lie."

"You do. You're lying to me right now. You know everything."

"No. I only know Amco's numbers didn't add up. More money flowed in than was possible."

"From where?"

"That's the big kahuna. There's a finite number of wells which, at max, pump a finite number of barrels that can be refined and sold, which dictates your maximum revenue, give or take for price fluctuations."

"So, you knew Amco's money was off, and your bright idea was to steal it from them?" Ray asks, his eyes narrow, skeptical.

"I wanted to help," Wilbur confides. "I think Agent Dancourt knew that. You don't mess with a guy like Mika Salko unless you think you're already dead. I thought I had nothing to lose."

Ray considers it. "Yeah, well something else doesn't add up—Dancourt."

Wilbur looks at him, confused. "Meaning?"

"You're a fugitive in a foreign country," Ray says, glancing back and from the road to Wilbur. "Feds would have sent US Marshals, not him. And more than one guy, along with support from the country's own agents."

Ray and Wilbur, unsettled and baffled about what it all means, return to silence as the maroon Ford Fiesta rounds another bend.

THIRTY-TWO

Two and half hours pass before the box truck cruises into the next town and the driver pulls down an alley off a side street and lets Phil out.

Fucking guy's lucky I'm down here illegally, Phil thinks to himself as he hops off, his clothes rumpled, his eyes bloodshot, his torn-off shirtsleeve pressed to his red and swollen nose. From the force of the blow, Phil knows there's no way it came from Wilbur and figures he and Dawson must have rendezvoused somewhere along the way.

"Good Lord," he says when his cell rings.

"GUATEMALA . . . STOLE YOUR FUCKING CAR!" booms Callahan's enraged voice after Phil picks up. "You on drugs, Phil? You better be on drugs, 'cause if you're not, it means YOU'VE LOST YOUR FUCKING MIND!"

As soon as Phil rounds out of the alley and starts down the street, he spots the maroon Ford Fiesta parked across the street in a roadside carnival parking lot.

"WHERE THE FUCK IS WILBUR?" Callahan's voice rages.

Phil tosses the bloody sleeve atop an overflowing trash can and scans the area.

"PHIL! PHIL, GODDAMMIT!"

He hangs up on him, heads over, and finds the keys are on the driver's seat. And on the passenger seat is a folded piece of paper addressed to

Secret Agent Man. He grabs both and unfolds the note. Above a smiley face, it reads "So close!"

"Motherfuckers!"

Fuck Callahan too, Phil thinks to himself as he gets behind the wheel. *Bottom-feeding swamp rat.*

After the brutal last few hours, the last thing he needs is an earful of shit from the boss who sent him here.

Twenty years in the field and this fucking mess is the nail in my maroon Ford Fiesta coffin.

His mind spins, fast and furiously.

Year after year . . . Pounding it out with my life on the line and little to show for it.

He tries to discern when the job, the life, went from "Let's do this," to "Let's get this over with."

Is it boredom? The been-there-done-it blues.

Or is it physical? The relentless slow creep of aches and pains where none had been before.

Or is it mental? The gradual slide to a time when the negatives out-pace the positives.

All of it—constant reminders of the losing battle with shit I can't control as my number marches on into the fog to a place where a warning blares on an endless loop: "YOU ARE NOW ENTERING THE HIGHER-RISK ZONE."

Higher risk of a heart attack, stroke, or terminal illness. Higher risk of losing friends and loved ones to them. Higher risk of no financial security when it is most needed. Higher risk of who the fuck cares.

Risk. Risk. Risk. Risk. Risk.

It's all I hear.

Where's my fucking reward? And don't tell me it's the journey. Fuck the journey. The journey is the past. I'm here and now, so where the fuck is it? Because, like Lorena, I may not be here tomorrow.

Since the accident, Lorena's memory is his reflexive go-to, and the web of thoughts ushers in the memory of her unshakable faith in God. It drove her positive outlook, something that died in Phil when she did.

Will I ever get it back? he wonders.

Her memory's calming effect is swift. And the more her spirit fills his heart and mind, the more the hows and whys no longer seem to matter. The more it reminds him he's still one of the lucky ones. He's still here. Still above ground. Still in the fight against all odds. Still a chance for a payoff. A chance to succeed. A chance to see his daughter again. A chance to walk her down the aisle. Chances to be grateful for.

A half mile up the road, Phil rolls into a small town and parks along its main drag. He can't help but take a moment to admire the two-hundred-year-old Spanish church across the way with its weathered baroque facade.

Like the church, the town has a colonial Spanish feel. Three-wheeled tuk-tuks abound and weave through traffic. Pedestrians and shoppers—many of whom are descendants of Mayans and dressed in vibrant indigenous garb—fill the street on the hunt for deals in textile and craft shops and clothing stores. Others stock up on local produce at a busy central market or dine in the various cafés nearby.

Phil can't look more conspicuous as he makes his way up the street. Most of the pedestrians and local shopkeepers ignore or avoid him, even as he holds up Wilbur's wanted poster and a pic of Ray for their perusal. Those willing to look shake their heads. Still undeterred as he nears the end of the street, he heads into the small café on the corner.

"Man . . . It smells good in here," he thinks aloud as soon as he enters—loud enough to draw looks from the cook, the waiter, and other patrons. He smiles and ambles about, the pic and poster held up on display. But he fares no better, his only consolation the delicious aromas coming from the kitchen area behind the counter.

Sitting at a table by the café's front window, his face relaxes the moment the waiter sets down the plate of tortillas, sweet corn rice, and refried beans with beef. Even his red, swollen nose seems more subdued. And with his first delicious bite, his whole body relaxes. Still, he can't help but be intrigued by the colorfully painted old American school bus that pulls up in front of the pharmacy across the street and picks up a hoard of passengers.

"It's called a 'chicken bus," the cook says in perfect English he learned during his years in the US on a work visa. "There is no limit on the number of passengers, and they're often crammed in like a load of chickens."

Two minutes later, his plate clean, Phil strides across the street and heads inside the pharmacy. Despite the line, he sidles up to the clerk who sells the tickets and learns Dawson and Bailey had been there earlier in the day.

"My nose was busted, and I'm halfway across Guatemala. In other words, I was fucked," Phil says to the trainees and waits a moment for the laughter to settle. "From here, they hop a bus north, and make it across the border to San Paraiso, a resort town in southeast Mexico."

On the map, the yellow line expands from the blue star northward into Mexico, and another blue star marks the spot.

"By now, thanks to social media, word of our reward, and the ten million Salko offered of his own, had gone viral. Sightings of Wilbur popped up around the globe." He pulls up several photos drawn from various social media. The first is a shot of Bigfoot wearing canvas shoes. In the next, Wilbur is behind Rick Steves, standing guard at the Vatican in a full-dress Swiss Guard uniform. And in the third, he's in the UFC octagon in canvas tighty-whities and covered with tats—the "17" across his face the most notable.

The group howls again. "It all seems funny now, but . . . not at the time," Phil says. "The bloodshed at the cornfield was horrific and brought with it a tenfold increase in the danger of being exposed, the danger of being imprisoned for life, of being badly hurt or killed. And local authorities also jumped in. They figured if the US was offering five mil and Salko another ten, Bailey must be worth at least thirty."

His nerves still raw, Phil pauses and takes a sip of water. "The last thing I needed was for them to get wind an American agent was down there hunting without a permit. And one thought crept in and gnawed at me." He fires up his e-cig and gazes about the room at the young, eager faces. "Why didn't Bailey and Dawson kill me?"

The vapor cloud billows as he expels the long pull of Banana Nut Bread.

THIRTY-THREE

To call San Paraiso a resort town is a bit of a stretch. Put another way, it wouldn't make Wilbur's list of the "TEN HOTBEDS OF INTERNATIONAL TOURISM." The main drag is lined with all the basic stores a small town needs to exist, alongside others abandoned due to economic decline. But beneath the facade is a well-off-the-beaten-path charm that's rich in Mexican culture and an easy, tranquil vibe that feels welcoming and a world away from everywhere.

Phil sticks out here even more than he did in the last town, but he couldn't care less. His only interest is whether Dawson and Bailey are still in the vicinity, and he spends the next hour going through the same rigmarole up and down the street, showing Wilbur's wanted poster and Ray's pic to anyone who will stop and listen.

Again, the search proves futile—until a mail carrier looks at the pics and nods.

Phil can taste victory as he hightails it back to his car to make the quarter-mile trek up the main drag to the Motel de Buena Fortuna.

With its colorful motif, the motel has a rustic charm with a traditional Mexican flair.

Ray hustles down the second-floor hallway with a bag of groceries, enters room 22, and sets the bag on the small table by the window.

Everything about the spacious room, from the natural wood floor and breezy fabrics to the stone walls with tile inlays, gives it a quaint and stylish feel. Everything except for Wilbur on a chair along the far wall—one hand cuffed to the radiator while the other flips through an English copy of *About Town* magazine.

Ray frees him, and within seconds of shaking off the stiffness, Wilbur, eyes swelling with disgust and contempt, watches Ray pull out a plastic bag of white paper plates, a plastic bag of white bread, plastic-wrapped cured chorizo, a plastic-wrapped pickle, plastic-wrapped brownies, and two cans of iced tea.

"Might as well eat chemo."

Ray looks to the heavens, exasperated, and pulls out a can of Pringles and a pack of gum.

"That's seven of ten foods one should never eat."

Ray scoops out a handful of mayonnaise and sweet-and-spicy sauce packets and tosses them on the table.

"Nine," Wilbur says, and he comes over and picks up the gum. "You aware the sodium stearate in this is used to make soap, latex paint, and ink?"

Ray winces. "No. You aware it freshens bad breath?"

Wilbur flips the gum back onto the table and picks up a can of iced tea. "The sweetener in this . . . also used to make antifreeze."

Ray holds up the other can and points to the slogan on it—Be Cool on a Hot Day. He pulls the tab and sucks down several big gulps.

Wilbur's lips break into a sneer of incredulity, and he snatches a plate and holds it up. "You at least know they bleach these, right?"

Ray tears open a couple of packets of mayo and sweet-and-spicy sauce with his teeth.

Wilbur tosses the plate back onto the table and flicks at the other items with his finger. "Loaded with mono- and diglycerides, trans fat, partially hydrogenated oils, gluten . . ."

Ray squirts the mayo and sauce onto a couple of slices of bread and smears it around with his finger.

"And I'm lactose intolerant," Wilbur says, reluctantly sitting.

"You don't shut up, you're gonna be oxygen intolerant."

"Would it have hurt to get one organic, air-chilled, non-GMO fed, cage-free-running chicken?"

Ray eyes him, briefly, at a loss for words. "You know . . . If right now I was still a cop, I'd quit to become a murderer." He reaches into the bag, pulls out a small bag of organic kale chips, and tosses it across the table. "Enjoy."

Wilbur's face softens. But as soon as he flips the bag over to the list of the ingredients and related info, much to his chagrin . . . "These expired eight years ago."

Ray tears open the wrapped chorizo and pickle with his teeth.

Wilbur starts to vigorously scratch himself. "And the nitrates leeching off whatever's in those BPA-infested plastic wraps ravage the body and emotional well-being."

"Yeah . . . Well, lucky for me, you're the one emotional being no one should ever listen to." He makes himself a double-decker sandwich and loads up on Pringles.

"Go ahead, wreak havoc on your gut flora."

Ray stuffs a few Pringles in his mouth and chomps them down. "I've dealt with every kind of freaked-out psychopath, killer, rapist, you name it." He grabs the pickle and points it at him. "But you . . . You're in a category all your own." He chomps off a piece of pickle, tosses in a Pringle, and crunches away.

"Really, tough guy?" Wilbur says. He snatches a handful of mayo and sweet-and-spicy sauce packets and rattles them at Ray. "Try taking down polysorbate 80 in a dark alley."

Ray washes it down with a few gulps of iced tea. "And don't ever say flora again," he says, gnawing off another huge bite of his sandwich and a piece of pickle, and he crunches away.

"Suit yourself. Just trying to help you become a happier person."

"Happy go screw yourself," Ray says, and washes it down with another gulp. "Hey, it worked. I'm feeling happier already." He gnaws off another huge bite, stuffs in a good pinch of Pringles and a piece of pickle, and crunches away.

Resigned, Wilbur tears open the bag of kale chips, pulls one out, and gives it a once-over, a sniff test, and a forearm scrape to assess any immediate allergic reaction. And when none surfaces, he pours the chips onto the table, finger-flicks away the particularly alarming-looking particles, and chomps on his chips as if to out-crunch Ray.

Amused, Ray attacks his sandwich, pickle, and Pringles and drains it all with the last gulps of iced tea. "Ah . . . That hit the spot," he says as he unwraps a brownie, and flicks his head toward the *About Town* magazine. "Any shows in town? I could go for a good musical."

Wilbur pops the other iced tea, takes a swig, gargles, swooshes, and spits it out into the bag. "One. It's called our way out." He grabs the *About Town* magazine, tears a corner off the back cover, and slides it over to Ray. "I hear it's . . . ebullient."

Ray smirks, stuffs the brownie into his mouth, and gives it a look. It's an ad for Air Adventures, a local travel company offering tourists an opportunity to admire unbeatable views on one of their Cessna tours. Ray smiles.

"Not bad, Wilbur." But again, as if by a switch, his smile disappears, and his focus shifts out the window to the maroon Ford Fiesta pulling up out front.

THIRTY-FOUR

The atmosphere inside the motel's lobby reflected the town: relaxed and lazy. Neutral wood tones. Low-key artwork. Local accents. Aztec patterned rugs and tile work provide a pop of color, as does the far wall's framed centerpiece: a vivid and colorful replica of a mural painted on a wall in Mexico City by renowned Mexican muralist Diego Rivera. It all comes together for an authentic Mexican feel.

Behind the front desk, the attendant, a clean-cut, gangly guy in his twenties, swiping through Tinder profiles, nearly jumps out of his skin when Phil barrels in, flashes his badge, and holds up Ray and Wilbur's pics.

Without hesitating, the kid turns and grabs the key for 22 from the cabinet.

The moment Phil bounds up the stairs and pulls his gun, thoughts of Emmi flood in. They always do when his next move is to bust through a door. Ever since Lorena died, the risks of the job seem magnified a thousandfold, and dark thoughts of his demise and its impact on Emmi quickly became his greatest fear—one he prays doesn't manifest as he makes his way to room 22, slides in the key, and flings open the door.

"Freeze!" he shouts, only to find Ray and Wilbur are gone.

Muttering "Damn," he scans the room and runs his fingers through his hair, taking with them another eight to ten strands. His eyes, though, are soon drawn to the *About Town* magazine with its corner torn off. But his intrigue turns to "Oh, shit," when out the window, he sees Wilbur smiling and waving bye-bye from the passenger seat of his maroon Ford Fiesta.

Seven seconds later Phil barrels out the motel's front door. Unfortunately, it took Ray just six seconds to hot-wire the car, take off, and disappear around the next turn.

"Motherfuckers!"

Phil darts back into the lobby and, seconds later, reemerges with a copy of *About Town* and pulls out his badge to flag down a passing vehicle. None stop, but across the street, he spots a woman in her eighties with a limp and a cane as she hobbles to her old Dodge Caravan and labors to get in.

His face says it all—he can't believe what he's about to do.

Above the English translation in smaller print, a weathered hand-painted sign reads Aventura Aérea.

In contrast, the small Spanish-style bungalow which serves as the airfield's office is relatively modern. Out front, a handful of cars dot the makeshift parking lot, and beyond, two twin-engine Cessnas sit beside the grass runway.

In one plane await the pilot and his passengers, an Indian couple, Arjun and Aarushi Sahoo, and their fifteen-year-old son, Narian, while a mechanic changes a tire.

At the other plane, the pilot—a high-strung, fast-talking American expat in his forties, with two days' growth on his face—hastily stuffs kilos of coke from a duffel bag through a makeshift hatch in the fuselage.

It jostles the Asian couple sitting inside, and he pokes in his head and shouts, "Just a little ground turbulence, folks—nothing to worry about. We'll be outta here in a coke-fueled minute." He jams the last one in, when from behind him, someone calls out.

"Excuse me."

Startled, he slams the hatch door shut and wheels around to see Ray and Wilbur, his carry-on in tow, hurtling toward him. He points toward the bungalow. "Office is thataway, gentlemen."

Ray's eyes flash the second he sees the pilot's face, but there's no time to waste. "We're in a bit of a hurry, and—"

The pilot cuts him off and thumbs at the Asian family on board. "Would love to help you boys out, but the flight's sold out."

But no sooner do the words leave his mouth than Wilbur whips out a wrapped stack of hundreds.

For the second day in a row, back at Houston's IRS headquarters, Callahan grills dozens of agents and rank and file about Phil, laying a foundation to insulate himself with plausible deniability as the mission he sent Phil on goes sideways and devolves into chaos.

Beyond honed ass-kissing skills, another of Callahan's main attributes, which helps account for his rapid rise to the corner office, is his ability to cover his ass regardless of who gets tossed under the bus. Nevertheless, by late afternoon a shitstorm is brewing.

The CBS anchor drones on Callahan's office TV as he strides in and heads into his private bathroom to take a piss. "The stock rose twenty-two percent after MeatEX announced its researchers have engineered the first plant-based bone-in ribeye, and are confident that, with the additional 3.4 billion dollars in government grants, they are on track to engineer a full steer by 2029. Shifting to a business story you don't need an MBA to enjoy, and mind you, these are real names. Michigan-based home builder STD Contractors is set to merge with Virginia-based Hooker Furniture. The new company, STD Hooker, will shed two hundred and three employees and relocate its headquarters to Fingerville, South Carolina."

Callahan settles in behind his desk to wolf down his third Potbelly Mama's Meatball sub in as many days as the CBS Breaking News theme chimes in. "Now to breaking news on the hunt for Wilbur Bailey and former NYPD detective Raymond Dawson. Moments ago, TikTok lit up when fifteen-year-old Narian Sahoo from Mumbai, India, posted a shocking video he shot while vacationing in Mexico with his parents."

Callahan sucks on his Dr. Pepper and locks in on the video footage of Ray, Wilbur, and the pilot that Narian shot through the other Cessna's window. It freezes on the pilot taking the cash from Wilbur, and a thumbnail mugshot of him appears.

"The pilot, seen here taking a large sum of cash from Wilbur Bailey, is Eddie Santoli, an ex-con fugitive who disappeared five years ago after being charged with drug trafficking. He is wanted by US Marshals."

The footage resumes, and Callahan stares in disbelief as he watches Santoli yank the irate Asian couple out of the plane before he, Ray, and Wilbur jump in and the plane starts to roll.

"As you can see, after Mr. Santoli physically removes Ping Yun and his new bride, Aiko, he, Dawson, and Bailey board the plane. Seconds later, a third unidentified man arrives."

In the footage, the old woman's Dodge Caravan skids up. Phil jumps out, his face obstructed from view, and he runs alongside the plane and tries to yank the door open while Wilbur waves bye-bye at him.

"We're told that the vehicle the man arrived in had been stolen a short time earlier from an eighty-three-year-old diabetic woman recovering from a stroke."

A glob of meatball-and-sauce-laden spittle runs down Callahan's chin as he watches Phil, unable to hang on as the plane accelerates, faceplant into the grass, and the footage ends with Phil's muffled scream bleeped.

"Mother—*beeeep*!"

"The unidentified man fled the scene soon after, leaving the vehicle on the runway," the anchor continues. "A company spokesperson claims the incident was a misunderstanding due to overbooking and offered the Yuns twenty percent off a future air adventure."

There's no need for Callahan to look at the ID when, two seconds later, his cell rings. "Governor—"

The ass-reaming is fast and furious, and despite Callahan's feeble attempt to reassure him he has it under control, Hargrove casts doubt on his nomination as state finance secretary and hangs up.

"Fuck him," Callahan thinks aloud and stuffs in another meatball. "Fuck them all."

THIRTY-FIVE

"Folks, from the flight deck," Eddie says as the Cessna cruises low over the Gulf. "In the unlikely event we hit unexpected turbulence, please remain seated, and keep your seat belt securely fastened. In the interim, please enjoy the in-flight entertainment, snacks, and crazy-ass views."

To anyone in the US who knew him, or knew of him, whether they were in law enforcement or among those trying to outrun it, Eddie Santoli was thought to be a two-bit hustler and a wiseass. There was good reason for it—he's a two-bit hustler and a wiseass. But when it came to drug trafficking and evading arrest, all agreed he went the distance to get the job done. And what he did five years ago is still legendary.

Late one night the feds, in concert with Boston SWAT, thought they had Santoli dead to rights until they busted through the front door of his house.

The homeowner whose yard abutted Santoli's told them he had let his old dog out to pee about five minutes before they arrived and saw Eddie pile his scuba gear into his pickup and take off—as he had seen him do many times before.

Soon after, they found Santoli's pickup near a remote pier in Boston Harbor. Within minutes the Coast Guard sealed off the harbor, had

divers in the water, sent alerts to every vessel in the area, and had choppers equipped with thermal imaging cameras overhead.

Unfortunately for them, while they were performing a full-tilt canvass of the harbor and surrounding coastline, Eddie, compliments of
the CDN cartel, was in his scuba gear under a mound of potash and
manure in the back of a flatbed cruising down the interstate.

"And if the cabin loses pressure," Eddie continues, "place your hands
over your nose and mouth, clench your sphincter, and breathe nor-
mally."

Ray studies his face and tries to pin the voice. And when Eddie banks
hard, his attention drawn out his door's window, Ray tracks his gaze
to a lone speedboat—drifting, waiting—and it all gels when he peeks
around the tarp behind their seats and sees the kilos of coke. "What are
the odds?" he mutters to himself.

"Whatever you're thinking, Raymond—not a good time," Wilbur
says in a hushed voice.

Ray pulls out his badge. "How've you been, Eddie?"

Eddie's eyes flash. "Folks, the captain has turned the seat belt sign
off. Please feel free to move about the cabin." In the blink of an eye,
Eddie flings his door open and bails out, and the plane rockets skyward
with Ray and Wilbur pinned to their seats.

Down below, the thirty-foot, modified, matte-gray cigarette boat
rumbles over to Eddie, and a cartel thug with *CDN* tatted down the
side of his neck hoists him onto the deck.

"Gracias for the lift, fellas," Eddie says, and points toward the plane.
"Dos americanos. Policía—though one looked a little peaked, if you
know what I mean."

The thug signals the driver, and the six 250-horsepower outboard
motors scream while, overhead, the plane spirals out of control.

Ray scrambles into the pilot's seat while Wilbur, terrified, yanks his
seat belt so tight the bolt that fastens it to the seat snaps off. Disgusted,
and at his wit's end, he thrusts his finger at Ray. "In a plane crash with
him, Wilma?" he cries out to the heavens. "You bitch!"

As if on cue, a hail of bullets rips through the plane, but Ray manages to level off. "Christ, Wilbur . . . A little faith. I flew models as a kid."

When it comes to flying, Ray likes to say he learned on the fly. For the most part, it's true. But he did a bit more than fly models as a kid. His love and fascination with planes go back as far as he can remember, and had he not been destined to be a cop, he would have been a pilot.

By the time he turned seven, plane spotting was his favorite pastime. When he was out with his mom, he scanned the skies and pointed out every plane he saw. And at home, he often sat by the apartment's front window, his eyes fixed on the patch of blue sky between their building and the one across the street.

His favorites were the planes that were no more than a dot but left contrails. Those were the ones he knew came from somewhere far away and could be going somewhere even further. Those were the ones close to outer space. Closer to heaven. Those were the ones that sent his imagination soaring—especially when, one day, his mom brought home a pair of secondhand binoculars.

Weather permitting, he loved to lie on the roof of the building, sometimes for hours, and scan the sky, amazed at the thought that in less than an hour the people on board would be hundreds of miles away. Still, he always waved in case someone on the plane had binoculars and was looking down.

By the time he was eight and a half, he knew the names of almost every airline flying into and out of JFK and LaGuardia and was equally adept at identifying the type of plane from the sound of its engines. And by age ten, his collection of die-cast model planes was vast, with only a handful given to him as gifts. The rest he bought with the money he earned from odd jobs for local shopkeepers.

Each plane was lined up on runways and taxiways and around terminals he and his mom painted on a four-by-four-foot piece of plywood she found next to a dumpster. Alongside the DC-9s and 10s, 737s, 747s, and L-1011s were his favorite military aircraft, among which was the replica of the B-25 Mitchell bomber flown by Jimmy Doolittle and the SR-71 Blackbird he scored on a visit to the Smithsonian.

It didn't stop there. While most kids read comic books after they finished their homework, Ray immersed himself in everything from the basic principles of aerodynamics, airspeed, attitude, pitch, and yaw to how to keep a heading, situational awareness, and keeping a mental picture of the location. But the one rule of flying, the one he thought was most important, was knowing when to break the rules.

At seventeen, at the helm of his model AP456 Spitfire, he took the top prize at the tristate area's largest model airplane combat flying competition and repeated it the following year. But the real crash course came years later during his last tour as a Raider.

The massive Boeing C-17 Globemaster III sliced through the late-night sky on a transport flight into Iraq to meet up with members of the Eighty-Second Airborne. There was no loadmaster on the flight since Ray, Joe, and their unit were the only cargo. It gave the guys ample room to bang out their touch football rubber match and gave Ray the chance to ride up front with Kurt, the pilot in command, and Rick, his second, both of whom knew him well.

It was Ray's third cockpit ride, each of which he considered the equivalent of winning tenth-row seats on the fifty-yard line for the Super Bowl. Best of all, it allowed Ray to tap into his childhood fantasies while Kurt schooled him on everything from the plane's avionics and the correct yolk pressure to how the trim tabs keep the correct pitch. By the second ride, Ray was already boasting he could fly "the Beast" with his eyes closed. And this flight was no different.

So he thought.

Two seconds into their initial descent into Baghdad, an explosion rocked the plane, and the first fire alarm blared.

Kurt and Rick never lost their cool, and Ray never missed a word while he watched them move through the dizzying array of digital screens, switches, gauges, and knobs with surgical precision. Two seconds later a second alarm screamed.

With two of the four hydraulic systems out, Kurt shut down the autopilot and took control, and as the plane pitched into a steep descent from fifteen thousand feet through the undercast, a second blast tore through, and the third alarm chimed, "*TERRAIN. TERRAIN. PULL UP . . . TERRAIN. TERRAIN. PULL UP.*"

Still they took it all in stride. Kurt pulled the plane into its maximum sixty-degree bank angle to align with the runway, but the plane dipped six miles per hour below stall speed, triggering the fourth alarm.

Still they remained unfazed, and if not for the sparks, the fire, the smoke, and the deafening grinding noise, it was no different from any other landing of a massive jet after enemy surface-to-air missiles take out half the main landing gear, two of the four engines, two flaps, and the lower rudder and put a football-sized hole in the vertical stabilizer.

"Piece of cake," Ray later said when they all kicked back over a few beers and some laughs. "Lucky I was there to oversee it. OORAH!" And to this day, the four-by-four-foot plywood airport sits in Ray's den, a model C-17 Globemaster III leading the charge.

Ray spots the boat closing in. "Folks, from the flight deck," he says. "Please return to your seats and buckle up for the remainder of the flight. Things are gonna get violent." He banks hard, and another volley rips through the fuselage.

Wilbur, his eyes closed, meditates in silent, peaceful prayer—until he lunges at Ray and grips his neck in a choke hold. "Thanks to you, I can't even die with dignity."

"Not a good time, Wilbur," Ray squeaks out between gasps. He slams the yolk forward, and when the plane lurches into a dive, he nails Wilbur in the face with his elbow.

Stunned, Wilbur jerks his hands away from Ray's neck, and he grabs his nose, horrified by the trickle of blood on his fingers. "I think you broke my nose," he says, pinching his nostrils. "I'm gonna have you arrested for assault and battery."

Ray glances over. "Wait'll the sharks get a whiff of that."

Another salvo blows out the Cessna's back windows, and while Ray struggles to stay airborne, Wilbur slips the cuffs off Ray's belt and slaps one on Ray's wrist and the other on the yolk's steering column. "Yeah . . .

Wait'll they do," he says, and leans into Ray's ear. "Dead. You hear me, Ray? Dead."

No sooner does Wilbur settle back into his seat than another barrage of bullets sets one of the engines ablaze and rocks the plane into a vertical bank.

Down below, the boat cuts a turn at ninety miles per hour and rockets twenty feet high off a swell, oblivious to the buoy in the swell's trough. The impact two seconds later obliterates the boat, and everyone on it, in a massive fireball.

THIRTY-SIX

Back in the DC swamp, politicians on both sides of the aisle are not about to let the Dawson and Bailey crisis go to waste, and it doesn't take long for the House Committee on Foreign Affairs to pull together their top-shelf dog and pony show.

After being summoned to appear, Joe and Stephanie make the two-and-a-half-hour Amtrak ride from New York to DC together, though Joe's not scheduled till the following day. She knows Joe would be Ray's only call when he's in a major jam. She also knows Joe will honor the request Ray surely made to not tell her. But the nine-thousand-pound gorilla in the room is what it is.

"It's the last time I heard from him," Joe says about the first call Ray made to him from the hotel bathroom in Costa Rica.

"Yeah," she says. "Before he told you not to say anything to me."

Joe chuckles. He knows she knows the routine. "You gotta at least admire his dedication and commitment, Steph. It might be hard to see it, but the same applies to you."

The truth is, she does see it. And feel it. Always has. Ray's integrity and commitment to a goal, no matter how great the struggle, are qualities Stephanie shares and loves most about him. It's one of the main reasons their divorce never made sense or felt right to either of them.

A half hour later, with her faith that Ray is still alive and okay renewed, she enters the Capitol chamber and takes a seat at the witness table.

The tension in the packed house is palpable. Reporters and photographers line the floor. Their cameras softly whir while sixty-five-year-old Blanche Wolf, the stone-faced woman in the center seat, bangs her gavel to settle the gallery. The plaque before her reads MS. WOLF, CHAIRWOMAN, above the Twitter logo next to @HouseForeign.

The gentlewoman from Portland wasn't always stone-faced. Then again, maybe she was. But when she first arrived on the DC scene thirty-five years ago, she was carved in sandstone: porous, easy to work with. Today she's a weathered, jagged chunk of granite: cynical and untrusting, but no less power-hungry.

"Thank you for coming in on such short notice, Ms. Dawson. I'm sure this isn't easy for you."

Stephanie acknowledges her with a nod.

"But, as you may well understand, in light of recent events, it's hard to believe your ex-husband and Mr. Bailey crossed paths randomly."

Stephanie shrugs. "July fourth . . . It's always been Ray's lucky day."

"Lucky?" Wolf scoffs.

"Yes. It's the day he came home from Afghanistan. The day he made detective. The day he divorced his first wife. And the day I, his second, said yes—the first time."

"I mean no disrespect, Ms. Dawson, but so far"—she reads off her tablet—"your ex-husband violated three treaties, eight laws of three different foreign countries, twelve United States federal laws, nine New York State laws and statutes, and used his 'second chance' with you to go after Mr. Bailey and leave you, the woman he claims to love, at the table during dinner. Sound lucky to you?"

"It's just his nature," Stephanie says, her eyes sharp, irritated by Wolf's brusque manner and insinuation.

"I'm sure," Wolf says. "I understand Mr. Bailey sent over a twenty-eight-hundred-dollar bottle of champagne. A bit excessive under the circumstances, wouldn't you agree?"

"I found it . . ." She searches for the right words. "Naive yet intimidating." Wolf eyes her, confounded, and while chuckles permeate the chamber, Stephanie glances at the gallery and winks at Joe, who's sitting in the back.

Undeterred, Wolf grinds on. "And you claim this is when Mr. Dawson recognized him?"

"Yes. Mr. Bailey was at the bar without the hat he had on in the elevator."

"Hmm . . . A foolish mistake," Wolf says, her tone mocking.

Stephanie sips her coffee. "Any cop will tell you, sooner or later they all make one."

"Yes, they do. Makes you wonder what the odds are Mr. Bailey's first would be with an ex-cop who had recently lost his job and pension and happens to be at the same hotel in a foreign country on vacation."

A slight smile crosses Stephanie's lips. "I already told you, Congresswoman . . . It's his lucky day."

Wolf, irritated, bangs her gavel to eighty-six the chuckles from the gallery and a handful on the committee. "You left Costa Rica early—why?"

"Wasn't my first Ray Dawson rodeo."

"Meaning?"

"I had a feeling he might be gone awhile."

"A feeling?"

"Yeah. A bad one."

"I'm sure," Wolf replies, and takes a more conciliatory tone. "Ms. Dawson, we are all aware Mr. Dawson is credited with more felony arrests than anyone else in the NYPD. We're not here to discredit him or his record. But did you ever witness him take any illegal drugs himself?"

"I've never seen Ray take so much as an aspirin."

"Answer the question, please."

"The answer is no."

"What about selling them? Ever see—"

"No. Never."

Determined, Wolf glances at her notes. "Three weeks before you and Mr. Dawson left for Costa Rica, is it true you were notified by your superiors you'd be receiving a ten percent pay cut?"

"As were all of us at the foreman level—to help make room for more hires."

"Still, it must have been troubling."

"That's life in the private sector, Congresswoman. You ought to try it."

All eyes turn to Wolf, sure she'd be infuriated by such a challenge. But from the glint in her eyes, it appears she's satisfied to have pierced Stephanie's armor.

"I'll take that as a yes, Ms. Dawson. My point is that it's hard not to imagine Mr. Dawson wasn't also deeply troubled after killing a defenseless child and losing his job and pension."

"And the point of your point is?" Stephanie says, unsure where this is going.

"Did it ever occur to you that Mr. Dawson was merely using you as a ruse for his rendezvous with Wilbur Bailey? Or that you were his safety net in case things went south?"

Stephanie's eyes sharpen. "What a load of crap."

Outraged, Wolf fires back over the chorus of grumbles and snickers that permeate the chamber. "Another outburst like that, and I'll hold you in contempt."

"Any more crap like *that*, and I'll hold you in a choke hold," Stephanie says, now a mama bear before a wolf who has entered the den. Save for Joe, who does little to conceal his knowing smile, the rebuke stuns everyone in the chamber.

But no one is more furious than Wolf, and unable to contain herself as the gallery's chorus rises in a crescendo, spittle shoots from her mouth as she bangs her gavel so hard the head snaps off.

THIRTY-SEVEN

Ray somehow manages to keep the bullet-ridden, windowless Cessna airborne long enough to make it back over land. Smoke pours from the one remaining engine as the plane wobbles and sputters and rapidly descends toward a rocky dirt field.

"That look to you like an appropriate place to land, Raymond?" Wilbur contemptuously asks.

"No," Ray casually says. "But the good news is we won't burn to death—we're out of fuel."

The propeller on the remaining engine snaps to a stop.

Wilbur clenches his jaw, mumbling, "At least you had an eye on the gauge."

The plane comes in hard, and Ray drops the landing gear, unaware there's also nothing left of the tires but a few chunks of rubber, all of which, on impact, snap off, and the fuselage tumbles in a cloud of dust and dirt.

When the brownout settles, there's not much left of the Cessna except a smoking pile of twisted metal. It's hard to imagine Ray and Wilbur survived. But a moment later, Ray's door creaks open, and out he stumbles—a few more bloody cuts and bruises, but none the worse for wear.

"Woo-hoo! You still got it, Ray," he cheers, exhilarated.

Soon after, Wilbur's door snaps off its hinge, and he flings his carry-on out—taking himself with it. Dazed, with his face flushed and nose bleeding, he looks around and tries to get his bearings, unable to believe he survived—then looks at his cuffed hands and can't believe that either.

Ray comes around and gets in his face. "You, of all people, should know the two things never to do with handcuffs. One . . . Never cuff the pilot of an out-of-control airplane to the steering column. And two . . . Never cuff the guy with the key." Wallowing in defeat, Wilbur slumps, and Ray uncuffs him and grabs a handful of paper towels from the plane. "For your nose."

"I mean, holy crap. Callahan's head exploded, but I gave him the good news—I got the car back," Phil says, and again, laughs with the trainees. "Still, doubts kept creeping in. But by then, I was on a mission."

The truth Phil doesn't tell them is that, at the time, the mission was becoming elusive and uncertain, increasingly shrouded in a fog.

He could feel it beginning to roll in, patchy at first, as he stood before the bloody massacre at the Honduran cornfield. Sitting in his maroon Ford Fiesta in a Guatemalan carnival parking lot with a busted nose and an earful of Callhan's bullshit, it thickened and began to swirl. As he sped away from the Air Adventure airfield to a destination unknown, it became so dense his mind's eye could barely see through it.

"How the fuck did I get *here*?" he asked himself.

But catching Wilbur wasn't what was on his mind. It was his life, and his thoughts funneled back to his local pub on a Sunday afternoon last year.

It was another brutal season for the Texans, but *at least they're playing the Jets*, Phil thought as he made his way to the local pub to watch the game over a couple of beers. It was the one cog in his weekly routine that afforded him a respite from his daily grind, and more importantly, it beat watching the games at home alone.

The minute he got out of the car and strode to the pub's entrance, he winced when the occasional mild twinge of pain shot through his knee. Sometimes it was his shoulder. Other times, his lower back. But nothing he couldn't still power through.

The first twinge happened a couple of years earlier, not long after his forty-seventh birthday. He got out of bed early one morning, and the first words out of his mouth on his way to the john were, "Ugh . . . What the fuck is that?"

Over the next couple of years, the aches and pains seemed to migrate at will to other joints and muscles. And the attacks weren't merely physical.

"Welcome to the club," his doctor told him. "You've got some lumbar disk degeneration, a bit of arthritis here and there, but nothing too serious."

"Yeah, well, it pisses me off, so how do I get rid of it without pills?" Phil said.

"Get younger," his doctor said, and smiled. "That's the thing with pain. It's in a category all its own. There are a lot of other ailments and illnesses out there that are far more devastating, but pain has the unique ability to alter your personality."

"Damn right," Phil said, ruminating on how it often left him irritable and frustrated—each pang a constant, ferocious reminder his body's gears were starting to grind, and it was only a matter of time before they failed.

He had already been having nagging thoughts and anxieties about other aspects of his life that felt out of control, or more to the point, out of *his* control: his health, financial security, finding love and companionship. It all fused to ignite a slow, methodical burn of what was left of the once happy-go-lucky young guy.

It made him realize how, outside of an unforeseen work incident, his daily life had become rigidly routine. His daily routine was the one thing he had command over, and it gave him a sense of order, of stability, of being in control.

But as time went on, the walls of his routine began to feel like they were closing in, a prison of his own making, and the warden was the devil he knew. *I'm like Shawshank's Brooks*, he had thought, half joking, a reference to a character in his favorite movie. The prison bars, the bells, the beatings, the yellow line, the routine—after a while, they become more tolerable, more acceptable, even comforting. To the point where without them, you're lost. Out of control. Afraid. The outside becomes cold and foreboding, even treacherous and untrustworthy. Ready and willing to plunge a shiv into your heart the moment you step off the yellow line. But the bars, the bells, the beatings—always there. Never failing. Comforting.

It was an epiphany to Phil at the time, one that hits most people at some point. The big cliché. That Father Time was on his tail. That his time left was shorter than his time spent. That the job he was once so enthusiastic about was a distant memory. That the once certain was now uncertain. The once calm was now chaotic. The once confident, now anxiety riddled. The once fervent, now a mutated, routine ground-and-pound exercise in survival. And that's all he was trying to do—survive. Survive alone.

As soon as Phil entered the pub, the bartender knowingly set a Bud Light before him as he took his usual seat at the bar. A moment later, Ben, another local in his mid to late sixties, came in from outside and took his usual seat next to him, where his beer, cheeseburger, and fries awaited.

"It would take six mangoes, four kiwis, a dragon fruit, and a pound of kale every day for me to get the same shit in these capsules," Ben said.

Phil looked over and watched him unwrap a balled-up piece of toilet paper.

"And not full-grown kale, but that baby crap the millennials eat," Ben said. "Loaded with antioxidants. Good for the heart."

"Tell that to your cheeseburger and fries," Phil said.

Ben chuckled and sucked down the five three-quarter-inch-long capsules with a long pull on his beer and lifted a small bottle from his shirt pocket. "Ashwagandha. Want a hit? You could use it. Great for mood and stress management."

Phil shook his head. "I'll go with a shot of tequila. Does the same thing."

Ben filled the dropper and squirted the load into his mouth. "Suit yourself. But all this stuff keeps me young and balanced at a cellular level."

Phil motioned to the bartender. "I'll take that shot now."

"Laugh all you want," Ben said with another chuckle. "They're potent. And you gotta be careful. I once took some shit called Yohimbe, a tree bark, before I took a Viagra. I sweat for two days and tried to fuck a cactus. I assure you . . . you end up in the ER for trying to fuck a cactus, they take you right away. And then they call the house shrink."

Phil laughed. "At least you got laid."

"That's what I love about you, Phil," Ben said. "You're a weekly re-minder of what it's like to succumb—the reason I don't need to go to church and still feel better about myself come Monday."

"Yeah?" Phil said. "Remind yourself of that when you head back outside to smoke another baby cigarette."

Ben stood and gulped down the rest of his beer. "I'll keep that in mind," he said with a smile, and he headed outside.

Despite the lighthearted banter, Phil couldn't get Ben's comment out of his head. *Succumb to what?* he wondered. And the answer hit him.

He'd lost count of how many times he had told friends and col-leagues to knock it off when they would spin on the doom and gloom of aging. *The big fucking cliché*, he had thought. Yet here he was, doing the same. And with the dam breached, the flood of thoughts poured in, fast and furious.

There is no "How to Get Old" guidebook.

No "Disturbing Content" warning on your college alumni magazine when those on the memorial pages are from your own class.

No line-item deduction on the tax return for the ever-growing number of up-and-comers in your business you don't know—nor they you.

No fine print in the driver's manual that spells out how what you've worked like a dog to achieve will soon be worth shit as you motor, on cruise control, into the abyss of irrelevance.

No bold print to announce that after forty or more years of pounding it out, the payoff is an extended stay at the This Blows Inn.

What the fuck!

What's next? Self-help books and YouTube videos of self-professed gurus of inner peace?

TV evangelists out to remind the flock they're overcomers whose best days are ahead?

Tell that to the person who's fine one day and on the next is told they have a terminal illness and their life is now measured in extra innings.

Tell that to the person on life support after a head-on crash leaves them with no chance of a better day. No chance to say goodbye to loved ones, or for them to say it to you.

Round and round . . .

One thing is for sure, he realized. Getting old is an unstoppable beast no matter what. At least with Lorena, they could have fought, and lost, the battle together—another ritual that would have made the distaste palatable. But alone on the battlefield . . .

Phil knew, then and there, it was decision time. He either take control of his thoughts or he'd become them. That, he decided, was not going to happen, and he drained the rest of his Bud Light and affirmed that he wasn't on life's descent but at the pinnacle of his game, just catching his stride despite the lines on his face, the hitch in his step, the social obstacles. Affirmed that experience matters, that it was only the third quarter and there was still plenty of time on the clock. That the best *was* yet to come.

And as Ben came back inside, Phil ordered another round.

"Thanks to social media posts, we were able to pinpoint where the plane came down," Phil says to the group, and another blue star appears on the map marking the spot in southeast Mexico. "For the media, it was another field day."

He pulls up footage of the ABC News anchor's report. "According to an eyewitness, who wishes to remain anonymous, the two survivors, who fit the description of Raymond Dawson and Wilbur Bailey, took off before authorities arrived, leaving behind a stash of cocaine and fentanyl with a street value of several million dollars. Eddie Santoli was nowhere to be found. Authorities believe a dispute may have broken out on the plane, after which Dawson and Bailey killed him and dumped the body somewhere out over the Gulf."

Phil taps the news report off. "Can't make this stuff up," he says as he takes a seat on the stool and sucks down a gulp of water while the laughter subsides. "Turned out Dawson and Bailey hitched a ride to an old rail depot a few hours away. I figured, with a full tank and a little luck, I'd catch up to them by nightfall—which brings me to the second takeaway from this case."

He fills his lungs with Banana Nut Bread and looks about the room at the ambitious faces as he exhales. "Just when you think a shitstorm can't get worse . . . If you're not already dead, there's always worse."

THIRTY-EIGHT

The mint condition 1980 El Camino rumbles through the Mexican countryside, past the grazing herds of cattle and sheep, mango trees and orange groves, and fields of sugarcane. In its cargo bed, Wilbur curiously watches Ray as he haphazardly folds his baggies of coffee beans.

"My dad was killed when I was four," Ray says, feeling Wilbur's stare. "My mother took a second job doing the books for a coffee importer. They shipped in these expensive coffee beans from all over the world. The manager paid her some dough under the table, the rest in beans." Ray's eyes smile. "She loved coffee and treasured those beans. Would take books out of the library and learn how each was grown, the aroma, the taste. And she mixed her own blends and taught me."

Wilbur's eyes soften, and a slight smile crosses his lips. He motions for Ray to hand them over, which Ray does, and he watches Wilbur expertly arrange and roll them together into one perfect packet.

"You're lucky, Ray. You know the true answer to why our paths crossed." Wilbur puts the beans in his carry-on. "I'm done running."

Twilight underscores that the old rail depot's glory days are long gone. Its rails are lined with overgrown weeds and strewn with trash swirling in the wind. Beyond, abandoned carnival rides stand frozen in time—rusted metal skeletons keeping vigil over the few remaining businesses on life support.

Migrants of all ages and genders stream toward the one dilapidated freight train in the yard, climbing atop each car and maneuvering for a free spot to sit and sleep. For many, the dangerous trek has been made numerous times before. For some, it would be their last.

"It's called the death train for a reason," Wilbur says as Ray hustles him along. "Death. Amputations. Beatings. Rape. Disease. That's five of the million reasons for us to find a more suitable means of travel."

"Texas border. One reason for us not to," Ray says, and yanks him along faster to the last car.

Wilbur plants his feet. "I'm not going up there."

What a pain in the ass, Ray thinks. He whips Wilbur around and gets in his face. "You have an ex-boss with Russian mob ties, who'd like to chop you into pieces. An IRS agent, out for vengeance, on your ass. And one of the world's most violent gangs tried to kill or capture us, and odds are they'll try again. And this *train* is your problem?"

"Well, when you put it that way," Wilbur says, the flippant sarcasm in his tone clear. In the distance, the engine's horn blasts, and the train starts to roll.

Ray raises his clenched fist. "Three, two . . ."

In no mood for another number one, Wilbur wheels around, and they dart to the train and scoot up the ladder. From the moment they step onto the roof and claim their small piece of open space, all eyes are on them, wary of two gringos who've gone astray.

The train rounds the bend and clanks off into the night.

Empathy. Sensitivity. Nonjudgment. Altogether they compose one of Wilbur's most loved attributes—compassion. Often to a fault. And sometimes misguided. It's not like he hasn't been accused of having wounded bird syndrome before. His desire to be needed has never been as strong as it's been since Wilma died. But his heart is always in the right place—which is where it is while he studies each of the migrant's faces, his eyes humbled by theirs, which bleed with the fear and danger they endure for a shot at a better life.

Ray's gut churns out distress calls. "Whatever you're thinking . . ." Ray says softly and shakes his head.

"I got this," Wilbur whispers and pats Ray on his knee. He stretches out his leg, sticks his hand down his pants, fidgets around his thigh, and pulls out a wad of hundred-dollar bills. Several blow away in the wind.

"Bad idea," Ray says, grabbing Wilbur's hand.

"Christ, Ray . . . A little faith." He removes Ray's hand, stands, and smiles as he shuffles to a young boy sitting with his parents. His mother, nervous and suspicious, pulls her son closer.

"¿Están sus padres en casa?" *Are your parents home?* Wilbur says to the boy and hands him a hundred-dollar bill. "Buenos días," *Good morning*, he says to his parents and hands a bill to each.

His pace quickens as he meanders across the roof and doles out the bills—each with a riff of his rudimentary knowledge of common Spanish phrases. "¿Tienes un lápiz?" *Do you have a pencil?* he says to one. "Estoy bien, gracias," *I am fine, thanks*, to another. And to a third, he asks, "¿Dónde está el baño?" *Where is the restroom?*

Just when I thought I'd seen it all, Ray thinks. But his short hairs spike when Wilbur approaches two menacing-looking guys at the far end of the car.

The guy on the right is a dirtbag named Diablo Cortez. But in these parts, most who know him, at least those who are still alive, know him as El Corbata, or "The Tie." It's a moniker he's earned over the many years of murders he has carried out using the "Colombian necktie"— his preferred form of execution. The heinous method, where a person's throat is slashed and their tongue is pulled out through the wound, dates to the late forties and fifties, when guerrilla warfare plagued the Colombian countryside. Its main purpose was to scare and intimidate. It's the undisputed champ at both.

The filthy punk next to him is Malvado Alvarez, but most know him as Madre, or "Mother," because he tortured his for several weeks before he took a pneumatic nail gun and shot her 183 times with rusty roofing nails. Other than that, he was a loving son.

"¿Hay especiales esta noche?" *Are there any specials this evening?*
Wilbur says to Diablo and offers him a bill.

Diablo strikes a match and lights a cigarillo before he snatches it and
reaches out for another. "¿Uno más para mi perro?" *One more for my dog?*

Wilbur smiles politely and hands one to Malvado. "¿Va a llover?"
Is it going to rain?

"Sí señor. Sangre." *Yes, sir. Blood.*

Wilbur smiles. "Muchas gracias." *Thank you so much.*

"See . . . All that worry for nothing," Wilbur says to Ray as he retakes
his seat. He looks around at the faces, many of them smiling. "Look at
the smiles . . . A momentary respite from despair, knowing tomorrow
will be a little better than today. Is that so bad?"

"No. What's bad are the two guys at the end who, at some point,
are going to slit your throat to get the rest of the cash."

Back at the old depot, it's desolate save for the swirling trash as the
maroon Ford Fiesta rolls up and stops by the rails. Phil gets out and
stands there, frustrated, tired, and unsure of his next move, when from
afar, the faint sound of the train's horn blast carries in on the wind,
and—*smack!*—a hundred-dollar bill plants on his face.

"Motherfuckers!"

THIRTY-NINE

The ride through the night is long and arduous. But at last, the halo of predawn bursts over the horizon. Diablo strikes a match and sucks in his first puffs of another cigarillo.

Most on the freight car's roof are still fast asleep. Those who aren't know enough to stay out of his path as he makes his way across the car, especially when he extracts a nine-inch bowie knife from the back of his waistband.

These are the moments Diablo lives for. The sense of power. Control. They intensify as he squats beside Wilbur, who snores, out cold, and he relishes the moment with another puff on his cigarillo. But as soon as he thrusts the knife at Wilbur's throat, he jerks to a stop and slowly looks down at the barrel of Ray's 9 mm pressed against his balls.

With a smile and another puff, Diablo stands up and backs away, all the way across the car. But the moment he settles back in next to Malvado, the train lurches, and its brakes squeal from the rapid deceleration.

Ray pops up, his eyes drawn to the faint strobe of flashing blue lights on a cluster of trees way ahead in the distance, and he shakes Wilbur, who drifts in and out.

"I'll drive, Wilma," Wilbur says, entrenched in a dream.

Ray pulls him close. "No, moron. It's me."

Wilbur's eyes snap open, and he winces. "Any gum left?"

"It's our stop."

Wilbur looks around and tries to clear the cobwebs. "We're still moving."

"Exactly. Let's go," Ray says. He thrusts the carry-on at him and pulls him up and over to the edge of the roof. The thick brush below flies by.

"I am not jumping off a moving train," Wilbur says adamantly.

"Two reasons why you are. One . . . It beats Mexican jailhouse torture. And two . . ." Ray shoves him over the edge, and he lands in the thick brush with a crunch. "It beats being *pushed* off," he says, and leaps himself. But he sails through a small bare patch in the brush and hits the dry, hard ground with a thud. "Ugh, Christ. What are the odds?"

Further back, Wilbur, his carry-on planted on his face, lies suspended, entwined in a thicket of thorny branches and twigs. "Where's the forgiveness, for Chrissake?" he bemoans to the heavens. "A little stolen money and you stick me with a psychopath who repeatedly violates no less than ten of the twelve non-detrimental ways to punish? Did Wilma put you up to this?" Spent and defeated, his body sags. "You win, God. I'm tappin' out."

But no sooner does he tap his hand on his carry-on than Ray, scratched and bruised but otherwise intact, reaches in, yanks him out, and helps him up.

"If anyone needs forgiveness, it's your parents," Ray says. "Let's go."

Meanwhile, Phil, unable to take any more of the Spanish hip-hop tune's pounding beat as he motors along, knuckles the maroon Ford Fiesta's radio off and pinches the bridge of his nose to ease the other pounding in his head. It's been twenty-four hours since he's slept but, between his rumpled clothes and tired, bloodshot eyes, it looks more like it's been seventy-two.

Amid the welcome silence, Tony Bennett's tranquil "I Left My Heart in San Francisco" meanders into Phil's mind—a welcome lull from the mental chaos. Thoughts of home flood in as he softly sings along, and it hits him how, out of all the crazy shit he's done in his life, *this is stupid crazy*.

He sucks down another 5-Hour Energy drink and tosses the vial in the back among the others—his fifth in as many hours. Anything to stay awake. Anything to stay focused.

Five seconds later, *anything* happens.

A blast of adrenaline shocks Phil's system, and he slams on the brakes, cuts the headlights, and pulls off the road, straining to focus across the tall grassy field and through the thick brush and trees.

Pay dirt—it's the train!

A deep breath does little to allay the churning in his gut and throbbing in his chest. In the past, *crazy* was enough to put the brakes on. *Stupid crazy* would have been enough to go full stop and reanalyze—not push forward on a wing and a prayer. Especially in a fog.

The acid in Phil's gut simmers, and his doubts gnaw at him.

It doesn't add up.

Bailey and Dawson could have killed me at the truck yet didn't even take my gun.

And they made sure the driver took me to the next town.

And left the car in plain sight.

It doesn't add up.

Still, when he clicks open the maroon Ford Fiesta's door locks, the look on his face is undeniable. It's as if he knows he is about to make a terrible mistake.

The gnawing thoughts intensify as Phil runs across the field toward the tree line, oblivious to the Mexican cops who, with flashlights lit and guns ready, methodically move from one railcar roof to the next, checking faces against a photo of Ray and Wilbur's IRS wanted posters while Ray and Wilbur slink past through the trees and brush on the other side of the train—Diablo and Malvado not far behind.

But as Phil makes a final dash for the brush and trees that border the track, he pulls up, disconcerted by a black Range Rover with its lights off, barreling down the tracks to the back of the train.

"Oh shit!" he thinks aloud when six heavily armed CDN thugs pile out of the car—unaware that six more have piled out of an Escalade at the front of the train.

Within seconds, bullets fly, and all hell breaks loose.

Frantic and knee-deep in a place where he shouldn't be knee-deep, Phil scrambles to a tree for cover. But no sooner does he pull his gun and drape his badge around his neck than he's lit up in a flashlight beam and wheels around to find his gun trained on Eduardo Díaz, a twentysomething Mexican cop whose own gun is pointed back at Phil.

Caught short by the sight of a white guy in a suit with a badge, Díaz hesitates. And in that split-second hesitation—*BAM!*—a CDN thug's bullet explodes through his head and launches him backward.

To Phil's horror, Díaz is dead before he hits the ground, and he blows away the thug who pulled the trigger and scurries back into the tall grassy field.

Further ahead, in the refueling station parking lot, Ray hot-wires an open-air jeep, and he and Wilbur rumble out of the lot as the owner barrels out of the station, his .30-30 Winchester levered. But it's the last thing he ever sees and never gets off a shot.

Diablo's blade nearly takes his head clean off, and Malvado bashes out the window of a Ford Bronco.

Winded, sweat-soaked, and desperate to make it back to his car unscathed, Phil is only halfway across the field when he spots the fast-approaching jeep, and he ducks low.

"No fucking way," he mumbles, and rubs the sweat from his eyes. "No fucking way," he says again as he watches Ray and Wilbur speed past, and he makes a mad dash for his car.

If not for the half-buried log, he might have had a shot. But instead, he faceplants with a thud.

"Motherfuckers!"

FORTY

By late morning in New York, the "Fox News Alert" theme chimes on the *America's Newsroom* set, and the floor director cues the anchor.

"Earlier today, a massacre occurred when Mexican police raided a freight train in the northeast stronghold of the Cartel del Norte after receiving a tip that former NYPD detective Raymond Dawson and fugitive Wilbur Bailey were aboard. But less than a week after members of MF-17 murdered six Honduran police officers, members of the notoriously violent CDN cartel ambushed the Mexican officers, killing all ten of them. It's believed one police officer, twenty-eight-year-old Eduardo Díaz, a devoted husband and father of twin baby girls, captured an image of his killer on his bodycam before the bullet to his head took his life. Warning—the footage is disturbing."

The image on the monitor changes to Díaz's rocky, whipsawing bodycam footage as he maneuvers through the brush, trees, and bullets. It steadies when he lights Phil up and freezes when Phil whips around with his gun aimed directly at him.

"Díaz's alleged killer, seen here, has been identified as Philip Dancourt from Houston, Texas, where he's a special agent with the Internal Revenue Service. Mexican authorities believe he is the same man who, days earlier, carjacked an eighty-three-year-old diabetic woman recovering from a stroke, and was later seen in fifteen-year-old Narian Sahoo's viral video trying to board the moving Cessna carrying Dawson, Bailey, and ex-con fugitive Eddie Santoli. According to an unspecified IRS source, Agent Dancourt has been leading a multiyear secret investigation of Amco Oil—the company that formerly employed Wilbur Bailey."

"I mean, holy moly!" Phil taps the footage off the screen and laughs along with the group. "As soon as the story broke, the horde of swamp rats on the Hill swarmed. And it took Governor Hargrove less than an hour to pull together his buttoned-down generic defender-of-the-little-guy presser with Callahan and the usual cadre of local panderers. It was quite a show."

Phil settles in on the stool and grabs the water. "For twenty minutes straight, the media suckles on Hargrove's cliché teats—how the honorable, God-fearing citizens of Texas deserve to know who knew what, and when they knew it. And how he and Texas stand ready to assist Mexican authorities in any way to help facilitate their capture." He sucks down a huge gulp and takes a deep breath. "All it did was fuel a Cat 4 shitstorm that me, Dawson, and Bailey were in cahoots."

Phil goes on about how Callahan couldn't wait to step up to the plate. "Going in, he figured once I took Bailey into custody, no one, including Hargrove, would care if he cut a few corners. But that was then. With shifting winds and horrible headlines, he quickly changes his tune to a little country ditty called 'My Lyin' Lips Will Cover My Ass.'"

The group bursts out laughing. "He denies any knowledge of my actions or whereabouts," Phil says with a smirk and fires up his e-cig. "And after he assures the citizens of an internal investigation, he announces to the world that I've been under a great deal of financial strain and expresses his heartfelt thoughts and prayers for my daughter, Emmi."

While the laughs linger, it strikes Phil how comical it sounds now but didn't when he had first heard it, and he detonates another blast of Banana Nut Bread and ejects the cloud.

"Funny, yes," he says when they settle down. "But let us not forget it was also tragic. Many good people lost their lives that night. And the real carnage was still to come."

FORTY-ONE

The late morning sun is blistering as the open-air jeep speeds down the unmarked narrow road somewhere in northeast Mexico. It's the kind of road often seen from airplane windows. The kind that cut through barren, dry, dusty rolling hills, and seems to come from, and go to, nowhere.

Keep moving, Ray tells himself again. *In uncharted waters like this, always keep moving*—like a great white shark, the undisputed heavyweight champion of the seas. Otherwise, you're the prey, just trying to survive.

Still, despite his focus, Ray can't help but feel a bit of déjà vu.

It was his and Stephanie's first cross-country road trip together. They took a southerly route through Nashville and Memphis—the perfect way to treat themselves to some great music, barbecue, a tour of the King's Graceland estate, and, of course, to see the Lorraine Motel where a bullet took out the other King.

From there, they continued west and made a dozen or so other stops along the way, one of which was to see an old friend who was still in the Marine Corps Reserve at Naval Air Station Joint Reserve Base Fort Worth.

The familiar sense of pride hit Ray the moment they drove through the gate. And after a quick tour of the base and a great lunch on Lake Worth, he and Stephanie cruised into New Mexico, spent a night at a charming B&B in Albuquerque, and took off early en route to a couple of sinful nights in Vegas, baby. But it was the excursion they took on the home stretch to SoCal that was on Ray's mind: a road-trip-within-a-road-trip that took them through the Mojave Desert. It sounded fun at the time.

The landscape was beautiful and otherworldly, but the heat was suffocating. The few towns—if you call a cluster of buildings a town— had names such as Badwater, Furnace Creek, and Stovepipe Wells. And all it would take to end up in a life-threatening situation was one wrong turn.

Their car was dangerously close to overheating as the outside temperature rose another 2 degrees to 119. For the third time, the tire pressure warning light flashed, and Ray pulled over to let out some more air so they wouldn't explode. And to top it all off, they had no water or cell service.

It's no wonder they call this place Death Valley, Ray thought.

The road he and Wilbur are driving down has an eerie Death Valley feel.

"There was a hybrid Kia two spots down. Would it have hurt to steal that instead?" Wilbur says as he pulls the last splinters from his forearm.

"Would it have hurt if I had let him slice your head off?"

Wilbur shrugs him off, stands, and checks behind them. For as far as he can see, the Bronco is nowhere in sight. "I don't see them," he says, and when he swivels back around, his eyes sharpen and lock onto an oddly shaped, crudely camouflaged radio tower atop the next hill. "Once we're over the next hill, pull off the road." He plops back into his seat and points out Ray's window. "That way."

"Why? You ready to die?"

"Three reasons why you should. One, if they are back there, they won't see us when we're on the other side, and we'll be long gone before they realize we turned off. Two, this road is taking us east. We need to go north. And three, there's an oil pipeline about twenty miles out, which we can follow north to a pump station that's only two miles from the border."

"You know this how?"

Wilbur points out the front window. "That radio tower . . . I know where we are. And I also know where every inch of pipeline in the northern hemisphere is. It's our best shot."

Ray looks out his window at the barren nothingness. "It's too wide open."

"For once, Ray, follow my lead," Wilbur says, exasperated. "Just do it."

Ray weighs Wilbur's knowledge of the radio tower and pipeline network against the potential danger of being sitting ducks out in the hills. It's the first time he's ever even considered tactical advice from someone outside of the military or law enforcement, let alone a perp he apprehended. But after a brief hesitation as they come over the crest, he cuts the wheel, veers off the road, and they speed off into the distance till they're nothing but a speck in a vast dry, dusty sea.

As the miles go by, the stillness of the passing surroundings and quiet within the jeep provide a peaceful respite after the death and mayhem of the early hours.

Wilbur stands to feel the wind rush past. It's cathartic. It's alive. It relaxes his face and enlightens his eyes, and he turns around and again checks behind them as far as he can see. "We lost them, I'm sure of it," he says, and sends Diablo and Malvado—somewhere out there—his best tough-guy Italian arm curse. "Take that, muchachos!"

But his exhilaration is short-lived.

The jeep's engine sputters and dies—out of gas—and he plops back down as they roll to a stop.

"Driving, Raymond . . . It implies keeping an eye on the gas gauge."

Two seconds later, from out of nowhere, the Ford Bronco skids up in a cloud of dust and rocks. And when it settles, Diablo and

Malvado are standing in front of them, each with a massive .44 Magnum hand cannon.

"Being sure we lost them, Wilbur . . . It implies being sure."

"Caballeros," Diablo says, a sly smile firm on his lips.

FORTY-TWO

BANG. BANG. BANG. BANG.

Congresswoman Blanche Wolf hammers away with her gavel till the gallery settles, and she gives the floor to the gentlewoman from Oklahoma.

A fifth-generation Oklahoman, Delaney Gray grew up on a farm, mostly wheat, among the rolling hills, grain silos, red barns, and white churches. Her great looks brought early attention, and she could easily have gone the beauty pageant and modeling route. But the family's moral compass set her on a different path. Perseverance is in their blood. And despite the fierce competition to excel, brought on by six older brothers, the work ethic her parents instilled in her lived up to the state motto: *Labor Omnia Vincit.* Labor Conquers All Things.

Pageant looks aside, she's a constitutional attorney, a rising star in her party, and a former decorated marine with firsthand knowledge of what it means to selflessly put your life on the line for others.

"Thank you for coming in today, Detective Wallace," Congresswoman Gray says to Joe, who is now at the witness table and acknowledges her with a nod. "And thank you for your willingness, along with the rest of your fellow officers across the country, to allow us, the public, to call on you twenty-four seven when in need. Because of a few bad apples, that's often forgotten today."

"Thank you, ma'am," Joe says as he leans toward the mic, relaxed. "Oops. My apology, Congresswoman, for calling you ma'am."

Amused rumblings fill the chamber, a welcome moment of levity in the tense proceedings.

"Maybe I'm old-fashioned, but you can call me ma'am anytime— once I'm out of my forties," she says, and waits for the gallery to settle down before she dives back in. "Ever kill someone, Detective?"

"Yes, ma'— Yes, Congresswoman. In the Marines."

"But not as a police officer?"

"No."

A warm smile crosses her lips. "As a former marine myself, I, too, am aware of the life-changing impact of taking another human being's life. I think you'll agree it never leaves you."

Joe nods, and his eyes wash over the other committee members. "I've never known a cop who ever woke up hoping to take a life that day, no matter the skin color. Especially a kid. Especially a cop like Ray Dawson."

"Meaning?" Delaney asks, further opening the door.

"Meaning that for those of us who had the privilege to work with him, he was Ray 'Angel' Dawson—one part brutally tough, one part extremely compassionate. But whether he was your guardian angel or your angel of death depended on which side of the line you chose to live."

From the sighs and fidgets of Delaney's "friends" across the aisle, it's clear Joe has struck a nerve. And with accusations sure to fly, she paves the way for him to cut them off at the pass. "You saying he was both judge and jury?"

"No. Like the other 99.9 percent of all cops, Ray Dawson was, and always will be, dedicated to the sanctity of life and to helping to save the lives of total strangers whether or not it could cost him his own." He shifts his gaze across several of the more damning and con-frontational committee members. "A cop who is as much a cop at the core of his being as he is a man." He chuckles. "Sorry. I don't mean to laugh, but as far back as the academy, the word on Ray was that as soon as his head popped out of his mother's womb, he looked at the doctor and said, 'Hands where I can see 'em, asshole'—which, by the way, is the same thing Stephanie said to him on their first date."

Raucous laughter erupts throughout. Joe turns and winks at Stephanie, who's sitting in the back of the gallery, while Congresswoman Wolf, irritated, vigorously hammers the chamber to silence, and Delaney jumps back in.

"As the chairwoman previously stated, we're not here to adjudicate Mr. Dawson's record. It's impressive," she says, and glances at her notes. "But he was also cited ten times for insubordination, twenty-three times for excessive property damage, and thirty-one times for reckless endangerment of his *own* life."

"He had just cause."

"Please . . ." Delaney says, again leading him where she knows he'll go.

"The thirty-one lives saved."

While some in the gallery grumble, the applause from the rest again triggers Wolf to bring down the hammer. But from the look Delaney and Joe share, it's clear Delaney has the chamber where she wants it, and their trust builds.

"How long have you known Ray Dawson?"

"Practically my whole adult life. Four tours together in Afghanistan. Together through the police academy, and partners until—"

"Would you agree some might view his methods as excessively violent?"

"Yeah, some. But they don't understand that on our side of the badge, violence is relative to the situation you find yourself, or others, in—often without warning." Joe's eyes canvass the media spread across the floor. "And what's never covered in the press is that every year, thousands of kids, some as young as eight or nine, are suspected of, or charged with, gun crimes." His gaze shifts back to the committee. "So, no. I have never seen Ray Dawson be overly violent, and that includes the Isia Serante case."

Joe knows he just drove the spike into the heart of the elephant in the room, into the hearts of those in the chamber, and in the media, who are out to further vilify Ray—those willing to do and say anything to fan the flames, justify their actions, satisfy constituents, or move their ratings along with the most hits, likes, and shares.

And though the chamber is silent, the committee members' faces denote the party lines: the sharp glare of contempt from one side, the soft gleam of gratitude from the other.

"Even though after weeks of searches and countless witness interviews, no gun was ever found?" Delaney asks.

"Despite thousands of years of searching, we've never found Jesus either, yet millions believe."

The comment again draws sharply contrasting reactions from both sides.

"Isn't it true, though, Mr. Dawson was violent within your department? That a physical confrontation with two other officers left them, collectively, with . . ." She grabs her tablet and reads off the notes. "Four broken ribs, a cracked pelvis, a ruptured spleen, and a shattered cheekbone."

"They got off lucky."

"How so?" she asks, somewhat surprised.

"Ray nailed them before me and the rest of the department."

"Meaning?"

"They were assholes," Joe says. "The kind of cops you can't have on the force. The kind that blow in the wind. You never know where they stand. Or if they have your back when your life is on the line—and it could cost them theirs." His gaze again drifts across the committee members. "I imagine that, for those who are prisoners of political winds, it's a tough notion to accept, let alone live by. But the only reason Ray Dawson ain't a cop today—and New York City streets are less safe as a result—is because, like those two asshole cops, many of you folks blow in the wind."

With nerves already frayed, the chamber erupts in a mix of outrage and accolades. And while Congresswoman Wolf lets her gavel fly, several on the committee whisper to their assistants to monitor social media and track how Joe is trending.

Joe leans into the mic and talks over the din. "Believe me, if any of you ever find yourselves on the wrong side of the fan when the shit hits, you'll pray to have a cop, a man like Ray Dawson, beside you."

FORTY-THREE

Ray is beside Wilbur. They're bruised, bloodied, and buck naked except for their shoes. But by the grace of God, they're alive.

Still, Wilbur's chest heaves in distress when Malvado tosses his carry-on in the back of the Bronco atop the rest of his and Ray's belongings and the rest of the cash.

"That's a red line," Wilbur mutters, and glances at the heavens. "Wilma, a little intercession with the man upstairs, please?"

"Unless Wilma's packin', you might find a better use for your last moments on earth," Ray says, his voice low, his eyes fixed on Diablo, standing guard a short distance away.

Diablo relights his cigarillo with a flare before he tosses it into their jeep, which ignites within seconds.

"Be careful. The sun's a bitch," Diablo says, his Spanish accent thick, and his shrill cackle carries in the wind as he and Malvado hightail it out of there.

Great. Just fucking great, Ray thinks to himself as he hustles to the burning jeep, grabs bottles of water from the console, and sets off on foot to continue toward the pipeline, Wilbur in tow.

Within ten minutes, he knew the trek naked across the dry, dusty rolling hills in the blistering heat would be the easy part. Trying to tune out Wilbur's unrelenting chatter . . . *Just fucking great.*

"And I told my doctor my urine looks more yellow than usual. His only question was if I had a will. Crazy, right? Everyone knows a will is not enough. You need a living trust."

Twenty minutes out, Ray avoids all eye contact and pretends he's cleaning underneath his fingernails.

"Corn on the cob. A healthy vegetable for most. But if you're a dog owner . . . Watch out. You eat the corn. The dog eats the cob, can't digest the hemicellulose and lignin fibers, and voilà—three hours later, little Jimmy Chew is under the knife."

Ray tries counting his steps, getting as far as 732 before he loses count.

"Twelve hundred milligrams per day of acai pulp can cut cancer risk by up to sixteen percent, but ingesting more than eighteen ounces of red meat per week pulls the risk up by fourteen percent. Sure, consuming cruciferous and green leafy vegetables every day offers a hefty twelve percent dip, but more than two ounces of alcohol per day, a fifteen percent pop. And God forbid you have an omega-3–to–omega-6 fatty acid imbalance. Might as well inject concrete into your jugular."

After forty minutes, Ray hums "99 Bottles of Beer on the Wall" for the fourth time.

"One day enjoying an innocent, leisurely swim in a serene country lake. The next . . . necrotizing fasciitis, the flesh-eater. Yesterday you were six foot three; today, three foot six."

After an hour, Ray tries visualization, imagining he's back on the beach in Costa Rica with Stephanie.

"It explains your strife with words, Ray. Words have a feeling. Take *vomit.* A Mona Lisa of words. It alone can cause nausea. Magnificent in scope and brilliance. Right up there with *phlegm, mucus, moist . . .* And how about *puss?*" Wilbur shudders as he says it.

Ray performs a deep-breathing exercise he learned eleven years ago when his first wife, Aileen, convinced him to try Headspace.

"And the legal jargon in the document . . . Herein, therein, hereof, thereof, hereunder, wherever, whether now known, not known, in perpetuity or a place beyond perpetuity if not now known, that might be known whenever."

As another thirty minutes tick away, Ray focuses on several of his most violent and bloody crime scenes.

"Take my neighbors. Real Bible-thumpers. I mean, try going into Walmart or Target these days and asking on what aisle you can find the armor of God. Cops will be there faster than you can say 'Can I get a witness.'"

Trudging along, naked in the desert, Ray's efforts to mentally evade Wilbur prove futile; time becomes indistinct.

"And the beignets were divine. Superior to any I've had before. Delicate . . ."

Unable to take any more, Ray wheels around. "Benyays? Divine?"

Wilbur, his skin beet red, jolts to a stop and holds his thumb and forefinger close. "Little French doughnuts served with the eggs *en cocotte.*"

"Three reasons I should beat you senseless. One, you're an imbecile. Two, your shoes suck. And three . . . you're without a doubt the whitest guy—ever. You're not even white, you're translucent." Ray shoots his hand up, cutting off any chance of a response. "Another word, and I'll benyay your divine head off."

Fortunately, it only takes another five minutes for them to reach the pipeline and find relief in its shade as they continue northward. By Wilbur's calculation, it's roughly a mile further until they reach the pump station two miles from the border.

But about halfway there, they come upon a small, clumsy pipe jutting out of the main line. Oil seeps from around the seam, and a thick pool of it sits below the pipe's hacksawed, jagged end.

"It's an illegal line," Wilbur says. "The drug cartels bore into the main lines, attach an illegal one, siphon off millions of barrels, and then sell the stolen oil on the black market for less than the price on the legitimate exchange." The moment he says it, the realization flashes in his eyes. "That's it!" he exclaims. "That's why Amco's numbers don't add up."

"Good for you, Wilbur. You can tell it to the feds," Ray says, and trudges on.

"C'mon, Ray, lighten up," Wilbur says as he hustles up alongside. "We're alive. If that's not lucky, then we're the two unluckiest guys in the world."

"No argument there."

"I had a thought—no, an epiphany is what it is—"

"Oh, Christ," Ray says, exasperated.

"—that since I lost Wilma and my company, I wasn't living, but merely trying to survive and stay relevant. Like you without your badge and Stephanie."

"I assure you, Wilbur—you're irrelevant."

"Wow. That hurts. For what it's worth, I . . . Never mind."

"'Never mind' is *never* your last word, Wilbur."

As much as Wilbur hates proving Ray right, he can't help himself. "You're right. But no matter how hard and crass and selfish you can be, Ray, I like you."

Ray looks at him, his eyes narrow, unsure where he's going with this. Their nakedness hits Wilbur.

"In a *friend* kind of way," Wilbur clarifies. "Underneath your bullshit, you're a good guy. The kind I always wanted to be friends with."

Ray can't help but take it down a notch. "Yeah, well, uh . . . Sorry about the shoes. And I do know a whiter guy—a murdered albino."

"You ever listen to yourself?" Wilbur asks. "The point is, there's more to life than just survival."

No sooner does Wilbur make his point than they jolt to a stop as, out of nowhere, a drone bearing the CDN logo swoops in and hovers right in front of them.

Its onboard camera swivels from Wilbur to Ray.

Ray looks off into the distance, his eyes drawn to the dusty rooster tail of a pickup speeding their way with half a dozen armed cartel thugs in the truck bed.

"There is more than just survival, Wilbur," Ray says. "An agonizing, painful death."

Back on the two-lane road, Phil's bloodshot eyes try to focus on the wrinkled map spread out on the maroon Ford Fiesta's roof. But it's clear he has no idea where he is or what he's looking for, and he flings the map aside.

Spent, he leans against the car and sees a red-tailed hawk soaring effortlessly above, a counterpoint to his thoughts chaotically spinning out of control.

And that's when a distant plume of smoke catches his eye.

FORTY-FOUR

"Can I get a *holy moly*?" Phil calls out to the trainees and cups his palm around his ear.

"HOLY MOLY!" comes the chant in unison, and laughter fills the room.

"What are the odds?" Phil says, and points to a female trainee sitting in the front row.

"Less than winning Powerball and Mega Millions twice in the same week," she calls out to more laughter.

"Bingo," Phil says, grabbing another bottle of water and chugging a few gulps. "Had it not been for a local farmer who saw the jeep blow past, odds are I would have never taken that road and would have lost Dawson and Bailey for good. And thanks to Callahan, it didn't take long for my daughter, Emmi, and her boyfriend, Matt, to become chum for the feeding-frenzied media."

He pulls up a series of clips of Emmi and Matt as they're swarmed by a crush of camera operators and reporters. In the first, they swoop in as Emmi comes out of the hospital's personnel door, their microphones thrust at her face.

"Ms. Dancourt, a word about your father's mental state?" asks one obnoxious reporter.

"Yes, he's smarter than you," Emmi says, and continues to her car.

"Is he seeing a doctor or psychiatrist?"

"Any truth to the rumors of meth use and heavy drinking?"

"Did you know about your father's debts? Are any from gambling?"

Laughter fills the lecture hall when the trainees watch Emmi ignore them and drive away, and next, Phil pulls up a clip in which the gaggle of press descends upon Emmi and Matt as they leave a local restaurant.

"How long has your father known Ray Dawson and Wilbur Bailey?"

"Have you ever met either of them?"

"Is it true Wilma Bailey was once your babysitter?"

"These alarming reports of your father-in-law's unhinged behavior must have come as quite a shock," another says, her mic pointed at Matt's face. "Any other red flags about him you've kept to yourself?"

Emmi and Matt share a resigned look and snicker as they make it to their car.

"Has your father contacted you since he murdered the Mexican police officer?" shouts another.

This question stops Emmi cold, and she wheels around. "My father didn't, and wouldn't, ever murder anyone—though I wonder if he should make an exception for trash peddlers like you."

Rousing applause fills the lecture hall, and Phil pulls up the final clip of Emmi pulling out of the garage in the back of her and Matt's townhouse in the morning, on her way to work. The familiar gaggle of press surrounds the car, cameras pressed to the windows.

"Do you know what drove your father off the deep end?"

Emmi lowers the window a crack. "Yes, asinine questions."

"If he's listening, is there anything you'd like to say to him?" shouts another.

"Yes," she says, with a smile. "Come home soon. I'll make more of my secret pasta."

Phil taps the footage off, and the room again erupts in applause. "First ten of you to make your stats join me for some of that pasta."

Taking another gulp of water, Phil pulls up a photo of the jeep engulfed in flames. "There was enough left of the burned-out jeep to confirm it was the one Bailey and Dawson stole, but they were nowhere in sight. And there were tire tracks of another vehicle, which meant I was back to square zero. But that's when I caught another break: two sets of footprints on a hill further out that hadn't blown away. So, I jumped back in the saddle and took off."

Phil takes a seat on the stool and sparks his e-cig. "Despite everything that had gone down thus far, I felt my luck had finally turned." He sucks in a lungful of Banana Nut Bread and exhales the cloud.

"A short time later, the shit hit the fan."

FORTY-FIVE

Dust devils waltz across the dry, dusty rolling hills. One dances over a pool of fresh blood, leaving no doubt that something horrific, something violent, something deadly, happened here. The blood drains off one side and dwindles to drops that end where Ray and Wilbur stand at the edge of a massive deep ditch—still buck naked but for their shoes, their hands bound behind their backs with extension cords.

A scorpion scurries across Wilbur's loafers and into the ditch, perhaps heading to its burrow under one of the countless vehicles that line it—most already carcasses, others partially stripped. Or perhaps it is on its way to a crevice inside the rusted shipping container on the far side, catty-corner to several rows of stacked oil barrels.

"One in three hundred thirty-seven million eight hundred fifty-six thousand four hundred and two. The odds our paths would cross—give or take," Wilbur says, his voice low and discreet.

Fixed straight ahead, Ray's eyes reflect stoic indifference. "One in one. The odds I'll kill you myself if you don't shut the fuck up."

A moment later, a dark-skinned CDN thug with a close-cropped beard, an assault rifle slung over his shoulder, and a bloody machete tucked in his waist, rises from within the ditch.

He stops before Ray and Wilbur, and his eyes dart back and forth between them as he holds up Diablo's and Malvado's severed heads by their hair.

Blood drips from their necks, and Diablo's lit, half-smoked cigarillo still dangles from his lips.

"These the men who robbed you?"

"He looks familiar," Ray says as he flicks his head toward Diablo. "Whadda you think, Wilbur?"

Wilbur leans toward Diablo's face and sniffs. "The cigarillo . . . is it a White Owl? I think it was the robber's brand." The cartel thug eyes him, his patience waning as Wilbur shifts his focus to Malvado's head. "I can't be sure," he says, taking a closer look. "Turn 'em around. I only saw them from the back."

Exasperated, the thug tosses the heads back into the ditch and withdraws his bloody machete. Wilbur drops to his knees and closes his eyes. "Yea, though I walk through the valley of the shadow of death . . ."

The thug rears the machete high, but just as he whips the blade toward Wilbur's neck, Ray whips around with a roundhouse kick to the crook of the thug's elbow, and the thug cuts his own head off.

". . . I shall fear no evil; for thou art with me."

Ray scoots over. "No, bonehead. *I'm* with you," he says and lays on his side as five thugs down in the ditch head their way. "Let's get our hands."

Wilbur's eyes snap open, stunned and fixated on the thug's head as it rolls into the ditch and settles next to Diablo's and Malvado's.

"Now, dammit!" Ray says.

Wilbur snaps out of it, scoots over, and lays on his side, facing Ray.

"Touch my ass, and your head's next, capiche?" Ray says.

Wilbur scoots closer, in no mood to be bullied.

Ray's body tenses. "That feel like a hand to you?" he says.

"It feel like one to you?" Wilbur asks with glib satisfaction. Intent on pinching Ray's vocabularic nerve, a sly smile crosses his lips. "I've had enough of your twaddle. Oh, I'm sorry. Did I say *twaddle*? I meant *drivel*. No, no . . . *poppycock*. Or was it *balderdash*? Or perhaps *mal*—"

An agonizing grimace contorts Wilbur's face and makes clear what part of his anatomy Ray has vise-gripped.

"Oh, sweet Jesus," Wilbur cries out. "Bunk," he struggles to get out, and Ray ratchets his grip a notch. "Ahhh . . . Bullshit."

Ray lets go. "*Bullshit*, yes. *Twaddle, drivel, poppycock, balderdash*, and whatever else, no. Now, let's get our hands."

Begrudged, Wilbur mouths *malarkey* and rolls over, and they untie the cords.

But as soon as they're free, gunfire explodes around them. Ray lunges for the headless thug's assault rifle and takes several of them out before he grabs Wilbur, and they tumble into the ditch and land by the Ford Bronco.

"Caballeros," they simultaneously say when they spot Diablo's and Malvado's headless bodies in the front seats, each a pin cushion for a hundred assorted cartel knives. They hustle around back and grab their stuff, but there's barely enough time for Ray to pull on his boxers, and Wilbur his canvas tighty-whities, before another hail of bullets sends them scooting into the maze of vehicles for cover, Wilbur with his carry-on in tow.

Despite the intense firefight, the cartel thugs are no match for Ray as he and Wilbur zigzag through the maze. It's not long before an eerie calm befalls the ditch. But as they near the shipping container, Ray motions to halt and directs Wilbur to get behind him.

The container's door is open a crack.

Ray nudges it open further with the rifle's barrel. There's no one inside, but as the sunlight reveals the container's contents, his stoic demeanor belies his shock and disbelief. "Looks like they're moving more than oil."

He and Wilbur head inside and check out the stacks of tightly wrapped packages, along with other assorted weapons, grenades, cell phones, tablets, drones, triggers, bolts, nails, wire—all the ingredients to make IEDs. But most alarming of all is the black flag with white Arabic text hanging on the back wall.

"Abu Sharia. They're an ISIS splinter group," Ray says. "Extremely violent. And committed."

"Oh, well . . . when you put it that way," Wilbur says, and heads out with a tablet while Ray videos it all with one of the cells.

A moment later, Wilbur expands the Google Maps' satellite view as Ray heads over. "This is us," he says, and points at the red marker on the screen. He slides his finger up a half inch to the Rio Grande. "Here's the border a few miles away, and this . . ." he says, sliding his finger to a bright, pebble-sized blotch a short distance across the border, "is Rio Bravo, Amco's refinery."

As he expands the image, the cluster of Rio Bravo's massive round storage tanks comes into focus. "There are ten of them, but this one, Tank One," he says, zeroing in on the tank closest to the river, the largest of the bunch, emblazoned with a huge, stenciled "1" on its roof. "It's the behemoth. The *T. rex* of tanks. Four hundred feet high, eighty feet across. Holds upward of sixteen million gallons of oil. And it's heavily guarded."

"The stolen oil?" Ray asks.

"Has to be," Wilbur says. "But given the amount, it would have to be piped in." When Salko took the reins at Amco, Wilbur never gave much thought to the specialized Russian construction crew Salko brought in to modify Tank 1 from its smaller size and capacity. Looking back now, it all makes sense—as do the bullets that shatter the tablet from his hand.

He and Ray scatter in different directions as a handful of cartel reinforcements pour into the ditch from a second pickup truck.

Within minutes, Ray takes three of the five out, but "Shit," he thinks aloud when he spots the remaining two hustling Wilbur out of the ditch, where they fling his carry-on aside, toss him in their pickup, and take off.

Ray hauls ass back to the container, fires up a drone, and spots the pickup on the remote's screen, a dusty rooster tail in its wake, when off to the side, he spots a second rooster tail speeding toward the pickup. As Ray zooms in, he can't believe what he sees—Phil's maroon Ford Fiesta.

"You poor bastard."

"Oh, Christ," Joe mutters under his breath when his cell pings with a text from a foreign number that reads "Found the head of Alfredo Garcia." But he's not surprised by Ray's message. He knew telling him to keep his nose out of catching a bad guy after he'd picked up the scent, was like telling someone not to collect their winnings after they'd won the lottery—the odds of it happening are zero. He locks himself inside the precinct's bathroom and calls the number.

"'Make sure they spell my name right,'" Joe scoffs when Ray picks up. "It's tough to misspell *asshole*."

"Captain know you're making this call, or are you hiding in the bathroom?" Ray says as he hustles to the pickup—a rocket launcher and cache of assault rifles, clips, drones, cells, tape, wire, and grenades wrapped in the flag slung over his shoulder.

Joe can't help but chuckle. "What're you doin', Ray? There's some serious shit floatin' around about you, Bailey, and this IRS guy."

"Fake news."

"Who is he?"

"Don't know. Think he's being hung out." Ray sets the rocket launcher and cache of goodies on the pickup's passenger seat and jumps behind the wheel. "Hold on a sec." He sets the phone down, grabs the rocket launcher, aims it out the window, and blows the shipping container to smithereens. "You still got it, Ray," he says to himself with a smile and tosses the spent launcher out the window, peels out, and jumps back on the line. "Hey, I'm back."

"I don't want to know what that was," Joe says.

"You're about to. I emailed you a video and a tell-all. Forward it to Bodie and Miguel—gonna need balls to the wall."

FORTY-SIX

". . . And I hear once you hit your seventies, forget about sex drive. Even when you wake up at three in the morning with one of those like-I'm-still-in-my-twenties erections, it's gone before you can remember how you got it. I mean, imagine . . . A Victoria's Secret model catwalks into your bedroom in nothing but her birthday suit, some feathers, and heels, and nothing—like you're watching a Holocaust documentary."

Phil, chained to a cinder-block wall in obvious discomfort, can't take any more. "Wilbur! Please . . ."

"Just making conversation," Wilbur says, chained next to him in his canvas tighty-whities, but upside down.

"How about making shut the fuck up."

There's a fleeting flash of regret in Phil's eyes. Neither brashness nor bravado is his style. Still, with a deep breath, he welcomes the silence. But in the silence, random thoughts plunge into deeper waters, thrusting those of how his life has been reduced to a cliché to the surface, to the moment he's often heard about: when someone on the precipice of death sees their life honestly as it flashes before their eyes—perhaps God's way of endowing a false sense of peace and control when all his fractured psyche sees is helter-skelter.

———

His descent begins with visions of Lorena. Love at first sight—a corny cliché, but that's what it was. Their first date. Their fourth, two weeks later. Their first kiss, a real kiss, *the* kiss—the one he felt he had waited for his whole life. Their wedding day. The peace and contentment that followed. The feeling of being home. The feeling that Lorena *is* home.

Man . . . She was beautiful.

With a jolt, the visions shift to the months they spent getting the second bedroom ready for Emmi's arrival. The fun they had shopping for baby clothes and toys. The nervous anticipation in the delivery room. The moment Emmi entered the world. *It's a girl!* he beamed. The joy two days later when they took her home. Her first birthday party. Her second, her third . . . *Emmi's smart and well behaved. You both should be proud*, her second-grade teacher said the day before they left for Florida.

What I wouldn't give for more of Emmi's pasta with her secret sauce.

Only in her twenties and will have no immediate family.

My last text assured her everything was okay and not to worry. My last words to her . . . a lie.

Did I tell her I love her?

"Take good care of her," he mutters aloud as his thoughts turn to Matt and how, every week since he lost his job, he swings by Tiffany's to make sure the ring his heart is set on hasn't been sold.

Is the ring still there?

I can't believe I won't be at their wedding.

I'll never know their kids, nor they me.

The dark thoughts anger him and shift to Callahan.

I'll find him, sir.

Finally get your wish to get off the field.

Fuck him.

Was any of it worth it?

Round and round . . .

———

"You're in deep doo-doo, Agent Dancourt," Wilbur says, snapping Phil back to the present.

"And you're in what—roses?"

"Touché. Well, at least now you know why the Amco numbers don't add up. And when this is over, we'll have helped take Salko down—done some good in the world."

"Yeah, I'm feeling all warm and fuzzy."

"Sarcasm. Number one of the four signs of hostility disguised as humor."

"You're lucky I can't move, or I'd show you two through four."

"Bullying. Number six of—"

"Enough of your judgmental bullshit," Phil says, cutting him off. "You shouldn't have stolen the money."

"You shouldn't have hit me with that cockamamie doctor scam."

"You know about that?" Phil says, surprised.

Wilbur scoffs. "Of course. You think I'm a moron?"

"That's exactly what I think," Phil says, and chuckles. "Look at that . . . We're finally on the same page."

"You're wrong about Ray Dawson too. He's a good man, with integrity. Unlike most people, who are chronic chameleons, Ray is who he is—always. And believe me . . . You don't want to piss him off."

With the help of a drone's bird's-eye view, Ray tracked the cartel thugs to a worn-out, walled-in warehouse complex near the US-Mexico border. Taking up position in an alley between the complex and an abandoned gas station next door, he launches a drone from the back of the pickup—the cache of other drones and weapons spread out on the truck bed.

Navigating the drone's camera, Ray scans the area surrounding the complex. All appears to be quiet, with the nearest noticeable activity at a cement plant about half a mile to the east. Just to the north, the Rio Grande peacefully drifts by for the seventy-five-mile final leg of its nearly two-thousand-mile journey from the Rocky Mountains to the Gulf of Mexico.

Ray swivels the camera past the river and US border wall to Texas beyond, and homes in on Rio Bravo. The camera shutter bursts as he zooms in on Tank 1, but Ray's focus is drawn to a cement patch alongside the tank where Mika Salko's security goon Logan boards a hydraulic lift with an assault rifle slung over his shoulder.

As soon as the lift descends, a four-by-four-foot concrete slab that conceals it slides back into place. Ray zooms out and swivels the camera back to the warehouse complex. The other pickup and Phil's maroon Ford Fiesta stick out among the faded sheds, stacks of pallets, and other tired equipment.

As Ray maps out the lay of the land, he spots a couple of armed thugs who spill out of the main building and hustle across the yard to a large shed.

When they swing open the doors, it reveals the tangle of pipes and valves of a high-pressure oil pump hidden inside. But seconds later, a four-by-four section of the concrete floor next to the pump separates, and Logan rises on a hydraulic lift.

Ray's eyes harden. He doesn't need to know who Logan is to know his arrival can't be good, and he pilots the drone along the main warehouse wall for a look through the windows. Other than more thugs, there's no sign of Wilbur or Phil—until the drone hovers before the last window at the far end.

The drone's camera shutter bursts. "These are going viral," Ray says to himself as he looks at the screenshots of Wilbur and Phil shackled to the wall on the drone's screen, and he pilots the drone home. The moment it touches down on the truck bed, he tapes grenades to its landing gear and secures a wire from the pins and safety levers to the camera mount. The other drones, fully loaded and ready to go, sit nearby, and one by one, Ray launches them skyward.

FORTY-SEVEN

"Walking my daughter down the aisle—the one promise I vowed never to break," Phil laments to Wilbur.

Pulling the wedding together would have fallen on Lorena's shoulders. Not that she would have minded. Ever since Matt asked for his blessing, Phil often thinks about how, by the time Emmi was five, Lorena would talk about Emmi's future wedding day; how Lorena had already pictured it. He loved her belief in the power of manifestation.

It's a torch Emmi now carries. He still smiles every time he thinks about how Emmi, by the time she was thirteen, had seen virtually every movie with *bride* in the title—from *Runaway Bride, Bridesmaids,* and *Father of the Bride,* both the 1950 and 1991 versions and the sequel, to old classics such as *The Bride Wore Boots, Seven Brides for Seven Brothers,* and everything in between. Of course, Emmi's favorite was *The Princess Bride,* which was okay with Phil—it was also Lorena's. To this day, it's still Emmi's favorite movie.

Emmi also loves and pores over the photos of her mom in her wedding gown, and she already pictures hers. But for Phil, Emmi's wedding conjures up just one thought: him walking her down the aisle.

———

"I'll never forget this one wedding I took her to," Phil says. "A colleague of mine. Emmi was only ten. You should have seen her eyes light up when the bride's father walked her down the aisle. Made me promise I would do the same for her one day. Twelve years later, one of her friends got married, and she reminded me she's never forgotten that promise."

"When is the wedding?" Wilbur asks.

"Her boyfriend—great guy—hasn't asked her yet. But he came to me, old school, and asked for my blessing. He'd been saving a long time for this Tiffany ring and was almost there. Then lost his job—through no fault of his own." Frustrated, Phil tries to yank the bolts off the wall.

"Christ, Phil, a little faith. It'll work out."

Phil chuckles. "My wife, Lorena, used to say that."

"Used to?"

"Died. Killed in a head-on with a kid high on weed and heroin."

"Sorry. Mine too. Head-on with cancer."

"Sorry. Truth is, I've never been able to fully grasp real faith," he confides. "I thought I did, but Lorena used to call me 'the man on the branch'—a story she heard from a TV preacher about a guy who fell over a cliff and managed to grab a branch jutting from the rocks. He looked down at certain death, then looked up and called out, 'Is anybody up there?' A voice from the heavens rang out, 'I AM here. Let go, and I will catch you.' He looked back down, then back up, and called out, 'Is there anybody else up there?'"

They both laugh, a brief but needed moment of levity. "Whatever faith I had left died that night too," Phil says.

"Try flying with Ray. You'd be amazed how much faith you can muster when he's playing pilot, it's raining bullets, and the plane is on fire."

Phil chuckles.

"Faith's a lot like love," Wilbur says. "It's easy when things are good. But when life throws you the inevitable curveballs—especially vicious sliders like cancer, loss of memory, and fatal crashes . . ."

Phil nods. "Amen."

"But there's one surefire way to get it back. Say a prayer."

"Yes," Phil says. "Let's thank God our faith has been rewarded with the peace of shackles before we're tortured and killed. Gimme a break."

"What have you got to lose?"

Phil hesitates, but at his wit's end, he closes his eyes, and his brow furrows as his thoughts drift back into the deep. And when he surfaces, he cries out: "HELP!"

The profound emotion hangs in the air, and the long-carried weighted pain drains from Phil's face as if he knows God is about to come through the closed door. But instead, in walks Logan, who, without saying a word, rips a vicious punch to his gut.

"Son of a bitch," Phil wails and glances at Wilbur. "So much for a loving God."

Wilbur shrugs. "Tough love."

Logan turns to Wilbur and presses his rifle's barrel into his chin. "Per Mr. Salko, your employment with Amco is terminated. Permanently." But no sooner does he issue the ominous forewarning than . . .

BOOM! BOOM! BOOM! BOOM!

The room shutters as the rapid-fire blasts jolt the complex.

Wilbur smirks. "Looking for Ray?"

Logan heads for the door, and without breaking stride, he rips another blow into Phil's gut.

Phil grimaces and fights through the pain.

"Motherfucker!"

BOOM! BOOM! BOOM! BOOM!

Four more rapid-fire explosions rock the yard as Logan spills out of the warehouse, enveloped in the smoke-filled air already thick with the fetid stench of flaming chemicals and burned metal and flesh.

BOOM! BOOM! BOOM! BOOM!

Two thugs hiding behind a forklift never see the next drone dive bomb in while its swirling camera pulls the grenade's pins and releases the safety levers.

Five more never see Ray coming, and with his route mapped out in his mind, his movements are quick, methodical, and silent.

BOOM! BOOM! BOOM! BOOM!

All Wilbur and Phil can do is wait and hope until—*BAM!* The room's window shatters, and Ray's face appears. He rockets another drone into a dive before he tosses the remote and hoists himself inside, one assault rifle at the ready, two more slung over his shoulder, his belt laden with knives and grenades—and a bolt cutter.

BOOM! BOOM! BOOM! BOOM!

"Hey, how's it going?" Ray asks. He strides straight to Phil, sticks a cell up to his face, and plays a brief cut of the Fox News segment. "Díaz's alleged killer, seen here, has been identified as Philip Dancourt, an agent with the Internal Revenue Service . . ."

"It's bullshit," Phil says. "I shot the guy who shot him."

"Why are you trying to kill *him*?" Ray says, flicking his head at Wilbur.

"You mean before or after spending an hour with him?"

Ray chuckles—confirmation his gut is right about Phil.

"That's funny to you?" Wilbur asks.

"No," Ray says. "But the fact I'm only cutting Phil loose is." Ray cuts Phil free and hands him an assault rifle and grenades. "They'll be waiting outside, and . . . sorry about the nose."

"We're even," Phil says, happy to be alive.

"Raymond, please," Wilbur pleads.

Turning to Wilbur, Ray gives a quick snort of derision as he snaps another photo of him. "You can't make this stuff up," he says. Wilbur's body sags. "Relax. It's not my nature." He cuts Wilbur loose and hands him the other assault rifle. "Don't point it at anything you don't want to kill." He hands him grenades. "Hold the lever, pull the pin, and toss it."

It's the first time Wilbur has ever held lethal weapons. Even as a kid at summer camp, he refused to go to archery. "That it?" he says, his unease apparent.

"No. Try not to kill us or yourself."

Wilbur tucks the grenades in the back of his canvas tighty-whities, and he and Phil follow Ray out the window. And as soon as they hit the yard, hell's round two erupts. Ray and Phil dart one way and let loose with a barrage of bullets and grenades, and Wilbur scurries for cover behind Phil's maroon Ford Fiesta. But when he peeks over the trunk, he spots a thug on the warehouse roof with a clear shot at Phil.

Wilma flashes through Wilbur's thoughts. Ever since she got sick, he's wondered if, in a dire situation, he would be able to muster up the courage, strength, and fearlessness she displayed.

Within seconds, it's as if her soul takes the wheel. The theme from Sergio Leone's Clint Eastwood classic *The Good, the Bad, and the Ugly* begins to play in his mind. His body straightens. His jaw sets. His shoulders arch back.

Head held high, Wilbur rises, steps out from behind the Ford Fiesta, takes an Old West duel stance, and with the assault rifle's butt planted on his hip, the baddest dude to ever don canvas tighty-whities empties the thirty-round clip into the air.

"Who's packin' now, motherfucker!" he shouts.

The thug whips around and unloads, and if not for Ray, who flies by and yanks him back behind the car, Wilbur would be the deadest dude to ever don canvas tighty-whities.

"Next time, try aiming at something."

"And kill someone?" Wilbur asks, put off as more rounds rain down.

"No, dimwit, just someone who's shooting at you. I'm sorry. Did I say *dimwit*? I meant *muttonhead*. No, no . . . *nincompoop*. Or was it *ignoramus* or *numbskull*? Stay put."

Ray weaves his way back toward Phil, taking out the guy on the roof and another goon who makes the mistake of trying to ground and pound him in hand-to-hand combat. But no sooner does the guy drop to an unconscious bloody pulp than Logan steps out from behind a crate and yanks Ray off the ground by his neck.

Ray's body jerks and his face swells, when Phil comes up behind Logan.

Like a batter swinging for the fences, Phil rips a steel pipe across

Logan's spine. The blunt force takes out Logan's wind and locks his body, setting Ray free, and Phil drops the goon with a vicious uppercut to his gut.

"Next round is on me," Ray says, his voice raspy, and he tosses over his cuffs.

"You're on," Phil says, and cuffs Logan to a pallet jack.

FORTY-EIGHT

"What is it?" Phil asks when the large shed's door opens.

"Our way to Rio Bravo," Ray says as he heads to the hydraulic lift.

Wilbur stands before the high-pressure pump, arms outstretched. "And this is the big kahuna."

"Not anymore," Ray says. He heads over and starts to crank a large purple valve. The pressure gauges above it quickly rise toward the red zone.

"Raymond!" Wilbur shouts. "There are three things you never do at a high-pressure pump, and turning that purple valve is all three of them. There are dissolved gases which need to be removed or they come out of solution and—"

"English, Wilbur," Ray says.

"It'll fucking blow."

"English enough for me," Phil says.

It's enough for Ray too. He reopens the valve and leads them to the lift. But at the last second, he puts on the brakes. "Wait," he says, and bolts from the shed. A moment later he returns with Wilbur's carry-on.

Flabbergasted, Wilbur leans in, his arms open. "A little love."

"Easy there, Canvas Man," Ray says, and shoots his hand up. "A little social distance. Just wanted my beans."

I can't believe it—it was Phil's first thought when Ray crawled through the warehouse window.

I can't believe I'm gonna make it out alive.

I can't believe the guys I risked my life to hunt down would be the ones to save it.

I can't believe it—it was Phil's first thought when they stepped onto the lift and started the fifty-foot descent.

I can't believe the payoff of a five-year tax fraud investigation lies at the end of a violent and deadly drug cartel's secret tunnel.

The thought triggers another that hits him in a far more profound way—on a level he's never been able, or willing, to acknowledge and accept, let alone receive in his heart.

Lorena was right.

For most, if not all, of his adult life, he's been the man on the branch. Capable of believing only in what he sees. Always positive the branch, whatever it is at the time, will snap, and he'll plunge.

It strikes him how often he's been proven wrong, yet how it never matters. But for the first time, he's certain this time it will matter. That it's time to let go of the branch. Time to surrender control of the uncontrollable. Time to venture off the path, away from the shore, and out into the deep waters. With confidence and courage.

This time, it's time to follow Lorena's lead and move forward in faith and not by sight.

By the time the lift reaches the bottom, Phil's spirits are lifted to a high he hasn't felt since the accident, despite the shitstorm they all know is sure to lie ahead.

Phil, Ray, and Wilbur—now in new canvas threads and his carry-on in tow—hustle off the lift and hop onto a Tesla-battery-powered mini railcar, and off they go for the half-mile-long ride to Rio Bravo.

The tunnel is both primitive and an elaborate technological marvel:

hand-chiseled stone walls reminiscent of those often seen at archae-
ological digs but lined with rail tracks on a reinforced concrete bed,
a sophisticated electrical grid, track lighting, and a ten-inch-wide oil
pipeline that runs the entire length.

Down here, it makes no difference how tough you are. It's a long,
harrowing haul through a potentially unstable narrow passage deep
underground—the worst nightmare for anyone claustrophobic. And
despite the vents, the air is thick and heavy with a pungent funk of
unrecognizable foulness.

Taken together, they remind Ray of the countless maggot-infested,
decomposing bodies he came across in caves and tunnels during his
years in the Marines and the Forty-First. And the memory makes him
wonder . . .

*What are the odds it would all lead me here. With Wilbur. With
Phil. Especially, Phil.*

Is it random, or are the three of us on an unseen predetermined path?

Up ahead, the tunnel's choppy gradient shifts to a noticeable
ascent, and Ray begins to softly sing "Summer Wind," Sinatra's version long his mindful go-to song to ease him into hyperfocus. But
no sooner does he croon through the first lyric than Phil cuts in and
finishes it.

"One of Frankie's greats," Phil says to Ray with a smile. "Up there
with Tony B's 'I Left My Heart in San Fran.'"

"Dino's 'King of the Road,'" Ray says.

"Sammy Jr.'s 'Something's Gotta Give,'" Phil says, and he and Ray
simultaneously belt out, "Nat King Cole's 'The Very Thought of You,'"
and Wilbur chimes in with "Air Supply's 'Even the Nights Are Better.'"

Ray and Phil stop cold and stare him down as if he has committed heresy against the music gods.

"'Making Love Out of Nothing at All?'" he asks, dumbfounded.

"Hey, he could've gone with 'Two Less Lonely People,'" Phil says to the
trainees as their laughter in the lecture hall subsides. "This brings us to
the last takeaway. Adages are old for a reason—they're true. And they

remind us of simple truths. You sleep with dogs, you get fleas. A bird in the hand . . . A deal too good to be true . . ."

He sucks down some water and takes a seat. "Those simple truths hit Salko the hard way. Slept with the cartel for millions worth of free stolen oil, laundered the revenue through countless shell companies, and sent it back to Venezuela to prop up the regime. But he had no idea the cartel had cut a side deal with Abu Sharia for weapons and cheap Middle East heroin, and in return, they landed what ISIS has coveted since the caliphate was destroyed—a below-the-radar way to move bombs and recruits into the United States." The thought still gives Phil pause.

"Then there's Wilbur Bailey. In his case, don't judge a book by its cover. The book is better." Some in the group chuckle, but most seem unsure about what he means. "Make no mistake. If being a pain in the ass was a crime, he'd be on death row. But what he did at the end . . . It took guts."

FORTY-NINE

Up close, in the warm glow of the magic-hour sky, Rio Bravo's massive Tank 1 is more impressive in scale, and more ominous in its presence.

The entire area is cordoned off with crime scene tape, including the cement patch alongside the tank where the four-by-four section of the concrete separates, and Ray, Wilbur, and Phil rise on the hydraulic lift.

The moment they lay down their rifles, Bodie, Miguel, and a dozen other heavily armed agents filter out from behind the maze of pipes and towers, each in their respective FBI, DEA, ATF, and US Marshal flak jackets.

On Bodie's signal, he, Miguel, and a marshal approach, and the marshal handcuffs Wilbur.

"There's a better way," Wilbur says.

Ray smirks. "Ignore him."

"Shoot him," Phil says.

Ray, Bodie, and Miguel hug it out.

"Hey, brother," and, "Still causin' trouble," Bodie and Miguel respectively say.

Though the three men speak every so often, it's been almost ten years since they've seen each other—the last time being when Ray, Joe,

Bodie, Miguel, and several others from their Raiders unit got together for a raucous weekend in Daytona Beach.

Ray smiles. "Whadda we got?"

"Two dozen in custody, but the tank's rigged," Miguel says. "Multiple triggers linked to pressure, temp, who knows what else."

"Daisy chain," Phil says, comparing the intricate setup to Amco's financial quagmire.

"To a hundred pounds of badass," Bodie says with a nod. "Take Bomb Squad a few hours to map it out, let alone whatever's in this place that's beyond their purview."

"The tank's the least of your problems," Wilbur says. "Pipes connect it to Unit 310—Alkylation." He points toward an area further in the refinery. "It's a hellish brew of chemicals and gases like methane and butane; solvents like benzene, and the granddaddy of them all, hydrofluoric acid."

"English, Wilbur," Ray says.

"A blast of that magnitude would take out 310 and unleash a toxic cloud that would put millions of lives at risk. Cancer. Reduction in blood cells. Sperm-head abnormalities . . . English enough?" Their silence provides the answer. "There's a way out," he says. "Safely backwash the chemicals and gases out of each station in 310 without raising their temperature or pressure or exposing them to air. One wrong move . . . Toast."

"Lemme guess. Organic, non-GMO, cage-free running toast," Ray says.

Wilbur can't help but smile. "I know every valve, lever, and switch in this place," he says, and casually adds, "Take me twenty minutes."

Resigned to the fact they have no better option, Miguel has the marshal uncuff him, and he hands Wilbur a walkie-talkie. "Every step, understand?"

"Christ, Ice Man, a little faith."

This time it's Ray who can't help but smile, but he still gets in Wilbur's face. "Anything stupid . . ."

"Yeah, yeah, straight to number four."

Ray wishes him Godspeed, and he, Phil, Bodie, Miguel, and the others clear out.

The moment Wilbur starts the four-minute trek to Unit 310 with his carry-on in tow, his nerves begin to tingle. It's not that he doesn't know his way through the maze of pipes. Nor does he lack understanding of the task at hand. But what he didn't tell them is that executing the complex task is way out of his domain, way out of his comfort zone. And he could cause the precise catastrophe he warned them about.

Once he enters the unit, two more minutes tick away before he makes it to the first station, which utilizes benzene—a harmful carcinogen that occurs naturally in oil and is used as a solvent to make other chemicals.

Prominent warning signs spell out its dangers, and another minute ticks by while he looks over the jungle of valves, switches, levers, pressure gauges, and most importantly, the emergency get-the-fuck-out-of-there button.

Wilbur can't help but wonder if the microscopic bolts of electricity shooting off his skin would be enough to trigger Armageddon. A silent prayer and deep breath do little to allay his pounding heart, and beads of sweat glisten as he rotates valves, flips switches, shifts levers, monitors gauges, and waits three agonizing minutes for the safety light to go from red to green.

Halfway across the refinery, atop Atmospheric Tower 16—the tallest in the refinery at ten stories—Ray, Phil, Bodie, Miguel, and the others are standing vigil on its large wraparound catwalk when Wilbur's voice squawks from Miguel's walkie-talkie. "One down."

Over the next twenty minutes, Wilbur zigzags through Unit 310, from station to station, and one by one, he backwashes the isobutane, methane, and naphtha.

Each time, his voice squawks the positive outcome from the walkie-talkie.

But despite the prior successes, the sign at the final station gives him pause: WARNING! HYDROFLUORIC ACID. No matter how hard he tries to forget about the potential for burns—or tissue necrosis, as it's known in the medical field—his mind reminds him that this highly corrosive shit is a vicious contact poison that not only dissolves metal, rock, and glass but can kill him in seconds if it penetrates his body through the skin, eyes, nose, or mouth.

How pale in comparison the pernicious groceries Ray bought in San Paraiso seem, he thinks, and he reflects on his beliefs and his fateful decision to work for Amco.

Why would any company, any human being, use this stuff and put the world in jeopardy? he ponders. But he already knows the answer. Money. When mixed with other oil by-products, it helps to make high-octane-value products. In other words, more money. And it's not only Big Oil. It's used to make everything from electronics, cleaning products, pharmaceuticals, herbicides, and incandescent light bulbs to the Teflon that coats nonstick pans and the cooling agents in air conditioners.

And that's when it hits Wilbur: it's us, we the people, who don't want it banned.

Yes, that's it. The same goes for processed meat, Pringles, sweet-and-spicy sauce and mayo packets, artificially sweetened drinks, bleached plates—all of it. We the people are hard pressed to give any of it up.

The high pitch of a compressor snaps him out of his reverie, and he approaches the station and executes the same process. Steam hisses, pressure gauge dials surge and release, warning lights strobe, and several minutes later the safety light turns from red to green.

"It's done," Wilbur's voice squawks.

The welcome news brings high fives all around.

Miguel grabs the walkie-talkie. "Good work, Mr. Bailey. Head to Tower 16. Copy." But the thrill of victory is tempered when there is no response. "I repeat. Head to Tower 16. Copy."

The second command also falls on deaf ears.

Wilbur's eyes are fixed on the unseeable abyss before him when he spots a dandelion growing in a crack in the walkway. A sense of peace that surpasses all understanding settles in over his face as he closes his eyes, makes a wish, and blows the white puffs of fluff into the wind.

Ray and the others are about to move out when Wilbur's voice squawks from the walkie-talkie. "That's a negative, Ice Man."

"Come again," Miguel says.

"I'm heading home to be with my wife," Wilbur says, his voice tinged with peaceful resignation. He sets the walkie-talkie on a pipe leading from a high-pressure pump and starts to turn a purple valve identical to the one he stopped Ray from turning at the warehouse. A barrage of thoughts, each prejudiced through the filter of what he is about to do, riot through his brain as the needles in the pressure gauges rise.

Ray grabs Miguel's walkie-talkie. "Wilbur. It's me, Ray. Whatever you're thinking . . . I'm asking you as your friend not to do it."

Deeply touched, Wilbur looks to the heavens, his eyes full, and he gives the valve its final twist. The pressure maxes into the red zone.

"Wilbur, please . . ."

KABOOM!

THREE MONTHS LATER

FIFTY

Like the death of a loved one or close friend.

No matter how long there is to prepare for the death of a loved one or close friend or if it happens out of the blue, the impact of death's arrival is jarring. The unsettling nature of its finality. The notion of a person, a body, being alive one second and gone for eternity the next is as difficult a concept for humans to grasp as the universe being infinite.

Nor is the impact of the life-and-death experience limited to the biological. Life's events, whether good or bad, have lives of their own. Especially if it's a once-in-a-lifetime life event that's un-expected, frenetic, harrowing, death defying, enriching—in other words, unforgettable. The kind of life event that leaves an imprint on the soul.

When an event like that is over, it's easy to embrace the immediate calm after the storm. But a deep sense of loss often lurks just below the surface. And it's just as powerful.

Like the death of a loved one or a friend.

That's how Ray often describes how it feels. And he's not merely refer-ring to Wilbur being blown to kingdom come, but the whole weeklong,

twisted cyclone of unimaginable, surreal insanity and mayhem. Then
there was an explosion, and it was over.

Poof. Just like that.

The loss hit Phil harder than Ray. For a while, he thought Ray's
time in the Marines and the Forty-First, dealing with a daily dose of
some of the world's most violent and evil, had better prepared him for
what went down during that crazy week. But before long, Phil couldn't
deny that the rush was what he missed.

Sure, my job carries its share of danger, he'd remind himself. *But never
as extreme and extraordinary as what I experienced during Case #1A.*

In time, Phil realized the experience affected him in ways he
could never have anticipated and may never fully understand. But he
knew in his heart what went down was a life changer. And it birthed
the central message he later drove home to the agent trainees: Shit
rarely, if ever, goes as planned. So be prepared, physically, emotion-
ally, and spiritually.

Phil catches a late afternoon flight back to Houston after a jubilant
trainee graduation ceremony. There's no denying he's shrouded in a
new sense of peace and purpose as he strides into IRS headquarters.

"Dinner at seven. Wouldn't miss it for anything," he says to Emmi
as he gets on the elevator. "Love you." He ends the call and knuckles the fifth-floor button as the doors close. But at the last second, a
hand shoots in.

The moment the doors reopen, Phil's body tenses. He doesn't need
to see her press the button for the third floor to know exactly who she is.

The desire to meet her digs in its claws. *How many times*, he
thinks, *have I wanted to say hello and ask her out but thought it too
risky in today's climate?* She takes a place in the corner, and Phil offers
a polite smile.

"Belated congratulations, Director Dancourt," she says, catching
him off guard.

Phil smiles again. "Thank you. All in a day's work."

"Not to those of us stuck in human resources."

The elevator stops at three, and she gets off. But Phil stops the doors from closing. "And it's Phil."

She smiles. "Lisa."

There's a spring in Phil's step as he enters the fifth-floor corner office. The new sign on the wall behind the desk reads I DON'T KNOW WHAT I'M DOING, BUT I'M GETTING GOOD AT IT. Replacing the motto was one of Phil's first actions after the IRS chief in DC canceled Callahan and handed him the reins.

He settles in at his desk and turns his attention to the ABC News report on the TV. "Though he denies any wrongdoing, former Texas governor Roy Hargrove was fined a quarter of a million dollars for campaign violations linked to donations made by then Amco CEO Mika Salko. Salko himself is facing eighty felony counts and other related charges in the wrongful death of Wilbur Bailey—who many now hail a hero. According to sources within the FBI, more charges are likely now that former Amco president and CFO Alex Zuyev flipped on his former boss early this week."

Phil had been briefed about Zuyev hours earlier, but the thought of the look on Salko's face when he found out still gives him a chuckle as he reaches into the lower desk drawer for a Banana Nut Bread refill—but finds only the empty box.

He can't take his eyes off it, locked in the embrace of Lorena's loving presence, a feeling so intense it's as if she's physically there with him. *It's a sign from her. A call to cut the tether and let go of the branch. An assurance everything will be okay.* And he at last understands. And her presence departs.

Poof. Just like that.

It takes him a moment to process the realness of the feeling, a feeling he would never have believed possible had he not just experienced it. He pulls the e-cig from his pocket, lays it in the box, and places both in the trash.

Man . . . She was beautiful.

The reverie is broken by a knock at the door, and a kid from the mail room enters and hands him a six-by-six-inch box addressed to him but with no return address or any other markings. "It passed security, Director Dancourt."

Phil thanks him as he heads out, and after he gives the box a quick once-over and a light shake, he opens it to find a Tiffany Blue Box, inside which is the stunning ring Matt had his heart set on. Above a smiley face, a handwritten note reads "Some things go exactly as planned."

A shiver runs through Phil, and he sits there stunned. *There's no way this could be a joke. Could it be from Ray? No way. I never told Ray about the ring.*

Round and round . . . Until he smiles.

"Motherfucker!"

Around the same time, up in New York City, a handful of young employees help Ray prep his new coffee shop—named The Mug Shot— for its impending opening day.

One arranges displays while others hang wanted posters from various law enforcement units, a handful issued by foreign countries. Another, with a steady hand, meticulously chalks the names of the offerings on the menu board. Among those already listed are On the Run, Armed and Dangerous, Fugitive, Suspect in Custody, and Freeze!— their iced elderberry and echinacea zing.

Behind the counter, Ray arranges a dozen large canvas bags of exotic coffee beans, above which the framed $5 million IRS reward check is proudly displayed.

A local mail carrier enters with a similar six-by-six-inch box for Ray, also with no return address. But unlike Phil's, a small stamp on the bottom reads "Made from 100% hemp and dung paste."

Ray's eyes twinkle as he opens the box and inside finds a Ziploc baggie of exotic coffee beans and a small card from Plantación de Bolivia on which is a handwritten note: "Sorry, Ray . . . Maybe next time."

As if on cue, a female employee comes out of the back office with a printout. "Just came in for you over the wire," she says to Ray and glances at the sheet of paper. "From Director Philip Dancourt, IRS,

Houston." She hands Ray the new IRS wanted poster for Wilbur Bailey offering a $10 million reward.

Beep. Beep. Beep. Beep.

The dump truck's alarm chirps as it backs into position while, beyond, the demolition crew continues to break down the tenement where Isia Serante, the kid Ray shot and killed, had lived.

Out front, Stephanie signs off on several forms and hands the clipboard back to the site manager. "Thank you, Tony. Good job. Have Mo run a second hose, and see if we can get everyone out of here early."

"You got it, boss," he says and heads into the site. A short distance in, he calls out to a guy in his twenties who's hosing down the area for dust control while the massive crane's basket scoops up another pile of the foundation's concrete slabs. "Hey, Mo . . . Hit a second line."

Stephanie heads for the site's mobile trailer office, when she spots Ray at the curb, leaning on her company pickup, looking over what's left of the crime scene that changed his life forever. She grabs a hard hat out of the truck and offers it to him. "You ought to be wearing a hard hat. It can be dangerous around here."

Ray smiles and dons the hat. "Ever been to Bolivia?"

She breaks out into her most winning smile while, behind them, the crane dumps the concrete slabs into a waiting truck. When the dust settles, jutting out from one of the slabs, barely discernible, is the butt end of a gun, and with its load full, the truck pulls away.

THREE WEEKS LATER

FIFTY-ONE

The dry, squeaky squeal of the windmill's metal blades intensifies as their rotation accelerates with the wind's gust. The needles on the gauge affixed to the frame bounce higher, measuring everything from voltage and resistance to amps and ohms. Thin green wires run from the gauge down the side of the frame and snake along the ground past another identical windmill a foot away.

Then another. And another. And another . . . All squealing in clangorous symphonic harmony.

It's the kind of big, vibrant, piercing sound expected from mighty giants. Yet each of the 120 windmills assembled on the secluded hillside in a meticulously layered grid stands no more than two feet tall. And the wires—coated with bio-polyethylene made from sugarcane instead of the traditional petroleum-derived polyethylene—coalesce through a system of bamboo gauntlets into one master cable that flows through the wall of a small but comfortable ecological love-fest of a cabin.

Save for the multiple satellite dishes on the thatched roof, everything else—from its straw-bale walls and rain-harvesting system to its recycled glass windows—defines a clean, sustainable tropical feel with a reduced carbon footprint. This is a home in concert with Mother Nature. The same goes for the interior's nontoxic, humidity-resistant bamboo floor, chemical-free furnishings, and natural accents.

Nestled in a nook off the living room, Wilbur, in a soothing light mauve and lilac canvas outfit with matching shoes, sits at his recycled rubberwood desk and wraps stacks of hundred-dollar bills in high-barrier alt-plastic sheets, half listening to the BBC World News anchor on the solar-powered TV. "Local authorities are looking to intervene amid growing tensions among the Amazon's indigenous groups and later generations of farmers, both worried about the escalating impact of deforestation. We now turn our attention to New York City and an update on former NYPD detective Raymond Dawson."

Wilbur cocks his head and listens with keen interest while he wraps another stack. "It's been roughly ten months since Mr. Dawson shot and killed fifteen-year-old Isia Serante outside his Bronx apartment," the anchor reports. "You may recall that despite Mr. Dawson maintaining the young man was armed, no gun was found, and he was forced into early retirement. However, several weeks ago the situation took a dramatic turn."

Wilbur wheels around to the TV. "Construction workers, razing the building where the young man lived, discovered a gun encased in a cement slab torn from the structure's foundation. Authorities were later able to pull a latent fingerprint and DNA that linked the gun to Mr. Serante."

Wilbur pumps his fist as the anchor continues. "In response to an offer to rejoin the Bronx's Forty-First Precinct, Mr. Dawson issued a brief statement, and I quote: 'Though I'm grateful for the offer, my top priority is getting a third chance to ask my second wife if she'll marry me again for the last time.' And in related news, early this morning the severed head of fugitive Eddie Santoli washed ashore at a beachside resort in Belize . . ."

Elated, Wilbur shuts the TV off, heads to the cabin's front window, and takes in the divinity of the countryside before him—now the master of all he surveys. Nestled in a magnificent tropical setting along the eastern slopes of the Andes Mountains in a band of jungles known as the

Bolivian Yungas, the view from this altitude of the lush Plantación de Bolivia is breathtaking.

He can't help but reflect on how their fateful journey left him enriched. Not only did it result in the nationwide arrests of over 150 would-be bombers and the seizure of enough bomb-making materials to kill thousands, but it also left Wilbur with a profound sense of purpose and a renewed spirit of faith and confidence that his life's second half will be okay. And though still alone, no longer lonely. No longer in need of a dog. No longer . . .

The reverie is broken when a faraway vehicle motoring down Yungas Road catches his eye. Infamously known as "Death Road," it connects the Yungas' coffee-growing region with Bolivia's capital, La Paz.

He grabs the binoculars off the sill, and as he brings them into focus, the vehicle is revealed to be a newer model beige Volkswagen Golf. A sly smile crosses his lips, but no sooner does he set the binoculars down than his smile vanishes and his pupils sharpen. It's as if he can sense there's someone no more than five feet behind him.

"Hello, Raymond. It's nice to see you," Wilbur says without turning.

"Sorry to barge in."

"It's your nature."

"So is this," Ray says, his gun trained center mass.

Wilbur turns to face him. "You of all people should know the three reasons why that's a bad idea. One, I don't allow guns in the house. Two . . ." He holds up his right hand. The grenade Ray gave him at the warehouse is clenched in its grip, the pin already pulled. "And three..." He holds up his left hand with the other grenade, its pin also pulled.

"You're right. I should've called first," Ray says, and sticks the gun in the back of his waistband.

"We did good. You should have left it there," Wilbur says, and lets the grenades roll from his hands.

Caught off guard, Ray backs away and lunges through a window one second before KABOOM! KABOOM!

The double blasts reverberate across the hillside. Flocks of birds scream as they take to the skies.

"Ugh, Christ," Ray moans as he sits up stunned, scraped, and entangled in a net of windmills and wires. It takes him a moment to get
his bearings as he stares in disbelief at the smoking pile of eco-friendly,
sustainable rubble. And no sooner does tranquility drift back in with
the breeze and all return to its natural state of quiet stillness than a pile
of rubble across the way begins to stir, and Phil's heads pop through.

"Motherfucker!"

EPILOGUE

Ray and Phil had tried to dig through the rubble to see if there was any chance Wilbur was still alive. But the fire was too hot. And by the time it was extinguished, there was nothing left.

It was a couple of weeks before Bolivian authorities found blood spatter matching Wilbur's on pieces of bamboo flooring that were blown down the hillside. But his body was never found, and from tiny bone fragments, it was determined he'd vaporized in the flames.

Weeks turn into months. But not a day goes by without Ray and Phil thinking about Wilbur. They speak from time to time, and Phil hopes Ray and Stephanie will one day take him up on his invitation to come to Houston and feast on his famous ribeyes.

Plus, he would love for them to meet Lisa. They've been dating exclusively ever since they first went out. Phil's convinced the romantic dinner he made at home on their third date, with a great bottle of wine and Emmi's special pasta, is what sealed the deal—though he's yet to come clean about the fact that it was Emmi who cooked it.

Ray, meanwhile, has his hands full with The Mug Shot. It opened to rave reviews and long lines, and there are already plans in the works for two more locations. Even better, he and Stephanie are thriving and have decided to move back in together at the end of the month, with her father's reluctant blessing. Things couldn't be more on track.

Sadly, though, after treating Alley for age-related chronic kidney failure, things took a rapid turn for the worse one evening a couple of weeks ago. Ray rushed her to the nearest animal hospital, where the doctor confirmed the end was not far and went over the options—one of which, given Alley's age and deteriorating state, he assured Ray was the right thing to do. He then left the room so Ray could be alone with her.

Ray held Alley close and whispered in her ear for the last time what he had told her countless times over the years. "I love you. I love you. I love you all the time. No matter what. Forever and ever and ever. That's the one thing you need to remember."

The doctor came back in, and one minute and twenty-three seconds later, Alley peacefully crossed the Rainbow Bridge at age seventeen.

Ray has loved animals for as long as he can remember—especially dogs. His father had instilled in him a distrust of anyone who doesn't love animals. "It's not that everyone has to have a pet," his father would say. "But anyone who doesn't love animals . . . their brain's wiring is off." Up until Alley, though, it never seemed like the right time to have one. Like he and Alley were meant to be. And he questioned whether he would ever feel that way again.

For anyone who's never been through it, putting an animal down, as the saying goes, is one of the most compassionate and gut-wrenching decisions to ever make. But, as Ray will attest, it's true—they have a way of letting you know they're ready and that everything's going to be okay. Gut-wrenching nonetheless.

It's a beautiful predawn morning, around 3:00 a.m., and Ray can't sleep. Without Alley, the apartment feels emptier, quieter, colder. He's not sure why, but as he stands by the window and sips his coffee, he feels her presence. Perhaps it's the dozen or so dirty paw prints still planted on the living room floor or the strands of her fur that manage to escape the vacuum.

Stop being so sentimental and foolish, he thinks. But compelled, he drains the cup, throws on his clothes, heads out, and walks the route he and Alley took every day for years to the park.

At this hour, the park is desolate and peaceful as he sits on the bench reminiscing and picturing Alley out there chasing the ball and squirrels and romping with her dog buddies. The memories are comforting—until his body stiffens.

From out of the darkness, a seventy-plus-pound mangy dog barrels straight for him. And as it closes in, it becomes clear the dog is mal-nourished and without a collar.

Ray knows enough not to run and increase the chances of an attack. Besides, there's no time. Within seconds, the dog, a Boxer-Doberman mix, is on him and knocks him over on the bench—and starts to breathlessly lick his face.

Many have told Ray he's lucky the dog didn't kill him, which is true. But so was the dog—Ray's .38 was in his ear.

A minute later, a frumpy middle-aged guy does his best to trot over and apologize. He tells Ray he was on his way home to Brooklyn when he saw the park and let the dog out to pee. He had found the dog a couple of hours ago on a pitch-black road in the middle of nowhere in Upstate New York and had taken him to a pound up there. "But they were going to kill him, so I took him. Gonna bring him to my local pound in the morning." The dog settles down and sits next to Ray.

"We're good, buddy. I'm fine," Ray says, and without thought, he drapes his arm over the dog and rubs behind his ears. "Maybe you shouldn't. Maybe you and he were meant to be. He's a keeper."

The man stands there, looks at the two of them, and smiles. Then without saying another word, he turns and walks away. Ray doesn't move. Doesn't call out. Doesn't stop him. Neither does the dog—both already bound by an undeniably deep, inexplicable, and powerful connection.

He names him Wilbur, and the rest is history.

What are the odds?

ACKNOWLEDGMENTS

Offering heartfelt thanks to the squad of people who helped make this book possible seems generic and underwhelming given everyone's effort. But for those who are reading this . . .

First and foremost, to Trident Media Group CEO Robert Gottlieb, for ushering the novel to his colleague Erica Spellman Silverman, my agent, the first to believe, the captain of the ship who deftly and tirelessly guided the material through choppy waters with support, encouragement, and great advice.

Special thanks to Marilyn Kretzer, Blackstone Publishing's senior acquisitions editor, the second to believe. Marilyn's editorial guidance and open-arms support kept me and everything else on course throughout the complex publishing process. And to my editor Dana Isaacson, whose insight pushed and guided me—and the novel—to new heights.

Many thanks also to Kristen Bertoloni (Erica's assistant and future Trident überagent), Michael Pintauro, and the rest of the Trident Media Group team. And to Josie Woodbridge, Kristen Gully (for her amazing book cover), Brianna Jones, Rebecca Malzahn, Michael Krohn, and the rest of the Blackstone Publishing team.

Last but not least, heartfelt thanks to friends who were willing to read *What Are the Odds* while it was a work in progress: Wendy Hull, for her encouragement and for allowing me to read it to her fifty times—over the phone! Harry Stein and Priscilla Turner, for their support, friendship, and guidance, and from whom I've learned much about writing. And Adam Berger, for his friendship and multiple reads along the way.

The input from all of you was invaluable.